D

THE HENLEY COLLEGE LIBRARY

This book is due for return on or before the last date shown below.

2 9 FEB 2024

D1343327

SHAKESPEARE AND COMPANY
KILOMETER ZERO PARIS

People Like Us

DANA MELE

G. P. PUTNAM'S SONS

G. P. PUTNAM'S SONS
an imprint of Penguin Random House LLC
375 Hudson Street
New York, NY 10014

Copyright © 2018 by Dana Mele.
Penguin supports copyright. Copyright fuels creativity, encourages diverse voices, promotes
free speech, and creates a vibrant culture. Thank you for buying an authorized edition
of this book and for complying with copyright laws by not reproducing, scanning, or
distributing any part of it in any form without permission. You are supporting writers and
allowing Penguin to continue to publish books for every reader.

G. P. Putnam's Sons is a registered trademark of
Penguin Random House LLC.

Library of Congress Cataloging-in-Publication Data
Names: Mele, Dana, author.
Title: People like us / Dana Mele.
Description: New York, NY : G. P. Putnam's Sons, [2018]
Summary: "When a girl is found dead at her elite boarding school, soccer star Kay Donovan
follows a scavenger hunt which implicates suspects increasingly close to her, unraveling her
group of popular friends and perfectly constructed life"—Provided by publisher.
Identifiers: LCCN 2017028973 (print) | LCCN 2017040563 (ebook) |
ISBN 9781524741761 (Ebook) | ISBN 9781524741709 (hardcover)
Subjects: | CYAC: Mystery and detective stories. | Murder—Fiction. | Boarding schools—
Fiction. | Schools—Fiction. | Secrets—Fiction. | Treasure hunt (Game)—Fiction.
Classification: LCC PZ7.1.M4692 (ebook) | LCC PZ7.1.M4692 Peo 2018 (print) |
DDC [Fic]—dc23
LC record available at https://lccn.loc.gov/2017028973

Printed in the United States of America.
ISBN 9780525516033
3 5 7 9 10 8 6 4 2
Design by Jaclyn Reyes.
Text set in Bodoni LT Pro.

This is a work of fiction. Names, characters, places, and incidents either are the product
of the author's imagination or are used fictitiously, and any resemblance to actual persons,
living or dead, businesses, companies, events, or locales is entirely coincidental.

For Luke, Sam, Mala, Floyd, Evie, Felix,
and all the other characters I have had to shelve.
Your name is in print, guys. You live.

And for Benji, who is real and patiently
allowed me to write this book.

1

*b*eneath the silvery moonlight, our skin gleams like bones. Skinny-dipping in the frigid waters of North Lake after the Halloween dance is a Bates Academy tradition, though not many students have the guts to honor it. Three years ago, I was the first freshman to not only jump, but stay under so long they thought I'd drowned. I didn't mean to.

I jumped because I could, because I was bored, because one of the seniors had made fun of my pathetic dollar-store costume and I wanted to prove I was better than her. I kicked down to the bottom, pushing past clumps of moss and silky strands of pondweed. And I stayed there, sunk my fingers into the soft, crumbling silt until my lungs twisted and convulsed, because even though the freezing water cut like knives, it was soundless. It was peaceful. It was like being encased safely in a thick block of ice, protected from the world. I might have stayed if I could. But my body didn't allow it. I broke the surface and the

THE HENLEY COLLEGE LIBRARY

upperclasswomen screamed my name and passed me a bottle of flat champagne, and we scattered as campus police broke up the scene. That was my official "arrival" at Bates. It was my first time away from home, and I was no one. I was determined to redesign myself completely into a Bates girl, and as soon as I took that dive, I knew exactly what kind of girl I would be. The kind who jumps first and stays under ten seconds too long.

Now we're the seniors and no first-years have dared to tag along.

My best friend, Brie Matthews, runs ahead, her sleek track-star body cutting through the night air. Normally, we would strip under the thorny bushes that line the lake next to the Henderson dorms. It's our traditional meeting spot after we pregame in one of our rooms and stumble across the green together, still in costume. But Brie received an early-recruitment offer from Stanford tonight and she is on fire. She ordered us to meet her at ten to midnight, giving us just enough time between the dance and the dive to ditch valuables, load up on refreshments, and deal with significant-other drama. Then she met us at the edge of the green wearing only a bathrobe and an exhilarated grin, her cheeks flushed and breath hot and sweet with hard cider. She dropped the robe and said, "Dare you."

Tai Carter runs just ahead of me, her hands pressed over her mouth to cram her laughter in. She is still wearing a pair of angel wings and they flutter with her long silvery hair twisting in the wind. The rest of our group trails behind. Tricia Parck trips over a tree root, nearly causing a pileup. Cori Gates stops running and falls to the ground, cracking up. I slow, grinning, but the air is freezing, and my skin is covered in goose bumps. I still get a thrill from the icy plunge, but my favorite part now is snuggling together with Brie under a mountain of blankets and giggling about it afterward.

I am about to make the final sprint across the patch of dead moss stretching from Henderson's emergency exit to the edge of the lake when I hear Brie scream. Tai halts and I push past her toward the sound of frenetic splashing. Brie's frantic voice escalates in pitch, repeating my name over and over, faster and faster. I tear through the bushes, thorns etching white and red stripes in my skin, grab her hands, and haul her up out of the lake.

"Kay," she breathes into my neck, her dripping body shivering violently, teeth clicking and chattering. My heart batters my rib cage as I look her over for blood or cuts. Her thick black hair lies damply over her skull; her smooth brown skin, unlike mine, is unbroken.

Then Tai grabs my hand so hard, my fingertips go numb. Her face, usually caught between a genuine grin and mocking smirk, is arranged in a strange blank stare. I turn and an odd sensation creeps over me, like my skin is turning to stone one cell at a time.

There's a body in the lake.

"Go get our clothes," I whisper.

Someone scampers away behind us, kicking up a flurry of dry leaves.

Fragments of moonlight lie like shattered glass over the surface of the water. At the edge, tangles of roots reach down into the shallows. The body floats not far from where we're standing, a girl with a pale, upturned face under about an inch of water. Her eyes are open, her lips white and parted, her expression almost dazed, except that it isn't anything. An elaborate white ball gown blooms around her like petals. Her arms are bare and there are long cuts up and down her wrists. I grab my own half-consciously, and then flinch as I feel a hand on my shoulder.

Maddy Farrell, the youngest of our group, hands me my dress. I nod stiffly and pull the loose black shift over my head. I am Daisy Buchanan from *The Great Gatsby*, but my dress was repurposed from the costume Brie wore last year and it's a size too large. Now I wish I'd chosen to dress as an astronaut. Not only is it freezing out, but I feel stripped and vulnerable in the gauzy fabric.

"What should we do?" Maddy asks, looking at me. But I can't tear my gaze away from the lake to answer her.

"Call Dr. Klein," Brie says. "She'll contact the parents."

I force myself to look at Maddy. Her wide-set eyes are glossy with tears, and dark, uneven streaks run down her face. I smooth her soft golden hair reassuringly but keep my own expression even. My chest feels like bursting and a siren is blaring somewhere deep in my mind, but I silence it with imagery. A room of ice, soundless, safe. No crying. A teardrop can be the snowflake that starts an avalanche.

"The school comes first. Then the cops," I say. No point in someone seeing on their newsfeed that their kid is dead before they get the phone call. That was how my dad learned about my brother. It was trending.

Maddy takes out her phone and dials the headmistress's number while the rest of us huddle in the darkness, staring at the dead girl's body. With her open eyes and lips parted as if mid-sentence, she looks so close to being alive. Close, but not quite. It's not the first dead body I've ever seen, but it's the first one that's almost seemed to look right back at me.

"Does anyone know her?" I finally ask.

No one answers. Unbelievable. The six of us, separately, probably hold more social capital than the rest of the student body combined. We must know nearly every single student between us.

But only students are allowed at the Skeleton Dance. At other dances, we are permitted to bring guys and other off-campus dates. The girl in the lake is our age and elaborately dressed and made-up. She has a familiar face, but not one I can place. Especially not like this. I lean over, clutching my arms to try to keep from shivering too hard, to get another look at her wrists. It's a grisly sight, but I find what I'm looking for: a thin, glowing neon tube.

"She's wearing the wristband. She was at the dance. She's one of us." I shudder at the words as they leave my lips.

Tricia studies the ripples in the lake without raising her eyes quite high enough to look at the body again. "I've seen her around. She's a student." She twists her silky black hair absently and then lets it fall over her perfect replica of Emma Watson's *Beauty and the Beast* ball gown.

"Not anymore," Tai says.

"Not funny." Brie glares at her, but someone had to break the tension sooner or later. It knocks me back into myself again a little. I close my eyes and picture the ice walls doubling, tripling in thickness, until there's no room for sirens in my mind, no room for my heart to thump chaotically off rhythm.

Then I stand up straighter and eye Maddy's costume, Little Red Riding Hood with a scandalously short dress and a warm-looking cape.

"Can I borrow your cape?" I hold out one finger, and she slips the warm shrug off her pale, bony shoulders and hands it to me. I only feel a little bad. It's cold and I'm a year older. She'll get her turn.

A wailing sound fills the air and a swirl of red-and-blue lights hurtle toward us from across the campus.

"That was fast," I murmur.

"I guess Klein decided to notify the cops herself," Brie says.

Cori emerges from the darkness clutching a bottle of champagne, her catlike green eyes seeming to glow in the dim light. "I could have called Klein. But nobody asked." Cori never misses an opportunity to mention her family's connection to the headmistress.

Maddy hugs herself. "I'm sorry. I didn't think."

"Typical Notorious," Tai says, shaking her head. Maddy glares at her.

"It doesn't matter. She'll be here soon." Brie wraps an arm around Maddy. The bathrobe looks thick and soft, and Maddy nuzzles her cheek to it. I narrow my eyes and toss the cape back to her, but overshoot, and it lands in the lake.

Tai stabs the waterlogged mass with a stick and fishes it out, dumping it at my feet. "I remember her. Julia. Jennifer. Gina?"

"Jemima? Jupiter?" I snap at her, wringing the cape out as well as I can.

"We don't know her name, and no one recognized her at all

at first," Brie says. "It would be misleading to tell the police we knew her."

"I can't look at her face. Sorry. I can't. So . . ." Maddy pulls her arms inside her dress, making her look like a creepy armless doll with her chalk-white skin and smudged dark eye makeup. "We should lie?"

Brie looks to me for help.

"I think Brie means we should simplify by saying we didn't recognize her and leave it at that."

Brie squeezes my hand.

Campus police arrive first, braking in front of Henderson and thundering out of the car toward us. I've never seen them move like that and it's scary in a sort of pathetic way. It's not like they're real cops. Their sole job is to drive us around and break up parties.

"Stand aside, ladies." Jenny Biggs, a young officer who often escorts us across campus after hours and turns a blind eye to our private soirees, ushers us out of the way. Her partner, a hulk of a male officer, barrels past us and wades into the water. A bitter taste forms under my tongue, and I dig my fingernails into my palms. There's no real reason for it, but I feel protective of the body. I don't want his hairy-ass hands touching her.

"I think you're not supposed to disturb a crime scene,"

I whisper to Jenny, hoping she'll intervene. She's been really nice to us over the years, joking and bending rules almost like an older sister.

She looks at me sharply, but before she can say anything, the real cops arrive along with an ambulance. The EMTs make it to the lake before the cops, and one of them dives into the water after Jenny's partner.

"Do not approach the victim," barks one of the officers, a tall woman with a strong Boston accent, jogging toward the lake's edge.

The campus police officer, now waist deep in the water, turns and crashes into the EMT.

"It's like the incompetence Olympics," Tai murmurs.

Another officer, a short Tony Soprano look-alike, nods dismissively to Jenny like she's a servant. "Get this guy out of here," he says.

Jenny looks a little miffed, but she waves to her partner, who reluctantly takes the EMT by the arm. They escort him up the bank, shooting daggers at the townie cops.

The woman officer, the one who called off the rescue mission, looks at us suddenly. She has a sharp chin, beady eyes, and over-plucked eyebrows that make her look sort of like a half-drawn Intro-to-Art exercise. "You're the girls who found the body."

She doesn't wait for a response. She leads us over to the water's edge as more officers arrive to rope off the area. Brie and I exchange questioning glances and I try to catch Jenny's eye, but she's busy securing the scene. Students are beginning to filter out of the dorms. Even housemothers—the adults in charge of each dorm—have drifted out and to the edges of the newly erected safety barriers and lines of police tape. The tall cop flashes a tight-lipped smile. "I'm Detective Bernadette Morgan. Which one of you girls made that phone call?"

Maddy raises her hand.

Detective Morgan whips a cell phone out of her pocket and shows the video screen to us. "I've got a terrible memory, girls, do you mind if I record this?"

"Sure," Maddy says, then darts her eyes to me with an apologetic expression. Detective Morgan seems to note this with interest and flashes me a crooked smile before turning back to Maddy. "You don't need your friend's permission."

Tai glances down at the cell phone. "Oh my God, is that an iPhone 4? I didn't know they still made those. Or that it was legal to record minors making statements on them."

The detective's smile brightens. "Witness statements. Do I have your permission, or shall we go to the station and call your parents in?"

"Go for it," Tai says, hugging herself and shivering.

The others nod, but I hesitate for just a nanosecond. Jenny is one thing, but I don't have much faith in cops otherwise. I spent half of eighth grade talking to various police officers and it was a hellish experience. On the other hand, I would go to extraordinary lengths to avoid involving my parents.

"Fine," I say.

Detective Morgan laughs. The sound is nasal and abrasive. "Are you sure?"

The cold is beginning to wear on me and I can't help impatience and annoyance from saturating my voice. "Yeah. Go ahead, Maddy."

But Bernadette's not finished with me. She points to Maddy's soaked, balled-up cape in my hands. "Did you remove that from the water?"

"Yes. But it wasn't there when we got here."

"How did it get there?"

I feel my face growing warm despite the cold of the night. "I threw it in."

The detective sucks her cheek into her mouth and nods. "As one does. I'll need to take it."

Shit. This is how it starts. Little things like that. I extend the cape to her, but she calls over her shoulder and a short man wearing blue nitrite gloves appears and places it in a plastic bag.

She turns back to Maddy. "From the beginning."

"We came out here to go swimming. Brie ran ahead. I heard her scream and—"

"Who's Brie?" Detective Morgan points the cell phone camera at us one by one. Brie raises her hand.

"—and we found a body floating in the water next to her. Then Kay told me to call Dr. Klein before the police," Maddy finishes.

"No I didn't." My voice comes out hard and shivery. "Brie did."

Detective Morgan turns to me and runs the camera over me slowly from head to foot, scanning carefully over my scratched-up skin. "You're Kay," she says, with an odd smile.

"Yes. But actually, Brie said to call Dr. Klein."

"Why does it matter?"

That catches me off guard. "Doesn't it?"

"You tell me."

I press my lips together tightly. I know from experience how police can take statements and then twist the words into something you didn't mean to say. "Sorry. Are we in trouble?"

"Did any of you recognize the body?"

I glance around at the others, but no one jumps in. Maddy is stiffly rocking from side to side, her arms still folded up inside her dress. Cori is watching the police down at the edge of the lake with an odd expression of fascination. Tricia's eyes are downcast and her bare shoulders are trembling. Tai just watches me blankly, and Brie nods for me to continue.

"No. Are we in trouble?"

"I hope not." Detective Morgan makes a signal over our heads to another officer, and I glance at Brie. She actually looks worried and I wonder if I should be. She makes a lock-and-key gesture over her lips and I nod very slightly and raise my eyebrows at the others. Tai nods evenly and Tricia and Cori link pinkie fingers, but Maddy looks seriously spooked.

Just then, I see Dr. Klein cutting a path through the crowd, a short but formidable woman, somehow impeccably dressed and composed even at this hour and under these circumstances. She brushes aside a police officer with a tiny wave of her hand and marches straight up to us.

"Not another word," she says, laying one hand on my shoulder and one on Cori's. "These girls are in my care. In their parents' absentia, I am their guardian. You may not question them outside of my presence. Is that understood?"

Detective Morgan opens her mouth to protest, but it's no use arguing when Dr. Klein has gone full headmistress.

"These students have just witnessed a horrific event and Ms. Matthews is soaking wet and at risk of hypothermia. Unless you're going to question them indoors, you will simply have to come back another time. I'll be happy to accommodate your schedule during school hours."

Detective Morgan smiles, again without showing teeth. "Fair enough. You girls *have* been through a lot. You go get a good night's sleep, huh? Don't let a tiny little tragedy ruin a great party." She starts to walk away and then turns back to us. "I'll be in touch."

Dr. Klein ushers us back toward the dorms and darts over to the water's edge.

I turn to Brie. "That was a bitchy thing to say."

"Yeah," Brie says, looking troubled. "It almost sounded like a threat."

2

*b*y the next morning, the news has infected the entire school. My dorm is on the other side of campus and I still wake up to the sounds of sirens outside and muffled sobbing from above. I open my eyes to see Brie perched at the edge of my bed, her face pressed to the window. She's already showered and dressed and is sipping coffee from my I ♥ Bates Soccer Girls mug.

Looking at it sends a jolt of energy down my spine. We have a crucial game on Monday and I've scheduled a long practice this morning to prepare. I jump out of bed, pull my thick, wavy ginger hair into a tight ponytail, and throw on a pair of leggings.

"Jessica Lane," Brie says.

A glacial frost laces over my skin, and my shoulders twitch. "What?"

"The girl in the lake."

"Never heard of her." I wish Brie hadn't told me her name.

It was nearly impossible to get her still, placid face out of my head last night as I lay awake next to Brie in my narrow dorm bed, and now I need to focus. I want to scrub every particle of last night from my mind. For three years I have been solid, and I will not crack and shatter over this. One snowflake.

"I did. She was in my trig class."

I get a rotten, gnawing feeling in my stomach. "Maybe it wasn't the greatest idea telling the police we didn't know her."

"Don't overthink it." She sits next to me and winds one of my curls around her finger. "I mean, I barely, barely know who she was. We couldn't tell the cops everything. They'd zero in on that and completely ruin our lives." Brie has her own, very different reasons for being wary of law enforcement. For one thing, her parents are top criminal defense attorneys, and she's heading in that direction. She probably knows more about criminal law than most first-year law students. Everything you say can and will be used against you. Since winning debate-club regionals last year, she has made a mantra of the quote "Dance like no one is watching; email like it may one day be read aloud in a deposition." For another, Brie has experienced racial profiling firsthand. Never at Bates, she said. But even I've noticed how different things are off campus. Once, when an off-campus party was broken up, a cop walked right past me, a minor holding an open bottle of beer, and asked Brie to take a Breathalyzer. She had a can of soda in her hand. They still made her do it.

I sigh. "And you can't tell Maddy anything unless you want the entire school to know."

"That's not fair."

Fair is beside the point. Last year, Maddy accidentally released the names of the new soccer team recruits online before we could "kidnap" them from their rooms in the traditional initiation ceremony. That tradition cements us as a team, and besides that, it's fun. When you take the fear out of initiation night, you take the exhilaration out of the moment you learn you have been chosen. You are good enough. But no. Maddy leaked the names I emailed her for the website and I learned Brie's mantra the hard way. Email like it may one day be read aloud in a deposition. Or posted in a school-wide community forum.

Maybe we're not completely fair to Maddy. A few weeks ago, Tai started this new "Notorious" nickname that I honestly don't get, but I'm not going to be the only person to admit it. Even Brie has been a little standoffish about Maddy lately, and I haven't been able to pin down exactly why. She isn't as witty as Tai or as studious as Brie, but she has a reputation among our group as being sort of the stupid one, while she's actually fairly brilliant. She has the second-highest GPA in the junior class, is field hockey captain, and she designs websites for all of the athletic teams.

She gains nothing from the time she puts into it, and it makes us look better. I think she just lacks a certain cynicism the rest of us share, and people tend to see that as a kind of weakness. She reminds me of my best friend back home, Megan Galloway. Megan's whole worldview was silver linings. That kind of vision is dangerous, but I envy it.

Sometimes it feels like all I see are dark spots.

"Anyway, her body's been identified. Parents called. All over the news." Brie points to the ceiling and I look up, slightly disoriented. The crying seems to intensify.

I clap a hand over my mouth and gesture up. "Was that her room?"

Brie nods. "I think so. The dorm's sectioned off with police tape and there's been crying up there for about two hours. I can't believe you slept through it."

"It's me." I'm a notoriously efficient sleeper—if and when I manage to shut my brain off—and no one knows it better than Brie. She was my roommate for two years before we got senior single privileges, and we still have frequent sleepovers.

She grins for a moment, and then her smile fades. "Bates hasn't had a suicide in over a decade."

"I know." She's tactful enough not to mention that in the past, when her mother attended, there was an epidemic. An entire wing of Henderson was closed for nearly thirty years.

"How did you not know her?" Brie says.

"Maybe she spent a lot of time off campus."

I pull a sweatshirt over my head and grab my campus ID and keys and then hesitate, my hand on the doorknob. I glance at the calendar hanging above my bed. My parents gave it to me in September with match days already circled heavily in red marker. Three scouts will be at Monday's game to see me play, and unlike my friends, I can't fall back on money if I'm not offered a college scholarship. I'm not the average Bates girl from a wealthy New England family. I'm here on a "whole student" scholarship, which is code for athletic, because my grades aren't enough to float me, and my family can't afford the tuition. Still, this is an extenuating circumstance and it might look bad to hold practice today. My parents might even understand.

I turn to Brie. "Should I cancel practice?"

She gives me one of her honestly-I'm-not-judging-you looks. "Kay, it's already canceled."

"They can't do that."

"Of course they can. We don't run the school. Athletics, music, theater, every nonacademic department is shut down while this is under investigation."

I drop back down on the bed, my head buzzing. "You've got to be kidding me. Monday is the biggest day of my life."

She puts her arm around my shoulder, drawing me into her warmth. "I know, sweetie. It's not over. It's just on hold."

I drop my keys on the floor and bury my forehead in Brie's shoulder, my eyes stinging. "I'm not allowed to be upset, am I?"

"You're supposed to be upset. You just haven't fully processed what you're actually upset about. Last night was traumatic."

"You wouldn't get it." I pull away from her and press my knuckles into my eye sockets. "I can't go home. Even if you weren't already signed, you have absolutely nothing at stake."

"That's not fair, or true."

I study her earnest mahogany eyes and perpetually furrowed brow. Her soft, cloudlike hair frames her face almost like a halo. She's always so neat and together. She doesn't belong in my nuclear mess of a room, or my life. She has brains, looks, money, and a perfect family. "You wouldn't get it," I whisper again.

"It's going to be open and shut," Brie says firmly, rising and gazing out the window again. "Clearly a suicide."

"What exactly are they investigating, then?"

"Whether there was foul play, I guess."

"Murder?"

"That's generally what they look into when someone dies a violent death."

The words echo in my brain. It was a violent death. She

looked so calm, so serene, but death is sharp and severe. It is violent by definition. "Here?"

"There are killers everywhere, Kay. In nursing homes and emergency rooms. Police stations. Everywhere you're supposed to be safe. Why not a boarding school?"

"Because we've been here four years and we know everyone."

Brie shakes her head. "Killers are people. They eat the same food and breathe the same air. They don't announce their presence."

"Maybe they do if you're listening."

Brie weaves her fingers through mine. My hands are always cold; hers are always warm. "It was a suicide. In a couple of days, athletics will be running again. You'll be recruited. No question."

The way the word *suicide* keeps rolling off her tongue with such ease is jarring. There's poison in it, eroding parts of me barely stitched together that I don't want Brie to see. "Now they're going to blanket bomb us with assemblies on warning signs and how not to kill ourselves and shit. Because that's so helpful after the fact." Which I guess it is to a point, when you consider Bates's history. It's better than nothing. But it does fuck all for the person who's gone and everyone who cared about them.

Brie hesitates. "Well, before the fact, we should definitely be nicer to people. You should think about that."

I gaze into her eyes and look for my shadow self somewhere in the depths. Maybe there is a better version of me somewhere out there, and if it exists, it is in Brie's mind. "Nice is subjective."

"Spoken like a true Bates girl. We are such a self-involved species. How into yourself do you have to be to not notice someone who's about to implode?"

For just a split second, I think she's talking about me.

But she isn't. She's talking about Jessica.

I breathe again.

"You're not running for president yet. It's not your job to be everyone's best friend. Just mine." I grab her into a big bear hug and tackle her.

She sighs and nestles her forehead into the nape of my neck. I allow one moment of serenity, breathing the scent of her hair, one moment in the alternate universe where I'm a good person and Brie and I are together. Then I force myself to sit up. "Did you try to call Justine?"

She pulls her cell phone out of her pocket, dialing as she speaks. "She isn't picking up. She sleeps late on Saturdays." Justine is Brie's girlfriend. Brie and I never date Bates students as a rule, so we mostly end up with students from Easterly, the local public high school. I recently split with *my* Easterly Ex, the eminently unfaithful Spencer Morrow. Tai had come up with that moniker while passionately disavowing him after we heard that he'd cheated, and for some reason it had cracked me up and become his nickname. I hear a faint, gravelly morning voice on the other side of the line, and Brie's face brightens. She pushes me off her and the room suddenly feels colder and emptier as she scrambles up, grabbing her coffee and darting into the hall. I wish Justine would sleep later on Saturdays. I wish she would sleep all weekend. I pick my way over to the window, careful not to trip on the land mine of clothes and textbooks and practice equipment. Laundry day isn't until tomorrow.

Outside, people swarm like it's moving-in day, but it's not just students and their families. A row of news vans lines the curb, beside which a handful of women holding clipboards pace anxiously and bark orders at tall guys with Steadicams strapped around their torsos. There are dozens of people wearing matching bright-blue T-shirts with a logo that looks like a cross between an infinity symbol and two linked hearts. Throngs of disheveled, homeless-looking townies mill around, bleary eyed, some of them crying. It's total chaos. It looks like the T-shirt people have set up a table and are providing coffee and bagels. Maybe I should head down to them instead of to the dining hall. It will be impossible to get to it in this mess, anyway.

I take the stairs two by two, hoping not to run into Jessica's family, who I assume are here to clear out her room. At the front door I find Jenny standing guard and I flash her a smile. "Get any sleep?" I ask.

She shakes her head. "Be safe, Kay."

"You want a coffee or anything?"

She smiles weakly. "That'd be great."

I hop over to the table where the people wearing the blue shirts are pouring coffees and handing out bagels and I grab two empty cups. I'm about to fill them when a guy standing behind the table yanks the cups out of my hand. I stare at him in shock. I know his face, but not his name. He's a student from Easterly, like Spencer and Justine, and a regular at their cast parties. Since Justine stars in most of their theater productions, I've seen him around quite a bit, but never onstage. He's probably a techie.

Sleeve tattoos cover his bare, muscular arms from wrist to elbow. His lower lip is pierced and his wavy dark hair tumbles over his eyes like he's just rolled out of bed. In skintight jeans and a torn-up black sweater, he looks like a washed-up rock star, complete with coke-chic sniffle and bloodshot eyes. Then I notice the balled-up tissue in his hand and wonder if he's not so much doing lines bright and early on a Saturday morning as he is crying.

My momentary sympathy dissolves the moment he opens his mouth.

"Bye-bye, now."

"I'm sorry, was I supposed to pay for those?"

He just glares. This guy's antisocial, a complete weirdo, even if he would be kind of hot without the tortured-artist vibe and holier-than-thou attitude. "They aren't for you," he finally says.

I look around, confused. "Who exactly are they for?"

He gestures wordlessly to the crowd.

"What?"

He sighs and his dark eyes narrow. He leans in close to me and whispers, looking embarrassed. "We're here for Jessica's people. The homeless."

"Oh." I straighten up. "I thought this was because of the crowd."

"That is the crowd," he says.

I look around again, and realize he's right. The people filling the parking lot don't just look homeless, they *are* homeless. Most of the people here are probably from shelters. I look back to sleeve-tattoo guy. "Why?"

"They're mourning a lost friend. Unlike some people." He flicks his hands. "Back to your lair."

I eye the coffee cups he took from me and then glance back at Jenny. "Could I just have one of those?"

He looks at me with contempt. "No. You can't. Go to Starbucks."

"Starbucks is a five-mile walk. And it's not for me." I point to Jenny. "That's Officer Jenny Biggs. She was on duty when the body was found. She hasn't slept since then. Can you imagine being up that long after finding a girl dead, a girl you'd sworn to protect?"

He sighs and pours a coffee, then hands it to me. "Fine. If I see you drinking that, I'll blacklist you."

I roll my eyes. "From your shelter?"

"Luck flips hard, Kay Donovan."

"Okay, Hank."

He looks confused. "My name is Greg."

I wink. "Now I know. And pull your sleeves down, it's freezing." I weave through the crowd and hand the coffee to Jenny, who knocks it back like a shot.

"I hope they figure this one out fast, kiddo." She flashes me an encouraging smile but doesn't look me in the eye, which is a little unsettling. I notice her tapping her phone against her thigh and wonder if she got news while I was talking to Greg.

"Is that likely?" I ask, knowing she won't answer.

She shrugs and gestures to the dorm. "Thanks for the coffee."

I head back to my room, wolf down a couple of energy bars and a Vitaminwater, then open up my laptop to google the news story. I learn that Jessica's family is local, and she started a nonprofit that helps the homeless find jobs and gives them basic computer training through an online learning program she designed herself. Pretty impressive for a high school student, even at Bates. Other than that, there isn't much. The news stories report that she was found in the lake shortly after midnight, cause of death undetermined. I read several more articles. No mention of her wrists.

None of the articles say foul play is suspected, but one says that her death is under investigation. I glance at the remaining match dates circled on my calendar. The clock is ticking. Each one of those dates is a desperately important deadline, and there is no reason to believe an investigation is going to be wrapped up in time for our games to resume so I can be scouted. My parents are going to flip.

As if on cue, my phone buzzes and I glance down at it. It's my father. I hesitate, but pick up.

"Hey, Dad."

"How was practice, buddy?"

"I had to cancel."

"Why?"

"Someone died. A student."

"Oh, buddy. One of your teammates?"

"No, someone else." I sit on the bed and draw my knees up to my chest. I usually check in with my parents on Sunday and it makes me a little nervous that he's calling off schedule. As if he's going to drop a bomb about something.

"Hmm."

"Is everything okay?"

"Maybe you should just stick to the routine. Keep up that stiff upper lip. You know, for the sake of the younger girls. To set an example."

It suddenly occurs to me that he probably read about Jessica's death already and that's exactly why he's calling. "It wasn't up to me, Dad. The school suspended athletic activities while the death is being investigated."

"What?" I hear my mother's voice in the background. Great. I should have known she was listening in. You can't mention death around my mother. I dig my fingernails into the back of my neck to punish myself for making that mistake. "Ask her about Monday." I hear her take the phone. "What about Monday's game?"

I curl into a ball and squeeze my eyes shut. "It's canceled. There is absolutely nothing I can do about it. I am no happier than you are. Believe me."

I hear my father curse in the background.

"That is unacceptable," my mother says. "Have you talked to Dr. Klein?"

"No, Mom. I did not reach out to the headmistress. I can't just call her and demand change. She's not Congress."

"You didn't even try? Do you want me to try? This is not the time to just sit back and hope for the best. We need to follow the plan."

"Someone did just die," I say quietly. But deliberately. Because I need this call to end.

She starts to say something but the words melt into a low sigh.

I bite my lower lip. There's a long silence. Then my mother speaks again, her voice unsteady. "Is there anything else you want to talk about, sweetie?"

"No," I say, holding my breath until it feels like my face is going to explode.

"Let's talk again soon," she says.

My father gets back on the phone. "Time to brainstorm, buddy. Make phone calls, write letters. Whatever it takes to get your offers locked in. You've worked too hard to let it all slip away. You ride this out like everything else. Right?"

"Right."

I hang up and let the breath out finally in an enormous whoosh, then punch my mattress and hug my pillow tightly to my chest. I wish Spencer wasn't eminently unfaithful. I wish Justine hadn't finally woken up so I could call Brie and vent. I wish my parents would just shut up and listen for once. None of that is going to go down the way I want it to. I can't play on Monday. I have no control over that. Damn you, Jessica Lane.

Then I sit up and force myself to take a deep, calming breath. I know the manner of death, I saw the body, and I know the family and her business are local. Cut wrists, high-pressure school. If the police can't open and shut a suicide case, it's because they're spread too thin. But I'm not. I've seen it happen. I've stood there helpless while it swirled around me, too slow to stop the moving pieces until everyone was in ruin. My best friend and my brother dead, my father devastated, my mother prepared to throw her life away, too. And me, encased in ice.

I close my fingers over my phone and turn it to silent, my mother's voice echoing in my head. I can fix this. I can. Before the next game is canceled.

A *ping* alerts me to a new email, and I glance over at my computer screen. The subject line reads "Athletic Scholarship Update." My heart begins to race and I pull my laptop over and open the message.

Dear Kay,

I regret to inform you that certain unsavory activities in your past have come to my attention and your eligibility for winning an athletic scholarship is at risk. I myself will be unable to attend college, so you have my sincerest sympathy. Therefore, if you agree to help me complete my final project, I may be able to overlook your transgressions.

Click on the link at the bottom of this email and follow my instructions. When you have completed each task, a name will disappear from the class roster. If you fail to complete any task within 24 hours, a link to the website along with proof of your crime will be sent to your parents, the police, and every student at Bates Academy.

If you succeed, no one will ever find out what you did.

Most cordially yours,
Jessica Lane

P.S. At the risk of sounding cliché, talking to the police would not go well for you, Kay. It never has, has it?

The email was sent from Jessica's Bates account. For a moment the thought that she's still alive runs through my mind and I don't know whether to laugh or cry. Maybe it's all been one massive, surreal mistake. Of course, that would also mean we left a bleeding victim alone in a lake. It would be a miracle, but we'd probably be guilty of attempted homicide or something. Oh God, I am dead meat. Then I talk myself down. I know, without a doubt, that she is dead.

It's possible that someone else sent the email from her account. But the idea is so twisted, I can't even entertain it. She must have written the message before she died and timed it to be sent now. The wording makes it look like she knew she was going to die. Her *final* project. Not attending college. Or maybe I'm reading into it. Finals are looming and there are tons of reasons people don't go to college.

This email might convince the cops that she wasn't murdered after all. I could take it to the police and possibly end the investigation right now.

But the postscript sends a chill down my spine.

There is a link at the bottom of the page that says jessicalanefinalproject.com. I click on it.

The screen goes blank for a long moment and then an image of a rustic country kitchen with a cast-iron stove appears. Letters slowly fog up on the glass window of the stove until the name of the site is crystal clear: *Revenge Is a Dish: A Delicious Guide to Taking Down Your Enemies.*

3

i click on the link frantically, but the site is password protected. *Revenge Is a Dish.* Jessica's final project was revenge. And she sent it straight to me. I make one more pointless attempt to open the site and then push my laptop as far away from me as I can. I can't take my eyes off it, though.

I wish Spencer hadn't screwed things up so royally. A devoted gamer as well as an athlete, he would be able to hack into the site effortlessly. I scroll down through my recent-calls list. He's never been more than one swipe down and it depresses me. I keep expecting him to call to apologize again, to check on me, to tell me something random reminded him of me. But apparently, nothing ever does.

I drop my phone onto the bed and turn back to my laptop. I log on to the school community network and scroll through the student body, looking for someone who might be able to help. Bates is a strong STEM school, and a decent number of students know at least some coding. Maddy, Brie, and Cori have all taken STEM-heavy course loads. I could try Maddy—she's taken the most coding classes—but I'm hesitant. Based on the threat in the letter, I don't want my friends anywhere near Jessica's project, and least of all Maddy. I would rather not have anyone I interact with at all involved. The less social credibility, the better. Just in case they learn something and it's my word against theirs.

Nola Kent. There's a little green dot next to her name, indicating that she's online. I hesitate before sending her a personal message. Two years ago, when Nola was a new transfer, Tai and Tricia and I had been a little hard on her. Mostly behind her back. We may have come up with a well-chosen nickname or rumor or two. But that was ages ago. She'd probably feel more awkward than I did if I brought it up. Not our fault if she dresses like a cross between a funeral director and a killer doll. And she's come to a few soccer games since then, so I figure no hard feelings.

Hey, you there? I hit enter and wait.

Her class picture pops up along with ellipses to show she's responding. She is very short and waiflike, with long, thick dark hair that seems to overwhelm the rest of her body. Her skin is porcelain white and she has bright-blue eyes that are so round, she always looks stunned. The word that comes to mind when I think of Nola Kent is *slight*. She's just not very much of anything, or so we thought when we started messing with her. But it turned out that she has an extremely valuable little quirk. She can wreak havoc with codes and systems. Hi.

I'm having trouble getting into a website.

Is it password protected?

Yes.

Do you have the password?

No.

Are you supposed to?

It's a long story.

Tell me.

I sigh. I need to know what Jessica thought she had on me, and what she meant by enemies and revenge. And Nola is my best shot at finding out and keeping the information contained.

Let's meet.

Where? Swarmed.

Library.

In five.

I slip out the back entrance of the dormitory to avoid the crowds and head down the hill to the library. Outside, the air smells like wood smoke and cider, the way it should on an early November Saturday. The sounds of the reporters and mourners still carry over from the front of the building. Some of them have begun singing hymns, while others continue to talk. It's like a cross between an outdoor wake and a giant tailgate. It's gauche and bizarre and creepy. Beyond the crowd of mourners, there actually aren't too many students out on the green between the dorms and the academic quad, and I slow my pace and kick at the dead leaves contemplatively. This was supposed to be a huge day. Practice until five, dinner with Brie and Justine, and then we were all going to make a definitive decision on whether Spencer could ever be trusted again. I mean, the answer is probably pretty obvious. According to Justine, an extremely reliable source of gossip at Easterly, he cheated on me with a Bates student at the café where we had our first official date. But people change. Everyone's done regrettable stuff in the past. Raise your hand if you haven't. Yeah.

I head to the top floor of the library, where I'm least likely to run into anyone else, and send Nola a text to let her know I've arrived. The top floor is totally retro. It houses VHS tapes, microfilms, and an old-school card catalogue. Everything up here must be valuable somehow or the school wouldn't hang on to it. But it's basically an old media boneyard, and I'm pretty sure no one is going to bother us up here. I find a comfortable, moth-bitten green corduroy armchair that's probably as old as the VHS collection and settle into it, unfolding my laptop on my knees.

"Hi."

A low shriek escapes my lips. Nola is perched atop a bookshelf just above my head, dressed all in black like the goddamned Raven.

"What are you doing up there?"

She leaps down nimbly and leans her chin over my shoulder, stretching a bony wrist out to type on my keyboard. "Waiting for your slow ass." She nudges me with her shoulder until I make room for her on the chair and surrender the computer to her completely. She inspects the revenge website and then turns her enormous eyes on me. "Why are we stalking a dead girl?"

I shift in the chair uncomfortably. This is too close for someone I barely know, and my idea now sounds completely stupid even to me. "Like I said, it's a long story. Can you just take it on faith that it's really important that I get into this website?"

She narrows her eyes. "Why?"

I hesitate for a moment. Jessica said not to go to the cops. She didn't say anything about Nola Kent. "Jessica asked me to."

She pauses. "Were you friends?"

There are moments for lies. "Close, but not best."

"Why didn't she give you the password?"

"Look. I need to read what's on that website. Jessica left me a message and I have no other way to access it. It's basically her last words."

She closes my laptop. "That's not very compelling."

"What do you want?"

"You don't have any money." She says it so matter-of-factly. If she'd said it more viciously, it would have stung less.

"You don't need any," I say. It's true. She's like the others. She may not dress like them or act like them, but her family is old New England money.

That seems to catch her off guard, and she hesitates before answering. "Put me on your team when you start up again."

My mouth drops open. "But—you've never even come to a tryout."

She shrugs, her face bland, expressionless. "I didn't say I was interested. I said I wanted in."

I gape at her. "I don't have that kind of power. Coach makes those decisions."

She is thoroughly unconvinced. "You have enough influence."

"I would have to cut someone who worked really hard to get there."

"Well," she says slowly. "That's the choice I'm offering you."

I consider this. I do have enough influence. As captain, I all but run the team. At Bates, teachers and coaches encourage students to take on full responsibility and leadership of our organizations. I hate the idea of cutting someone who earned their spot. On the other hand, I need Nola's help. I reluctantly give her my hand and she shakes it with cool fingers.

"Excellent," she says. "I've always wanted to be awesome." She shoots me a mocking look. "I can be awesome now, right?"

I allow her full rein over my laptop uneasily. "Don't close any windows."

"Got it." She opens it and taps her fingers lightly on the keys. Then she opens a new window and starts downloading something.

"Hey!" I grab for the computer, but she yanks it out of my reach.

"Relax. I'm not going to destroy your Jurassic operating system. I'm downloading a program I use all the time that's pretty good at cracking passwords. Jessica was a fairly sophisticated programmer, but the human mind can only dream up so many permutations . . ."

"Did you know her?"

"Only from comp sci classes. Never spoke." She runs the program and types furiously and then turns to me triumphantly. "See?"

The word *L@br@d0r* is highlighted on the screen.

I stare at her. "Could you figure out my passwords that easily?"

She hands the laptop back to me. "Don't ask if you don't want to know."

I click back on the blog and type in the password. The oven opens and inside, the title of the site appears again in seared red letters: *Revenge Is a Dish: A Delicious Guide to Taking Down Your Enemies.* I click on the title and six categories appear below: appetizer, first course, main course, palate cleanser, side dish, dessert. I click on appetizer and a graphic of a burned tennis ball appears with a recipe for Tai Burned Chicken. At the same time, an icon of an oven timer pops up, set at 24:00:00. It immediately starts ticking down. I click on the timer but there's no way to stop or alter it.

Nola tries typing a few commands and shrugs. "Maybe the link only stays live for twenty-four hours?" But I know better. That's the time I have to complete my task.

I click on the next recipe, but an error message pops up, reading, *Oven in use. Revisit kitchen when timer resets.*

"Adorable," Nola says.

As I scan the recipe, the corners of my lips begin to turn up. It has to be a joke.

> *Take a chicken, white and red*
> *Mock it till it's good and dead*
> *Brand it with a 3.5*
> *Burn it if it's still alive*
> *Stuff with Sharapova's shame*
> *Take her out and watch the flames.*

Nola looks at me out of the corner of her eye. "I'm no master of poetic imagery, here, but it looks like Jessica had some grand plans for Tai Carter. What did Tai do to her?"

I frown. "I don't think they really knew each other." When we found the body, Tai couldn't even remember her name. How much damage can you do to someone whose name you don't know?

Nola shrugs. "Poetry gives me migraines. The way everything means something else. According to Mr. Hannigan, anyway. But look at it line by line, Hannigan style, starting with the title." She runs a finger along underneath the text, assuming our English teacher's slight Irish lilt. It's unfortunate that she doesn't have his rugged handsome features, because that might soften the disturbing imagery. Her fingers are slender and delicate and her nails painted a glossy eggplant color, and the blue light issuing from my laptop just makes her look paler and thinner as she peers into the screen.

'Tai Burned Chicken,' she reads. "Thai's spelled wrong, unless it really means your girl. Burned. It's a food blog but it's about revenge, right? And chicken. Again, food, but also coward."

"Tai's no coward," I say.

She looks at me, interested. "Oh?"

I have zero interest in defending my friends to Nola Kent, of all people. "Trust me," I say.

Nola looks disappointed. "Okay," she says, rolling her

eyes elaborately. "I *trust* you." She moves on to the next line. "'Take a chicken, white and red.' Bates school colors, obviously. 'Mock it till it's good and dead.' Now, I don't know her as well as you do, but does your bosom buddy not have something of a reputation as a wiseass?"

I grin. "She does." Tai isn't just funny, she is incisively clever. It makes it that much more painful when she turns her acerbic observations on you. She'll be the next Tina Fey or Amy Schumer, there's no possible doubt about that. But even Tina Fey admitted she was a mean girl in high school. Not that I'm calling Tai mean. It's just that the truth hurts, especially when people laugh about it. And Tai is egalitarian. Everyone gets their turn. I'm the perennial borrower. That's her bit for me. A sort of icy wave of nausea washes over me when she begins a borrower routine, but everyone gets theirs. People laughed when I gave Lada Nikulaenkov the nickname Hodor, because she's about six feet tall and so shy you never hear her talk except to correct teachers on the pronunciation of her name. But I couldn't do it if I didn't also force a smile every time Tai pointed out that fact that I can't afford to buy the clothes I wear. It's a two-way street. Fair is fair.

"Also," Nola adds, "there's that insufferable 'mock' thing from *Henry V* Hannigan was harping on last month. Tennis balls, right?"

"Oh my God!" I tend to cram for exams and then let the

information whoosh back out of my brain, but Shakespeare did write a speech where he used the word *mock* repeatedly to imitate the sound tennis balls make smacking around the court. "So I guess Jessica did like poetry."

"Or Mr. Hannigan," Nola says, raising an eyebrow archly.

"Stop." I suddenly feel ashamed for discussing Jessica so casually, as if she were just another classmate we were free to bitch about. So what if she had a crush on a teacher? Hannigan is the clear choice if you had to pick one. He's new at Bates this year, extremely sexy, and at times flirtatious. There have been rumors about more than flirting, but no proof. I don't believe it. That accent, though. I turn back to the "recipe" and read the next line. "'Brand it with a three-point-five.' That's Tai's GPA." This is public knowledge. GPAs are posted in the Great Hall to motivate/shame us.

"'Burn it if it's still alive,'" Nola continues. She looks to me.

"A burn. An insult. Tai's specialty. Blurring the line between funny and painful."

"How is a burn different from a mock?"

"A mock is a sport. A burn is deadly."

"Then there's 'Sharapova's shame.' Which sounds like bad community theater."

"Seriously? Maria Sharapova is a tennis superstar. There was a huge scandal a couple years ago when she was suspended for doping. But it's complicated, because the drug she took is a legitimate medication, too."

"Whatever, I couldn't care less. What this says to me is your girl Tai is pulling a Sharapova. The question is, how did Jessica know?"

"Well, *if* it were true, all she would have to do is hack into Tai's email to know anything Tai ever mentioned there, right?"

Dance like no one's watching.

Nola nods. "Jess was a solid coder. Those computer skills training programs she built were legit."

"But I don't believe Tai did this. People like us don't use drugs. It's automatic expulsion."

Nola favors me with a slightly contemptuous smile. "People like you?"

I feel my face warm. "Tai could go pro someday. My friends and I have a lot to lose."

"How dreary to be somebody," Nola says.

I think about my brother. After he died, the newspaper articles focused on his athletic accomplishments and didn't touch the kind of person he was, the good or the bad. Megan's death was treated quite differently. She wasn't a star athlete or a student at a prestigious prep school. There were articles, but they didn't talk about her accomplishments, her hopes and dreams, everything that made her special. Only what happened to her.

"We all have a lot to lose," I say. "Bates is a golden ticket. You don't throw it away."

The sun is beginning to set outside, and pink and orange rays filter in through the attic window and illuminate Nola's pale face, making her eyes glow. "Why did Jessica?"

4

*b*efore I go looking for Tai, I stop by Brie's room to drop the *Gatsby* costume off. I pause outside before knocking to listen for signs that she's busy and hear muffled giggling. Justine is visiting. Great. I smooth out the fine, silky layers of fabric and leave it on the polished wood floor next to her door, then head for the stairs. I hate being the constant borrower (and occasional thief), relying on friends, acquaintances, and even random students to provide my wardrobe during the hours we're allowed to ditch our uniforms. But it's necessary. The *Gatsby* costume is one of the most extraordinary things I've ever worn. The fabric made my skin feel electric. Daisy Buchanan was an exciting person to be. Sleek and sexy and a little dangerous. I'm sad to return her to Brie, but it's too conspicuous of an item to "forget" to return.

When I step outside, the sun is bleeding over the lake, a bloom of fiery orange and red through the black knots of branches, giving the illusion that early autumn has returned. I head across the courtyard toward the athletic complex as the chapel bells ring out a tune I don't recognize, and gaze back at the silhouette of the main campus. It's stunning at sunset—like a cross between an Ivy League university and Hogwarts, with beautiful Gothic architecture, spindly towers, and quaint Elizabethan cottages.

Tai is practicing alone at the tennis court in the waning light. The school has indoor courts, but Tai likes to practice in all weather conditions because not all schools do. Her form is perfect as she elegantly swoops, arcs, and slices down on the ball. My chest muscles relax as I near the court, and I feel my shoulders drop reflexively. Tai has no reason to cheat. She is so far above the rest of the team that it's actually embarrassing to watch them practice. My heart sinks again. Why is she so good?

I throw my hands up against the chain-link fence and growl like a zombie, and she whirls around and hurls her tennis racket at me.

"What the hell, Kay? I thought you were that lake girl for a second." She shakes her damp hair out of her ponytail and combs it with her fingers. She's dressed in a spotless white tennis outfit accented with the signature Bates scarlet.

That wipes the smile off my face. "Too soon."

"Don't sneak up on me." She retrieves her racket and inspects it for scratches.

"Want to grab dinner?"

She makes a face. "People are going to be crying and acting all melodramatic like their mom died."

Quintessential Tai. Her mom did die freshman year, but she drops this line with a straight face, and she'd be furious if I showed an ounce of sympathy. I punch her arm. "Someone *did* die."

"But, like, no one important."

"Seriously, Tai."

She smiles, her lips cutting into a sharp, asymmetrical V shape. Tai has taut skin that makes it look like her hair is always being stretched back tight, even when it's hanging loosely around her face; a sharp nose and jaw; and eyelashes and eyebrows so light, they're invisible without makeup. "I am serious. Her friends should be sad. I remember this girl, though. She didn't have Bates friends. She was a townie."

"So we don't feel bad because she wasn't rich?"

Tai rolls her eyes. "That's not what I said. Jessica Lane was a thief."

I laugh out loud. "Everything I've read says she was Mother Teresa."

"Well, she wasn't. First year, we lived on the same floor,

and my mother had sent this really beautiful box of designer soaps from Provence."

"Jessica stole your soap?"

She grins, embarrassed, but I can see she's actually upset. She doesn't mention her mother very often. "I can't prove it. But they were gone and she smelled like them. And I didn't see my mother after that, or even hear from her again, so that was important soap."

I link my arm through hers as we near the courtyard and the dorms. "Okay. She was a thief."

She's quiet for a moment. "So I stole her hard drive."

"Why?"

"I gave it back. Just not until after our papers were due." She sighs. "It's the sort of thing that bugs you after someone dies. You remember little ways you wronged them. Even if they deserved it."

A breeze blows my scarf up into my face and I remove my arm from hers to straighten it. Now or never. Just ask. "I need your advice."

Misleading. Sometimes misleading is necessary.

"Sure."

I take a deep breath and gaze around campus. The sun has sunk just below the horizon, painting the Gothic architecture of the quad against a velvety blue background. The lights issuing from the lampposts that line the stone path are a soft glowing yellow, like jars filled with hundreds of fireflies gently swaying above us. "Would you ever consider taking a performance-enhancing drug?"

Tai runs her pale eyes over me with a trace of condescension. "Who wouldn't? If you weren't going to get caught, it's no different from drinking coffee so you can study longer."

My throat tightens and I try to conceal my anxiety. Her answer doesn't bode well. "It's a little different."

"For example, meldonium, the drug Maria Sharapova got caught taking. It's perfectly legal."

"Not in the U.S." I stick my hands in my pockets. I've forgotten how to act casual. Hands are the biggest obstacle. There's nothing for them to do. It was the hardest part of picking up soccer. My reflex was to grab at the ball, protect my face, flail. Hands are too much a part of us. They give us away.

"It's prescribed all the time in Russia. All it does is increase blood flow, which enhances your exercise capacity."

"Yeah, but it's banned for a reason. It gives you an advantage."

She stops walking and faces me, unsmiling. "You're not looking for advice."

I sigh and look her in the eye. "What do you want me to say?"

"Nothing. I'm not having this conversation." She begins walking away.

"You need to turn yourself in."

She whirls around, her eyes wide as moons in the lamplight. "Excuse me?"

"Someone knows. They're trying to blackmail me into doing it, and if you do it first, it's going to make you look better."

Her face turns white. "Look better? It's a zero-tolerance policy. I'll be expelled. I told you because I trusted you and I know you need to up your game, too. At first I thought you were asking me for help."

My mouth feels like it's made of the dry leaves we're walking on. "No. I'm sorry."

"Is this about Georgetown? I'll call right now and turn them down. We're not even up for the same sport, Kay. You get that, right?"

"It's not about that. I'm telling you the truth."

She shakes her head. "Wow. Kay, I know you're threatened by success, but this is next level."

"Or maybe you're too scared of losing to compete fairly." I can see a couple of people open their windows and I lower my voice. "I'm dead serious. Someone knows. How do you think I found out?"

"So name them." She towers over me. "Otherwise, I know it's you."

I shake my head. "I'd tell you if I could, but they have

something on me, too. Believe me when I say it's bad. Please, Tai. If you turn yourself in, the school might be lenient." There are all kinds of lies. There are self-preserving lies and anesthetic lies.

"If something happens to me, it's on you," she says, but there's pleading in her voice.

I start walking again toward the dining hall. I know if she says one more thing, I'm going to burst into tears.

But then she says it.

"Fine. But, Kay? No matter what happens to me, you will leave Bates with no honors, no scholarship, and no future, and you'll head right back to the hole in the ground you crawled out of before you got here. I can get thrown out and I'll still be headed to the Ivies next year. But hey, maybe if you didn't spend so much time borrowing my clothes and trying to get under Brie's, you would actually be a threat."

I turn slowly and face her, my thoughts running too quickly for me to catch one and process it. Say something. Say nothing. Ruin her. Forgive. "I *am* a threat," I say quietly. She has no idea.

She continues advancing until our faces are inches apart. "Everyone has their own priorities. Mine are succeeding and making a name for myself. Yours are playing dress-up and not having sex."

Gauntlet thrown.

AT DINNER, THE entire dining hall is somber and no one talks much. Saturday evenings are always pretty quiet because most upperclasswomen get advance permission to eat off campus, but tonight almost everyone stays home in solidarity. Mrs. March, our housemother, has been crying all day judging by her beet-red face and bloodshot eyes. She sits quietly in a corner and picks at her food. I feel like I should go and say something to her, but I don't know what there is to say. I'm not sure "I'm sorry for your loss" is appropriate, because it's not quite her loss. The administration and staff are always saying Bates is a family, but we're not really. We're more like a team, but even that's not completely true. We're two teams. The faculty and staff are one team, and the students are another. From there it gets even more complicated, and I say this with the measured authority of a two-year team captain. Despite what coaches hammer into your head from the time you're a toddler running frantically around a field kicking or swinging at air, not every team member is essential.

That's why there are cuts. That's why there are benches. That's why the constant fear of failure looms over you throughout the season, and over the summer, too, in the off-season, in the preseason, in your sleep the night before a big game. Even as a team captain, knowing that bad decisions can sink you and you can be rendered inessential in the blink of an eye. Mistakes matter. Jessica may have been part of the student team. But I won't feel her loss. I feel bad about that. More empty than bad.

After my epic blowup with Tai, I decide to sit alone and avoid further drama. Tai can have custody of our friends tonight. I don't have the energy for another battle. The round oak tables of the dining hall seat six and most of them are filled to capacity. I take a stack of five empty plates and spread them around the table to put people on notice that I'm not looking for company. A few soccer teammates offer sympathetic waves as they pass, and I get a couple of hushed "I'm so sorries" from random juniors and sophomores who probably assume I'm in mourning or something. For the most part, though, I'm left in peace. But after a few minutes, a pair of arms wind around my waist and I feel Brie's cheek against mine.

"How are you, lovey?"

The evil feelings dissolve. I smile up at her. "Terrible. Did Justine leave?"

She settles down across from me. "Rehearsal. Life goes on at Easterly. So I hear you attacked Tai in the courtyard."

I sigh into my hand. "Sure. I attacked Tai in the courtyard. With a candlestick."

She leans forward, her eyes practically glowing. The only thing Brie loves more than dark chocolate with caramel and sea salt is gossip. "Kay." She draws my name out seductively and my eyes focus on her lips.

"Tai's doping," I blurt out.

She drums her fingers on the table and chews on her lower lip. "Are you sure?"

"Beyond a doubt."

"I'm not calling you a liar . . . I just . . . it doesn't sound like Tai." She doesn't believe me. I don't blame her. I didn't believe it either.

"That doesn't mean she didn't do it."

"Let's play lawyer," she suggests brightly. This is one of Brie's favorite games. She gets to show off how clever she is and make it seem like fun. In her opinion, truth and justice naturally prevail. And generally, she wins.

"Fine."

"You prosecute and I'll defend."

"Okay . . ." This is going to be tough. I can't tell Brie about the revenge blog, and I don't have any other physical evidence. "Tai Carter is one of the most talented tennis players Bates Academy has ever seen. She outmatches every other player she's gone against. There's no doubt she has unbelievable natural talent. But she supplements it. I don't have physical evidence, though I'm pretty sure we can obtain it. The fact is, Tai has admitted to using meldonium, the very performance-enhancing drug that got Maria Sharapova a two-year suspension. And a confession is the most damning evidence of all."

Brie's mouth drops open. "The defense rests. But how did you know?"

"Anonymous email."

"That's creepy. Obviously the most likely sender is someone else on the tennis team. I wonder why they sent it to you, though. Why wouldn't they just turn her in?"

"They want me to turn her in. If I don't, they will."

"What are you going to do?"

I shrug. "I told her she should turn herself in. They're more likely to be lenient on her. That was the full extent of my so-called attack. She flipped out on me."

Brie glances over at "our" table. The rest of our friends are huddled together whispering. Tricia shoots me a reproachful look. "This isn't going to end well."

I want to tell Brie about the revenge blog so badly. This is just the beginning. But I can't risk involving her. I decide to throw wide.

"Did you know Tai knew Jessica?"

Brie raises a shoulder and rests her chin on her hand. "She said she didn't."

"She stole her hard drive and made her turn in a paper late."

"So what? You think Jessica's behind this? When did you get this email?"

"I didn't open it until today."

"And it was anonymous." She shudders. "That timing is unfortunate. Does Tai know?"

"If Jessica ever threatened her, Tai didn't think it went beyond the two of them. She was completely caught off guard when I mentioned it. *And* she seemed surprised that I thought there was anything wrong with it. Although I guess I led her down that road."

"Keep all that between us." Brie rubs her forehead wearily. "Tai's as good as gone," she says in a soft voice. "I don't think there's any way around it. You're right, though—it might be better if she's the one to turn herself in. Maybe if I talk to her." She turns back to me suddenly. "You didn't tell anyone else?"

"Of course I didn't." Tai would flip if she found out Nola knew. Not that she's ever going to forgive me anyway.

"Because Tricia and Cori will hound you. And especially Maddy." She makes just the ghost of a face.

"Why don't you like Maddy?"

She raises her eyebrows. "Don't put words in my mouth." She looks over my head and waves at a table of debate club members. They are the only people on campus who wear suits when out of uniform. It gives me a headache to look at them.

I hesitate. "Is it just me or does it feel a little like everyone is slightly anti-Maddy lately?"

She flicks her eyes back to me. "Anti?"

"It doesn't seem like she appreciates her new nickname."

Brie nods. "Maybe people will drop it now that Tai has bigger things to worry about."

"But, like . . . Notorious? B.I.G. or what?"

Brie bursts out laughing. "More like R.B.G. I think. Maddy isn't exactly a hip-hop enthusiast."

"What's Notorious R.B.G.?"

Her smile fades. "Ruth Bader Ginsburg," she says hurriedly. "The Supreme Court justice."

"What does that have to do with Maddy?"

"Ask Tai." Brie sighs, sinking her heart-shaped face into her hand. "I hate her nicknames. Can we just drop Maddy?"

I don't get Brie sometimes. She has zero enemies, and she rarely talks shit about anyone. But when she does, it's always the last person I would ever guess, and in such a roundabout way that I can never figure out what exactly they did to piss her off. It's like she's nudging me to guess so she doesn't have to dirty her hands. I'm not up to playing the game tonight. Luckily, I don't have to.

"Have the police followed up with you yet?"

I blank for a moment. "I didn't call the police."

"Good. Because that would make you look really weird. Maybe guilty weird. Just play it cool."

It occurs to me that she isn't referring to the revenge website, but the detective from the crime scene.

"So you think she'll follow up?"

Brie nods. "We were the only witnesses." My expression must reflect exactly how I feel about facing the police, because she pushes her tray aside and looks into my eyes. "Repeat after me: I am not going to prison."

I flick a balled-up paper straw wrapper at her. "You are not going to prison."

"Every one of us has an alibi."

"It's not exactly an airtight alibi," I point out. "We split up for a half hour between the dance and the lake. Tricia called her boyfriend, Tai went for more drinks, I went to change out of my sexy boots—"

Brie rolls her eyes. "Then we'd all be suspects. *If* there was a homicide. But there wasn't."

"Then why would they still be investigating?"

"Because it's been less than twenty-four hours, Kay. If that detective calls us again, we just all say we were together the whole time. Problem solved."

"Well, make sure everyone gets the memo, Brie." I hesitate. "Didn't it seem like that detective was kind of singling me out a little?"

"Paranoid. Anyway, I told you not to take this investigation too seriously." She pushes her chair back and glances across the dining hall. "I'm going to go talk to Tai."

I follow her gaze and see Nola lying down on a bench at the side of the room, laptop open on her chest. She raises a shoeless foot in an odd sort of wave, displaying black paisley stockings under her skirt.

Brie looks back at me quizzically.

I wave my fork at Nola and avoid Brie's eyes. "Homework help."

"Why didn't you ask *me*?"

"You lack the requisite skills." I grin flirtatiously.

"Is that so?" She shoots another glance at Nola. "Interesting."

"She's not that weird."

"Since when?"

"You're the one who said we should be nicer to people."

"To Necro?" Brie whispers.

I glance around the dining hall to make sure Nola isn't within earshot. "Tai came up with that nickname."

"You used it."

"You laughed."

She drops her eyes. "It wasn't funny."

"It was also ages ago, and no one says it anymore. Except you, apparently. So, do you have a problem with me studying with Nola?"

Brie laughs suddenly and I feel better. I'm physically incapable of seeing her smile without smiling back. It's biochemical. "God, no. I just feel bad. It's completely self-serving on your part," she points out.

"Not so," I say. "We made a deal. I'm—" I pause. Brie wouldn't approve of me persuading Coach to kick someone off the team to make room for Nola. "Giving her soccer lessons."

She looks thoroughly unconvinced, but raises a glass of milk to clink mine. "Well played, Kay." She takes a thoughtful sip. "But cross the hacker and it's your funeral."

At the next table, Abigail Hartford stops talking and glares at Brie for her poor choice of words, and then quickly looks down, blushing. People don't glare at Brie. She's too nice. But Brie looks mortified.

"You know what I mean," she whispers. She stands. "Okay, I'm going back to the other table."

"Yes. Speaking of which. Is Justine coming to the memorial tomorrow?"

Brie shakes her head. "I'm not subjecting her to that. It was bad enough just walking across campus this morning. Try cramming that festival of mourning into Irving Chapel."

"Should be fun."

"Why?"

"I wanted to ask her about an Easterly guy. He does theater. You wouldn't know him, but she definitely does."

"Try me, sexy."

"Okay. His name is Greg. He's tall, sleeve tattoos, annoying attitude, I think he might have known Jessica."

She grins. "You are so in the dark, it's adorable. Creepy Greg was Jessica's boyfriend. Even I know that."

"So you *did* know Jessica," I say, annoyed at her tone. "More than the fact that she took trig."

Brie's cheeks flush slightly. "Only through Justine. Anything else you want to ask me?"

"Guess not."

She leans across the table and plays with the friendship bracelet I always wear around my wrist. It's one of the few relics I allow myself to wear from home, a simple suede band with a heart seared on the inside. Megan made it for me one summer at camp. "Don't worry about Tai," Brie says. "We've all been there."

It always gives me emotional whiplash when she goes from talking about Justine to touching me. "What?"

"She isn't very nice sometimes. I mean, in her heart she is. But the things she says aren't. You can't just slap the label of comedy on anything and expect people to be okay with it. I've cried over some of the things she's said."

"Like what?"

She shakes her head. "I'm not repeating them. Ever."

"Why?"

She looks me straight in the eye. "Because if we fought, you'd know exactly what to say to destroy me. And if you said those things, our friendship would be dead with no chance of revival."

"I can't believe she hurt you that bad and you never said anything."

She swallows as if her mouth has gone completely dry. "You've come dangerously close to crossing that line yourself, Kay."

I break eye contact. I just can't. "But you and Tai are still friends."

She places her napkin on the corner of the table and begins to methodically smooth and fold it into smaller and smaller triangles. "That's the way it is with Tai. We all just kind of go along with it. None of us is any better. Everyone has a dark side."

I push my plate away, my stomach churning, panic beginning to rise as I wonder if my name could possibly be on the revenge blog. After all, Tai's was, and we're part of the same group. I'm guilty of some teasing and hazing, too, especially at the beginning of the year and tryout season, but I never do anything downright mean.

Almost never.

THAT NIGHT, I go for a run on the indoor track. I always prefer running the path around the lake, with the inviting scent of pines surrounding me, but tonight I'm too shaken to run out there alone. When I get back to my dorm, I grab my phone in the dark and dial Justine's number. She picks up and I can hear Sia playing loudly in the background.

"Hold on!" she shouts into the phone. The music quiets down. "Hey, Kay."

"Hi. I have a favor to ask."

"Are you all right?" Her soft voice is tinged with concern.

"Powering through. Do you have Greg's number?"

"Newman? Weiss? Vanderhorn?"

"Creepy Greg?" I cringe at the words.

"Lots of tattoos, lip ring, Dr. Glares-a-lot?"

"Yes! That's him."

She laughs. "You could have described him physically instead of throwing a random nickname at me."

"Sorry. That's what Brie called him. I assumed it was a thing. Can you give me his number?"

"Hold on. Let me grab the contact sheet." I hear the sound of ruffling papers. "What do you need with Judgy McJudgerson?"

"I just want to ask him a few questions about Ms. Lane."

Her voice softens again. "Oh, honey, do you need to talk?"

"No, I'm fine. I just want to jump-start things back to normal. Move the investigation along."

"Here we go." She reads the number to me.

"Muchas." I hang up and dial Greg's number. It rings five or six times and then goes to voice mail. I hang up and try again. This time he picks up on the first ring.

"Hello?" He sounds irritated and groggy.

"Hi. This is Kay Donovan looking for Greg . . ." I trail off, realizing I don't have his last name.

"This is Greg Yeun. It's not a very good time."

"Okay, I'm sorry."

"Wait. Kay Donovan?" He sounds annoyed. "How did you get my number?"

"From Justine Baker."

He groans loudly. "What do you want?"

"I'll call back."

"I'm awake now."

"It's eight thirty on a Saturday night."

"I've been up since four. You?"

I bite my tongue. "I'm so sorry to bother you. I've been thinking over how rude I was to you today. So I'm sorry for that."

"Sure."

"Also, I heard you were dating Jessica and I'm trying to learn a little more about her. I know this is the worst possible time, but—"

He sighs. "Are you a reporter for your school newspaper or something?"

"No. I'm conducting a personal investigation."

He snorts. "So you're a future detective."

"Not exactly. I . . . care a lot about what happened to Jessica. That's the truth. It may sound weird, but it's personal for me, even though we weren't friends."

"We dated but it was over."

The ex-boyfriend is always a suspect. Everyone but everyone knows that. "Can we meet by any chance?"

He pauses. "Now?"

I check my watch. "Sure." I don't have permission to leave campus, but I'm too amped up to care. Brie and I have slipped out to the street by the far side of the lake and hiked to town dozens of times. It's okay as long as we keep a low profile.

"Fine," he says. "Where do you want to meet?"

"Do you know the Cat Café?"

"Twenty minutes."

5

i spend a few minutes digging through my closet before heading out to meet with Greg. Fashion gets a reputation for being frivolous, but it's the one form of art I understand. It has the ability to transform bodies and environments, to conceal or seduce, to break hearts or make them sing. The first time I slipped into my school uniform, I almost cried. I locked myself in my mother's room and spent an hour examining myself in her full-length mirror from every angle. I tried on a dozen different postures, hundreds of expressions, even tones and pitches and cadences of speech. It technically fit my body, but not *me*. And when I finally packed the fitted navy blazer and plaid skirt, the white shirt with a strip of ruffled fabric along the buttons that was softer than any sheets I'd ever slept in, and the scarlet tie in my suitcase, I felt like a different person.

Now, if I dress a little bit like Greg, I might have a shot at earning his trust. It's a subtle subconscious thing. But it works.

People trust people who are like them. Accordingly, I select a pair of black Alexander McQueen patchwork jeans, which Tricia is never going to get back, and a dark collared shirt. I pull my hair into a tight bun, which makes me look slightly older and a little like a detective from a police procedural. I throw a notebook into my backpack along with my laptop and grab my reading glasses for good measure. I don't really need them, but they make me look studious. After a moment of consideration, I decide to wear my navy wool overcoat. I almost never wear it around campus, because it's way too big, has been torn and mended in several places, and generally looks like a thrift store reject. But it's warmer than the considerably more flattering Balenciaga bomber jacket Tai got me last Christmas, and I'm not planning on running into anyone who matters tonight. It also makes me feel safe somehow. It was my brother's coat, and I feel weirdly close to him when I wear it.

At the sign-out desk downstairs I smile at the security guard and write *library* in the destination box, and then once I sign in to the library, I sneak out the back door and head for the lake.

It's even colder tonight than it was last night, but I have the benefit of my warm wool coat now. The sky is clear and the moon and stars reflect sharply off the still water. I avoid the spot where Brie discovered Jessica's body and hurry around the shore, making sure to keep under the cover of bushes so I'm not spotted. Now would not be a great time to get caught sneaking out.

The Cat Café has always been my favorite clandestine meeting spot. It's within walking distance of campus, though not close enough to be frequented by many students or faculty. It's tiny and serves only plain coffee, tea, and decaf. There are seven other cafés in town, so this one doesn't get much traffic. It's a great place to not get caught. Plus, it's cheap. It is decorated top to bottom with kitschy paintings and figurines of cats, and old-timey big band music is always playing softly in the background. I push the door open and a recorded meow sounds. The air smells like coffee beans and incense, and Tiffany-style lamps filter the light so that it's warm and orange tinted. I glance around for Greg as a girl with jet-black hair in a pixie cut and dramatic eye makeup takes my order, but I don't see him anywhere.

"Be safe, sweetie." The clerk snaps her gum and hands me my coffee.

"Thanks." I take it to the counter and load it with cream and sugar. As I'm stirring it with a plastic stick topped with a grinning cat, I hear the recorded meow and turn around. Greg walks through the door, dripping wet. I hadn't realized it started raining.

He looks at me. "Fine night for a walk."

"I guess I just missed the storm."

"Maybe you'll catch it on the way out." He smiles unenthusiastically and finds a corner table without ordering.

I carry my coffee and backpack over and set up my laptop to take notes. He pulls a sandwich out of his own backpack and I eye him distastefully as he takes a bite.

"What?" he asks with his mouth open.

"You shouldn't bring outside food into a restaurant," I whisper with a surreptitious glance at the waitress, who's leaning against the counter and reading a snowboarding magazine.

"Why not? They don't serve food. I'm not competing with them."

"So you've been here before. With Jessica?"

He nods. "Among others."

I wonder who the others are. For some reason it surprises me that multiple Bates students would date him. He just doesn't seem like the Bates type. I poise my fingers over the keyboard. "So. How did you and Jessica meet?"

"Tinder." He watches me for a reaction, but I wave for him to continue. "I do a lot of volunteer work and I heard about her organization through a flyer at my church. I showed up at an event, and we got to talking."

I type as he speaks. "And when was that?"

"About a year ago. We didn't start dating until New Year's."

"Over the break?"

"We both live here year-round," he reminds me.

"Oh yeah." I pause. "What drew you to Jessica?"

He smiles slightly and brushes his hair away from his intense eyes. "Are you running an investigation or writing a romance novel?"

I keep a straight face. "It's all relevant."

"Okay, I'll play. She was kind. Generous. Impressive. She started her own company when she was fifteen. How many people do you know who can say that?"

I shake my head. "None."

"Beautiful, obviously, but so are a lot of people. The other things, pretty rare." He fidgets with the lip ring. "I liked talking to her and being with her. That's what really matters, right? And I guess it was mutual."

"Guess?"

"I'm not a mind reader."

"Why'd you break up?"

His expression darkens. "I'm not a mind reader."

"Fair enough. When was the last time you talked to her?"

"Last night."

"Last words?" He flinches and I cringe. "I'm sorry, I put that badly. I meant—"

"I know what you meant," he interrupts me. He takes his cell phone out of his pocket and shows me the screen and I can see the last fragment of their conversation, at 9:54 p.m. last night.

GREG YEUN: If you're sorry, why did you do it?

JESSICA LANE: I didn't say I regret it. Sorry doesn't mean regret. I'm sorry I hurt you. I'm sorry for you.

GREG YEUN: You pity me?

JESSICA LANE: You're putting words in my mouth. Stop it.

GREG YEUN: You know what I regret? Knowing you.

My heart begins to pound. Those are dangerous words. "How long ago did you break up?"

"Officially, three weeks ago. But you know how things drag on, don't you?" There's a pink flush in his cheeks and his eyes shine like they might tear up, but he holds a steady gaze. For a split second I feel a bizarre urge to reach out and stroke his hair, because I know that wild look. I've worn it a thousand nights alone in my room, staring into the darkness, trying to will myself into another person or place or thing. And by the morning, I always succeeded. But he doesn't know how to do that. It makes me want to rock him and whisper that even the worst things can be forgotten. You just have to keep forgetting over and over again.

"Nothing lasts forever," I finally say.

He swallows hard and nods.

"Spencer and I are about three weeks over, too," I offer. The conversation on Greg's phone looks hauntingly familiar. In the context of Jessica's death, it takes on a sinister tone. As awful as it sounds, I wanted to hear that Jessica may have been suicidal, that Greg could give the police a reason to cross murder off the list. This isn't going to do it. "One last question. Did she ever mention me? Or anyone else from Bates?"

He eyes me carefully. "No."

But he's always so hostile toward me. It doesn't add up. He must know something about the link between me and Jessica.

"Why did you agree to meet with me? Tell me all of this?"

"The cops are going to question me, probably sooner rather than later. I should be thanking you for giving me a chance to rehearse."

"They haven't contacted you yet?"

He shakes his head. "They will. But who knows? They may not consider me a top suspect. I wasn't there that night."

I stand woodenly and offer him my hand, and he takes it

with icy fingers. His eyes are blank as he shivers under his layers of wet clothing. "Thanks for meeting me."

"Good luck with your investigation. Hope you catch the killer."

"I hope there is no killer," I say in a slightly unsteady voice.

His eyes travel over my face carefully. "Jess was happy. She was so full of life; she was *luminous*. She had her life mapped out to the minute. And even *if* she ever hurt herself, it wouldn't have been like that. She was afraid of blades. She didn't even shave her legs. She wouldn't do this to herself. Someone else did. And it sure as hell wasn't me. I'd watch my back, Kay."

I press both of my palms onto the tabletop to hold myself steady. "Why me?"

"Who's the link between you and Jess?"

I shake my head.

"Spencer. The relationship wrecker himself."

6

i run the entire way back through the rain and drip mud onto the library floor as I sign myself out. I head straight to Brie's dorm and pound on her door. She's watching a movie with the lights dimmed and hurriedly invites me inside, tossing me a dry change of clothing.

"Spencer was sleeping with Jessica," I blurt out.

She looks dubious. "Are you sure?"

"Pretty damn." As I explain, I peel my wet clothes off and gratefully slip into a flannel button-down and boxers. "I just met with Greg. He said she cheated on him with Spencer. They broke up three weeks ago. Remember Justine said he cheated with a Bates student?" I give Brie a meaningful look. "And Greg says there's no way she killed herself. She was happy, she had plans, she hated blades."

"So that gives Greg a motive." She makes room for me on the bed.

"And me." She combs my knotty hair with her fingers. "Of every person in the universe, Spencer *had* to have sex with a dead girl."

"That's a morbid way to say it."

But when I picture Jessica, I see her as the body in the lake, and now I see Spencer there with her, her cold, white arms locked around his back, his hands slowly lifting her waterlogged dress.

I can't picture her alive. I don't remember seeing her around campus very much. After first year, we get to choose many of our own classes and Jessica probably took most of her electives in the STEM departments along with Nola and Maddy. Cori, who has been premed since kindergarten, also takes mostly STEM electives. Poets like Tricia and people like me who want something new every day tend to stick to the humanities. Tai's parents also force her to take what they've decided are all pre-prelaw courses, in case a pro career falls through. Brie has an overloaded course schedule because she's determined to pack it with humanities *and* STEM classes. It's part of how she manages to be friends with so many people without going out as often as the rest of us.

So even though it's a small school, it's still possible to miss someone. I try to blink the images away.

"Greg also showed me some pretty damning texts from the night she died. Between him and Jessica, I mean."

"What were you doing with Creepy Greg?"

"I'm not going to sleep well until this murder thing is dropped." It's never been easy to lie to Brie, and I hope I'm pulling it off. I *do* want the murder investigation to be dropped. I still need athletics to start back up. I need to earn a scholarship and keep my parents sane and at a manageable distance. But if I don't follow through with the revenge blog, none of that even matters. Because what Jessica had on me will destroy everything I've worked so hard to get.

I switch a light on and Brie shields her eyes. She wears sky-blue Ralph Lauren pajamas, and her hair is held back from her face by a matching headband. The light reflecting in her eyes makes them look even rounder and brighter than usual. Even in the middle of the night, Brie is beautiful.

She sighs loudly and pauses the movie. "Kay. You need to stop obsessing over this."

"Well, I think it's weird that you're not *more* interested in the murder of a fellow student. Whose body we discovered. And who we might be suspected of killing."

She touches a finger to my lips. "You're being paranoid again. No one suspects anyone of anything, and if they did, it would be Greg. Or maybe Spencer. We're golden."

The thought of Spencer doing it makes my skin crawl. "Why would Greg give me all that information if he was guilty? He said he wanted to rehearse for the police, but—"

"That's reasonable. Lawyers rehearse their clients and witnesses over and over to get their stories straight."

I shiver and pull my bare legs up under the sheets. "They had a huge fight right before we found her. Like two hours before." My hair is more or less smoothed now, and Brie is stroking my neck. I turn to look up at her.

"That fits the timeline pretty well. But we can't assume she was murdered without evidence."

"Greg did. She had everything going for her."

"No one has everything."

Our faces are close and I wonder how long she'll stay like this with me. My heart stops. My lungs stop. I am paralyzed this close to her, poisoned by longing, and for an aching instant I think she's going to kiss me. It's our broken record, the moment we are doomed to relive over and over. There's no outcome except to stop and start over.

She stands suddenly and begins folding the wet clothes I've discarded on her floor. I squeeze my eyes shut and force myself back into the role I've been assigned.

"You never know what's going on in someone else's mind. Sometimes people are just unhappy."

"You don't think she would have told him if something was wrong?" I pick up the towel I've drenched and roll it into a neat ball. She takes it from me, shakes it out, and hangs it up.

"Sometimes people don't feel like they can."

I take Brie's hand, a wave of fear washing over me. "You would tell me, wouldn't you?"

She hesitates only for a split second. "Yes."

"You said you couldn't tell me what Tai said that made you cry."

She gazes at my hand in hers and I follow her eyes down. She's taller and more muscular than me, but her hands are smooth and graceful while mine are dry and too big for my tiny wrists. I always feel self-conscious holding hands. "That's different."

"It's not. I'd never forgive myself if something happened to you and I could have stopped it."

She looks at me for a long time without saying anything. "If I didn't talk to you, I'd talk to Justine."

My eyes feel like needles are poking at them but I nod and stand abruptly.

"I'm not trying to hurt your feelings, Kay. I'm just saying we all have safety nets that cross over different people. I tell you some things and I tell Justine some things. You don't tell me everything, do you?"

Almost. Almost everything.

Brie is the only one at Bates who knows my best friend and my brother died, though she doesn't know how. She knows my mother tried to commit suicide, though she doesn't know it was my fault. She knows just about as much about me as you can reasonably know and forgive. And somehow, she makes me feel like my freak-show life is totally normal. I guess that's what I love about Brie. She makes me feel like everyone has secrets, and hiding them is just part of the human experience.

"I'm going to try to study before bed."

"Okay." She stands and gives me a hug. "Don't let this get in your head, Kay."

I read over my old texts from Spencer as I struggle to fall asleep. I wish I didn't sound so much like Greg and he didn't sound so much like Jessica. I think about texting Spencer to tell him what I found out, that Greg may be suspected of killing the girl he cheated on me with, that it's definitely beyond over between us, but that would be pointless. Every time I text him to say it's over, we end up getting back together.

Instead, I end up playing the one saved voice mail I have from him on repeat until I fall asleep. It's a birthday message from over the summer. It's fifteen seconds long. I'm embarrassed for clinging to it just to hear the sound of his voice. But I keep hitting replay until I drift off into darkness.

I SKIP BREAKFAST the next day in favor of an extra-long morning run to clear my head. After a brisk shower, I meet the others outside the dining hall to walk to chapel together. It's a crisp morning, and the sky is shockingly blue. It always feels jarring when there's a funeral or a memorial on a beautiful day. I link arms with Brie as we walk across the courtyard with the rest of the student body, an army of teenage girls dressed in proper black dresses with respectful hair and makeup. Since it's a memorial, we've been instructed to ditch our uniforms. Most of my peers probably haven't dealt much with tragedy at this point in their lives, but all of us have trained in formality. It's our way.

Tai isn't there, but as of this morning, her name is still on the class roster, and the oven timer on the revenge website is ticking down.

No one says a word to me until I finally turn to the others. "Can we talk about Tai?"

Tricia spits out the gum she's perpetually chewing. "Are you goddamn serious?" She looks, as usual, model gorgeous, with her hair swept up from her swanlike neck, her long lashes framing her usually warm deep-brown eyes. Right now they look cold as ice.

Brie waves solemnly at some of the track team members and then turns back to us. "Tai was exaggerating. Kay never attacked her."

"We had a fight; it's over."

Cori balances on one foot as she pulls a sagging knee sock

up her freckled calf. "I can't believe you're defending yourself. I heard she's leaving. For good."

I try not to react visibly. "Did she tell you that? When is she going?"

"No, she didn't tell me. She's on a total communication blackout. *I* know things."

Brie shoots me a look. That means the info came straight from Klein's office to Cori's parents. This whole thing went down lightning fast.

"Don't blame Kay," Maddy says quietly. "Tai doesn't back down. She would never drop out of school unless *she* had done something wrong." By now we have all stopped dead in the middle of the path, and everyone is staring at me. I wave them aside under a leafless willow tree to allow others to pass. Tricia hesitates at the edge of the path, gazing down at her Christian Louboutins. Then she takes them off and runs barefoot over the cold grass, scowling.

"You're hiding something." Cori twists a winding branch around her arm until it snaps. Her usually rosy cheeks look drained of blood. "Why won't you tell us what really happened?"

"Yeah, Kay. No secrets," Tricia says.

Brie places a hand on each of their arms. "It isn't Kay's secret to tell. It's Tai's."

Tricia's eyes well up for a moment, and then it evaporates.

"She's my best friend. If she'd really done something wrong, she would have told me."

I look at each of them in turn. "Are you saying I made something up to screw her over?"

No one says anything for a moment.

"Tai will be fine," Brie says firmly. "We'll all be fine. We don't even know she's leaving."

"Then where is she?" Tricia is hugging her arms tightly to her chest, her shoulders squared and rigid. She looks like she's about to fall apart. I want to comfort her, but I'm the one who did this.

The chapel bell begins to ring, signaling the beginning of service. "I don't know," I say wearily. "I can't say any more. I'm so sorry."

"Come on, girls." Tricia links arms with Maddy and Cori, turning away from me. "Time to honor the fallen."

EVERY PEW IN the tiny chapel is packed with students and additional members of the community, and people crowd into every corner. Jessica's family sits in the front row. They look like the prototypical Bates family, despite the fact that she was here on scholarship. Her mother is tall with broad shoulders and sharp features. Her eyes are puffy and bloodshot, but she doesn't cry during the service. Her father is stoic, his jaw clenched, posture hunched, and his fingers woven together, rough boating knots. There is a younger sister, not yet old enough for Bates, and an older brother, handsome, broken, his arm protectively slung around his sister's shoulder. There won't be a funeral here—that will be private and after the body has been examined—but there is a large framed picture of Jessica surrounded by cascades of lilies.

I despise lilies. They are the floral mascots of death and everyone knows it. I had to inhale their stench, mixed with the thick perfume of Catholic incense, during the funeral masses for all four of my grandparents, then Megan, and then my older brother, Todd, just two months later, the year before I started at Bates. I have no patience for lilies.

The service is longer than usual so that a variety of homilies, poems, and songs can be crammed in, and then afterward pastries and coffee are served. The room is thick with students and teachers, and I do my best to nod politely as they filter past one by one. It reminds me of Todd's wake, when we were forced to greet every mourner. Like we were hosting a party or something. I resented every person who showed up for making me feel like I had to entertain them. Now I sense the same resentment bubbling up as fellow students gather me into weepy hugs and professors offer handshakes and low words intended to be comforting, but probably repeated on a loop to every student in the room. Robot words. I eventually manage to pull Tricia and Brie into a secluded nook where we can speak uninterrupted.

I'm observing Jessica's family and nibbling a chocolate croissant when Maddy scurries over excitedly, pulling Cori by the elbow.

"Look likes Notorious has news," Tricia observes.

Maddy ignores her. "We need to talk about Tai."

"Didn't we already do that?" Cori says, straightening her collar in the stained-glass window.

"I know what *happened*," Maddy says meaningfully. She beckons us to incline our heads together and whispers into our ears, "She was doping."

"Was not." Tricia eyes my croissant and takes a sip of coffee. Tricia was extremely overweight her first year, and after a surgery and summer of extreme dieting, she's physically transformed. Now she refuses to eat outside her nutritionist's daily menus. She was stunning then and she's stunning now, but she's intense about sticking to her menu.

"Interesting." Brie tilts her head at me.

"Why did she always have so much energy?" Maddy points out.

"Because we basically shotgun six cups of coffee a day," I say.

"Yeah, but Tai was too good. No one plays that well and

has time for a social life." Cori drains her paper cup and slinks away to refill it.

Tricia bites her lower lip and then adds, "I'm glad it was that."

I eye her curiously. "Why?"

She shrugs. "I was afraid it had something to do with Jessica's death. It's so paranoid of me. But she definitely knew her better than she let on. She hated her."

"So you knew her, too," Brie says.

"Only that Tai despised her." Tricia flicks her wispy bangs out of her eyes. "Everyone has secrets," she says knowingly.

I glance at Brie, but her eyes are fixed on the other side of the room. Nola is balancing on one foot like a ballet dancer and licking the sugar off a beignet.

I wind my way over to her. "Hey."

She falls into a graceful plié. "Bonjour." Today she's wearing cat-eye makeup and dark mascara, and combined with her pale, almost colorless lips, it gives her a retro sixties look. Unlike the rest of the students, she has chosen not to wear a black dress, which is ironic considering her usual choice of clothing. Instead, she is dressed in the standard Bates Academy uniform.

"Did you hear about Tai?"

"I heard I was right and you were wrong."

"That's correct."

A playful smirk creeps across her lips. "Say it."

"I was wrong and you were right."

She nods and takes a bite. "Well, this is crap." She dumps her plate into the garbage and walks outside, and I follow her, pulling my tiny jacket on over my black dress.

There's a choppy breeze blowing up over the lake, whipping a few rogue paper plates and coffee cups over the chapel lawn. It stings my legs and teases tendrils of hair from my braid and into my face. "I need your help cracking the password for the next recipe."

"In exchange for . . . ?"

I halt. "We already had a deal."

"That was for the initial password. What will you give me now?" She takes a pack of cigarettes from her pocket and lights one, and I pull her behind the chapel. Smoking is strictly forbidden.

"I don't have anything you want."

She leans against the Dumpster and taps her feet thoughtfully. "Get me a date with Jessica's ex."

I blink. "Greg Yeun? I don't think he's probably open to dating right now."

"I'm not looking for love, I'm looking for a challenge."

Clearly, she's looking to challenge *me*. "I—I don't know if I can manage that. I'm not a pimp."

She shrugs. "The password software's pretty basic. You probably don't need me."

"Okay, I'll do it," I say hastily, regretting it as soon as the words leave my lips. I have no idea how I'll pull it off.

She sticks the cigarette between her lips and pulls her cell phone out of her pocket. "What was it, the delicious dish?"

"*Revenge Is a Dish.* Hold on." I open my email from Jessica, copy the link, and send it to Nola. Then I check the class roster, and Tai's name is gone. Task one, complete.

"Okay . . ." She pulls up the website and types rapidly for a moment.

"Do you have the code-breaking software on your phone?"

She casts me a withering glare. "What do you think?" She types for another moment or so and then turns the screen to me.

I look down at the list of dishes. Tai Burned Chicken was the appetizer. The next item is the first course. I click on it. The name of the recipe is Pulled Parck Sandwich. Tricia's last name is Parck.

> *Take a piggy plump and pink*
> *Trim the fat; select a drink*
> *Irish whiskey aged and iced*
> *Serve with papers, that sounds nice*
> *On a board with fancy trim*
> *Skewer her for screwing him.*

Nola whistles under her breath. "Your friends are deviants, Donovan."

I read the poem several times. Tricia. Irish. Screwing. "There's no way."

"That Tricia's sleeping with Hannigan? Because that is exactly what it sounds like. Irish? Aged? That piggy and plump shit is cold, but the rest is spot-on."

I feel sick. Tricia's extreme weight loss explains the cruel first couplet. But Nola's right. The rest sounds like a reference to Hannigan. And there was a rumor about a student back in September when he first started. We all trashed it as fake news, though, because no one came up with an actual name.

I shove the cell phone back at her. "I don't want anything to do with this."

"You know, we might be reading into it."

"Jessica was obviously a very messed-up person. Maybe she—"

"Had it coming?" Nola flicks her cigarette. She blows a wisp of smoke through her pale lips and then twists them into a prim smile, her blue eyes piercing. "Maybe. But you don't want to find out any more?" She looks at the screen. "Although, I have no idea what the papers or board part means."

I take the phone from her and tap the screen experimentally in a few places. The graphic for this recipe shows a bar napkin with a phone number scribbled on it. Tricia's number. I tap on the number and a pdf file opens. It's Tricia's early-decision application to Harvard, including her recommendation letter from Hannigan. On the final page is a screenshot of the Harvard admissions board, and one of the people listed has the last name Hannigan. Attached is a jpeg file of Tricia and Hannigan together in his office, her arms wrapped around his neck, his face tilting down to kiss her.

"Well, that doesn't look good," Nola says. The back door of the chapel opens and I duck behind the Dumpster, but it's only a caterer from the bakery carrying a towering stack of white pastry boxes to his van. Other than that, the small parking lot between the chapel and the trees lining the lake is completely deserted.

My head swims. "I need to talk to her." I race back toward the front of the chapel, my heart tumbling around my chest, and burst through the doors. The air is thick with the lingering scent of incense from the service, mingling with the sweet pastry and coffee smells. My stomach churns and I try not to breathe as I march over to Brie and Tricia.

Brie scrunches up her nose. "Were you smoking?"

I shake my head vigorously. "Tricia, I need to talk to you outside."

She follows me curiously. "What's up?"

I wait until we're out of earshot from the few students milling around the lawn. "I know this is intrusive, but you need to be honest with me. Are you having an affair with Hannigan?"

She doesn't even hesitate for an instant. "No. Gross."

"Don't lie."

She places a hand on my arm and laughs, the dimples in her cheeks appearing. "Oh my God, Kay. I'm not lying."

I draw in a deep breath. "You're always talking about how guys our age are basically preschoolers."

She shifts her eyes to the side for just a split second. "Some of them are. Look at Spencer."

"Trish."

She watches the students pour out of the chapel and head past us toward the dorms. "What do you have against Hannigan all of a sudden?"

"Nothing if it isn't true." Now I'm running through every time I stopped by his office to go over an assignment that didn't make sense to me. He had me read love scenes when I didn't understand the political speeches. Maybe he just wanted me to study what he was going to test. But it creeps me out now.

"Then why are you trying to get him fired?" She glances behind her reflexively, and we watch several of the professors lingering at the chapel doorway, chatting with students.

Hannigan is there with his wife, who looks remarkably like Kate Middleton. Tricia looks at me, and she seems to have shrunken.

"He sucks, Trish. It's an absurd abuse of power to sleep with a student."

She turns back to the chapel for a moment, and her elegant profile is striking. We're all dressed for mourning, but only Tricia's face reflects it. She and Tai were best friends, and I know that's part of it. The rest is heartbreak. "It's not like that."

"He's the one who's in the wrong, one hundred percent. But please be honest with me," I say softly.

She doesn't respond right away. "You're all about you."

"Someone knows. And they're going to go public."

She looks at me, alarmed. "Unless?"

"No unless. He's going to get fired, and I think they might want you to leave."

"Who's they?"

"I don't know."

"That's convenient. Is that what you told Tai?"

"I didn't force Tai to leave." But it's not true. I did.

"So why should *I* leave?"

"You shouldn't." I don't know what else to say.

"Neither should he. I'm eighteen. I can do what I want."

"That's not how it works. He's a teacher. He controls our futures. One failing grade—"

Her eyes begin to gloss over, but she grits her teeth. "You think you're so much better than me."

"I really don't. I'm just warning you. If there's any possible way to cover your tracks in the next twenty-four hours—"

"Now you're just threatening me. Look, I like him. I admit it. We've spent time together. But we've never actually had sex and I don't appreciate your judgment."

A sharp edge of doubt creeps into my mind. There are consequences to not believing your friends. That's how things fell apart back home. The moment when the chain reaction began that ruined everyone's life. When Megan told me what happened, what Todd did, and I hesitated, and said, "I'm sure it was an accident." That was the moment she spun away from me, and after that she was out of my reach; no one else was able to grab on to her again. And then hell descended.

I look at Tricia now, and all of the guilt I felt about Megan floods through me. It's too late to do anything about Megan. It's too late to help Tai. But maybe it isn't too late to help Tricia. And one thing is certain. If no one talks to me, I'm never going to figure out just what it is that Jessica wanted to get back at everyone for. "Did you know Jessica Lane?"

She shakes her head and then smiles as if we'd been talking about classes or sports or our futures, not our potential downfalls. "Nope." She turns back toward the chapel. "I'm really sorry games are on hold, Kay. Hopefully you'll manage to pull through with your grades." She pauses and then gazes toward the steeple with a saintly expression. "Miracles happen."

My mouth drops open.

And it's just at that moment that Spencer exits the chapel, an unlit cigarette dangling from his lips, looking—as always—like he just rolled in from an all-night party. His straight sandy hair blows wildly in the breeze, and he stops to shield his cigarette with one hand as he flicks a lighter to try to ignite it, squinting his pale blue eyes.

I freeze for a moment, stunned to see him, and then turn abruptly and head back toward my dorm. But not before he sees me.

"Katie D."

He knows I hate when he calls me Katie. I keep walking but he jogs to catch up with me and slings an arm around my shoulder in a one-sided hug. The feel of it makes me want to sink into him and push him away at the same time. I want to see him, but not now. And the fact that he would just show up for Jessica's memorial and act as if nothing had happened after everything that's gone down between us feels like a punch in the stomach.

"Long time no see," he says.

"Or call."

"You told me not to."

"With good reason."

We share a glance, and then he shrugs and takes a long drag. "What have you been up to?"

"The usual. Murder and mayhem. You?"

"Same." He hasn't shaved this morning and the faintest ginger stubble covers his jaw. It's a special Spencer quirk. His facial hair doesn't quite match the hair on his head. It matches mine.

We're almost at my dorm. The parking lot has been blocked off with barriers to make room for extra cars, but most of them are gone now. I feel torn. I want this conversation to end as soon as humanly possible. I also want it to go on endlessly.

It wouldn't be fair to say that we had a love-hate relationship. Love-hurt would be more accurate. We met the night Brie and Justine met, at the same party. Brie and I had gone together, back when we were still in a maybe phase. I had screwed up several times already, and this was the clear last chance. It was a cast party for some show Justine was in at Easterly, and it had seemed like Brie and I were getting really close to actually happening. I had finally persuaded her to go out with me. At least I thought so. I thought it was a date. Tricia spent two hours stripping my body of hair, covering me with fragrant goo, straightening my frizzy locks, and applying makeup with a horror movie special-effects level of skill. Tai loaned me a killer pair of Louis Vuitton boots and a cotton-silk Coach mixed-print dress. Not too much—just enough. That is, as long as it actually *was* a date.

Then at the play, everything fell apart.

The show was depressing to the point that I started crying and had to leave the theater. By the time I pulled my shit together, the cast party had already started. But when I got there, I found Brie off in a corner flirting with the star of the play.

So. Maybe not a date after all.

I found myself sitting on the couch alone, pounding vodka lemonades and pretending to text so I didn't look like a total friendless wonder.

And then this guy flopped down next to me like we were best friends, leaned in, and whispered, "Texting makes it look worse."

He totally stood out from the rest of the crowd. Bates students tend to dress to their status with a preppy spin, Polo Ralph Lauren and Burberry. The Easterly drama crowd favored a more hipster flair, with a lot of scarves, vests, skinny jeans, cardigans, and glasses. Spencer wore ripped-up jeans, a long-sleeved Red Sox ringer T-shirt, and a pair of scuffed Converses. But he exuded an air of confidence that struck me as both condescending and intriguing for someone so clearly out of his league. He looked like he rolled out of his bed and wandered over in the dark. I may have been abandoned on the island of misfit party guests, but I still looked awesome.

I placed my phone down. "Texting makes what look worse?"

"You're supposed to be with Burberry." He nodded at Brie.

"How do you know that?"

"It says so on her scarf." He tilted his bottle back and I shot another desperate look at Brie, but she was deep in conversation. She gets stuck in, thick. But only when someone really, really sparks her interest.

"That's not what I—"

"Because you keep looking at her, but she's not looking back." I turned back to Spencer, my face burning. "So you're stranded. And pretending you have something better to do at a party just makes you look sadder. First mistake, introducing your girl to Justine. Second mistake, acting like you don't care."

"So what do you suggest?"

"Make her jealous."

I laughed. "Not gonna happen, friend."

He shrugged. "Suit yourself."

I glanced around the room. More than one Easterly student was looking at us curiously, and there was unmistakable envy on some of their faces. I shot a glance over to Brie and Justine, and finally caught Brie's eye. She raised a brow as if to ask what

I was doing. I nodded to invite her over, but she shook her head and held her finger up like *hold on a sec.*

I turned back to Spencer. "Who did *you* come with?"

He grinned. "The question is who do I leave with? Want to help me decide?" He described a few of the girls in the room, gave me some pros and cons, and then, of course, made his pitch. "Or I could help you out with Burberry. You have two basic options. One, we grab a room. We can play blackjack and I Never all night, and no one will even know the difference. Two, we make out here on the couch. I know which one I prefer."

I flicked my eyes over to Brie again. She had repositioned herself against the wall so she had a full view of me now. But she made no move to end her conversation or even to invite me to join them.

I adjusted my position so that I was angled in toward both Brie and Spencer, and leaned closer to him. "Amateur."

An intrigued smile crossed his lips. "That's a treasonous accusation."

"Oh no. It's a fact." I took his beer and placed it on the floor and then pulled him to his feet and placed him at one end of the couch and sat down at the other, facing him, legs folded beneath me. "That's not how jealousy works."

His smile grew, but I also saw uncertainty and excitement flicker in his eyes. He was kind of cute. That didn't take the sting out of Brie crushing my heart for the millionth time, but there was something magnetic about his smile. It made it easier not to look at her, at least. "No?"

I shook my head. "It's a slow burn. We keep talking. Low voices, so no one else can hear what we're saying. And every time I smile. Or laugh. I come a little closer." To illustrate, I slid one inch toward him and lowered my voice to just above a whisper. "Just one little bit. You have to earn it."

His breathing quickened a little, and I couldn't help biting a smile. I had been waiting and wanting for so long with Brie, I had completely forgotten what it felt like to be wanted. It felt powerful. It felt sexy. He was sexy.

"What makes you smile?" Spencer asked, leaning in closer. There was something so tempting in his smile. Something dangerous and innocent at the same time. A paradox. This is why people like him, I decided. They can't figure him out. I realized suddenly that we must be attracting a lot of attention, and wondered whether I had finally caught Brie's. But I suddenly didn't want to tear my eyes away from Spencer's. Not even for Brie, especially after she humiliated me. I hoped she was watching.

"Back to your corner. This is the final rule. You don't get to kiss me until my lips are breathing distance from yours. That means if I was a Dementor, I could suck out your soul."

"Exquisite image. That's a lot of smiles for someone who looked like they were ready to explode when I first sat down."

"Challenge extended." I smirked.

"That's one." He grinned, and the boyish excitement in his eyes was contagious. He wasn't Brie but he would be a fun, sexy distraction.

AND HE WAS. He always was, right until the end. I never meant to fall for him.

I never meant to hurt him.

I certainly never thought he could hurt me.

Now he looks up at me from the bottom of the stairs with the most innocent expression, and I'm so tempted to ask if he wants to go for a drive that I actually take a step down toward him before he spins with a half wave and heads back down the path and I'm stumbling into his shadow.

7

i call Greg that night after a bit of studying. My first instinct was to call Brie to tell her about Spencer and Tricia, but if I don't force myself to study, it doesn't happen, and I'm anxious to settle up my debt with Nola.

Greg answers the phone, and I hear music blaring in the background. For a moment my breath catches in my throat. When Todd died, I stole his iPod and listened to his music nonstop—in class, in my sleep, while I ran endless miles. This album, *xx*, by the band The xx, was always the last to play, and when it stopped, so did I. It was so hard to press play again, to restart, to get out of bed.

"Hello, Kay Donovan. Am I under arrest?"

I breathe again. "No. I have a favor to ask."

He lets out a short laugh. "I didn't know we were on favor-asking terms."

"We're not, necessarily, but we have a lot in common. We

were both cuckolded by a lewd encounter between Spencer Morrow and Jessica Lane."

"That's a lighthearted way of discussing a pretty heavy matter."

"Yes, but it's life, and if you get too serious, you drown in it." I stretch out on my bed and kick my legs up against the wall, my feet landing on a poster of the U.S. Women's Soccer team.

"You're quite the philosopher."

"Not really. To the point. I would like to ask you on a date."

There's a pause.

"Not with me. With someone a little more you. She's quirky. And pretty. She has a certain je ne sais quoi."

"You haven't told me anything concrete."

"She speaks a little French, does a little ballet, and is a mean hacker."

He is silent and I check the phone to make sure the call hasn't dropped. "Kay, you remember my ex-girlfriend just died, right?"

"Like I said, this would be a favor." I search desperately for a more convincing argument. "It'll be a good distraction. Get out of the house. Turn off that depressing music."

"Don't quit soccer for cheerleading, Kay."

"That came out wrong. When my brother died, the single,

solitary thing that kept me sane was going out and doing stuff. I know grief is different for everyone, but..."

His voice is softer when he speaks again. "Sorry about your brother. I'm not a doer, though. I'm also a boring date."

"I think you would be a thrilling date," I say.

I hear a stifled laugh and blush involuntarily. It was a stupid thing to say. "You know I'm a person of suspicion in a murder case, right?"

"It's not officially a murder case, is it?"

"I don't know. They didn't use that word when they questioned me, but I've already been called in twice. That's not a good sign."

I hold in a sigh of relief. If they're focusing on Greg, they're not focusing on us. Maybe Morgan will never follow up after all. But I still owe Nola her date. "Also, I'm not greatly attached to the bachelorette in question."

He laughs. "You're a terrible salesperson, Kay Donovan."

"Maybe. But again. She speaks a little French and does a little ballet. And she's artsy, like you."

"Well, artsy people do congregate together. We're like crows."

A murder of crows. "So, do we have a deal?"

"No. That's completely one-sided. What do I get?"

I think. "Name something."

"Let's talk again. Not a date," he says quickly. "But let's meet up at some point and compare notes and scars. Will that work?"

I nod slowly, considering. "Yes." It will be an opportunity to size him up again, and to dig a little deeper about Jessica's blog. "But first, you have to follow through with Nola."

"Nola. Okay. Give me her info."

THE NEXT DAY, classes resume, and it feels strange being back in a classroom, taking notes and trying to focus as if the past weekend had never happened. Friday seems like a month ago. But it's only been three days since Jessica died. It feels surreal to be going through the motions of an ordinary day, and I text Tricia several times to see if she's still speaking to me. She doesn't answer, and she isn't at lunch. Brie tells me she wasn't in trig or Comp Lit, either. She's still on the class roster, though, and Hannigan is in his office when I walk by, so the task hasn't magically resolved itself. By the end of lunch, I have fifteen minutes before the timer on the revenge blog runs out, and I begin to panic. Even if I do somehow force Tricia to drop out of school now, her name isn't going to disappear that quickly.

I step outside and call Nola.

"Busy."

"Don't hang up."

"Hook me in one line."

"I have fifteen minutes left to get rid of both Tricia and Hannigan and I need your help. Fourteen."

Nola saunters out of the dining hall, spots me, and waves. "That's two lines. Why the change of heart?"

"Because I'm desperate," I whisper. I feel terrible. But this is a temporary fix. Hannigan has to go. There's no question about that. But then something occurs to me. Tricia's name just has to disappear. Not Tricia herself. The program is only going to register her name being removed, and Nola can totally make that happen. "I need you to take Tricia's name off the class roster."

Nola leans against a tree trunk and pulls her laptop out of her backpack. "That doesn't sound like skewering."

"I didn't make up the rules."

"And Hannigan?"

"I'm going to report him."

She nods. "Okay. My payment?"

"Nola, I'm in a time crunch. Let's just say I owe you a favor to be called in when you want. Okay?"

"That works."

She types while I scrawl out an anonymous letter calling out Hannigan as a teacher in a relationship with an unnamed student, and drop it in Dr. Klein's mailbox. I drop Hannigan a second anonymous note letting him know that if he doesn't resign immediately, I'll give Klein the name of the student along with photographic proof. Just as I'm about to leave the building, though, her administrative assistant calls to me from the top of the stairs and asks me to take a seat outside her office. I sit in the waiting room in a state of stifling dread, expecting to field questions about Tricia, but when I'm ushered into the office, Detective Morgan is waiting for me inside along with Dr. Klein.

"Sit down," Dr. Klein invites, pointing to an azure suede chair.

I sit and smile nervously. "Is there something I can help with?"

"Detective Morgan is going to ask you some questions, dear. I'm just here as your chaperone," she says.

I turn to Detective Morgan. "Okay."

She smiles. "How are you holding up, Kay? Rough couple of days."

"I'm all right."

"I saw they canceled your big game tonight. That's rough."

Rough twice in two sentences. Not exactly an impressive vocabulary. "It is."

"I understand you had some scouts coming to watch you play. Some recruiters."

The unblinking way she's staring at me is incredibly

unnerving, not to mention the level of stalking she's obviously engaged in. "Yes, that's true."

"Rough," she says for a third time. For some reason, this really irritates me.

"How can I help you?"

"Just a few questions about the other night, Kay. Can I call you Kay?"

I try not to let my annoyance show. "Everyone else does."

"You say you found Jessica a little after midnight."

"I didn't time-stamp it. We found her and then you guys showed up and we reported it right away."

She looks from Dr. Klein to me incredulously. "Now, I thought you told your friend Maddy not to call us."

"No. My friend Brie told Maddy to call Dr. Klein first. We didn't want Jessica's family to find out on the news or the internet that their daughter was dead."

She scribbles in her notebook. "So you told Maddy not to call us because—"

"Brie told Maddy."

She smacks her forehead dramatically. "Brie told Maddy not to call us to protect Jessica's family."

I can't help the irritation from edging into my voice. It feels like she's deliberately twisting my words. "I said she told Maddy to call Dr. Klein first. Then the cops."

Detective Morgan assumes an innocent expression. "My bad. To protect Jessica's family."

"Yes."

She flips through her notes. "So this in fact contradicts your statement at the scene that you didn't know who the victim was."

I blink. "No, I didn't know."

"You just said you wanted to protect Jessica's family."

"I did. I just didn't know it was hers."

She taps her pencil against the notebook skeptically. "Which is it, Kay?"

I draw in a deep breath and try to remain calm. "We wanted to protect the unknown victim's family. We were pretty sure she was a student and Dr. Klein would know who she was."

"Okay." Detective Morgan raises her eyebrows and writes this down. She doesn't look like she believes me. "So." She looks up at me again. "When I arrived at the scene, you were holding a soaking-wet garment and had scratches all up and down your arms."

My throat begins to go dry. I do not like where this is headed. "I dropped the costume into the lake, like I said. We had planned to go swimming. And I ran through the thorn-bushes to help Brie out of the water."

"Why not run around them?"

"Because my friend was screaming and I needed to get to her."

"How many seconds did you save by running through the bushes?"

"I don't know off the top of my head."

"Guess."

My eyes flick over to Dr. Klein. She nods encouragingly, but her hands are knotted together. "Maybe twenty?"

Detective Morgan notes this down. "You were with your friends all night?"

"Yes. At the dance."

"Were you ever alone?"

I hesitate for a second. Brie said we should tell the police that we weren't. But I don't know if she ever confirmed this with the others. I end up splitting the difference. "Not significantly."

"What's significant?"

"Not long enough to murder someone." The more I talk, the more I realize I'm digging myself into a six-foot-deep hole.

"How long does that take?"

"I don't know, I never did it."

She smirks. "Cute. To verify, you were never alone, for even a second, the entire night?"

Shit. "I went back to my room briefly to change my shoes before we met up at the lake."

"Right around the time Jessica Lane was killed."

"I didn't know she was killed." My eyes dart over to Dr. Klein again, but she is looking down at her desk.

"Now you know. Maybe knowing will help jog your memory." Detective Morgan taps her pencil on her pad. "You were dating Spencer Morrow for quite a while."

"Yes." I get another awful flash of him with her again, of *my* Spencer with dead Jessica. Dead but animate, cold but passionate. Why do I always have to picture her dead with him?

"You broke up when he began seeing Jessica Lane."

"I didn't know it at the time."

"You know it now?"

"I just found out."

"Convenient."

My face feels hot and my heart is pounding like it wants to burst out of my chest. I want to scream at Detective Morgan to fuck off. But that would just make me look worse.

"Just a couple more questions. When campus police officer Jennifer Biggs arrived on the scene, you told her not to touch anything because it was a crime scene, correct? There was a girl with slit wrists. Most people see that, they think suicide. What made you think crime scene?"

"I don't know." My voice creaks out in a dry whisper.

"Just now you acted surprised when I told you Jessica was murdered. But just before that you called her a victim and conjectured on how long it would take to murder someone. That's quite a performance, Kay."

"I didn't mean—"

"Is it true you've been in almost constant contact with Jessica's ex-boyfriend, Greg Yeun, since her death?"

"Not constant." I feel like I'm going to throw up. The room is spinning like a carousel, faster and faster.

"Were you in Jessica's room the night she died?"

I shake my head and the room tilts sharply.

"Is there anything else you'd like to tell me? Anything at all?"

I open my mouth, dry heave, and then lean forward and vomit on the floor.

UP UNTIL THE whole murder incident, this year's Skeleton Dance had been the best to date. As seniors, we ruled the scene. Tricia awed the room in her custom designer ball gown with her killer dance moves, and Cori dictated the playlist to the juniors assigned to the sound booth. The art club in charge of décor had completely transformed the ballroom into a glittering midnight forest swirling with mist and distorted shadows. Tai ran an underground cocktail bar from the bathroom, and Maddy flitted around taking pictures and uploading them to the event website while Brie danced, chatted, and took a selfie with virtually everyone in the room. Parties are always a little more difficult for me. I rarely settle into a function like my friends do. I feel like I need to be someone's date or guest or I just kind of melt into the corners. Dressing up helps, though. As Daisy, I was able to identify a Gatsby type, a junior rugby player dressed in an expensive-looking suit.

I swirled over to her tipsily, ignoring the redhead she was talking to, and smiled my brightest Daisy smile. "Hello, Jay."

She looked confused, but pleased at the attention. "Flapper."

"Mrs. Daisy Buchanan."

"Ah. Wrong Leo. *Wolf of Wall Street*."

She offered me her hand, but I took the drink out of her other one—a ginger ale and lime with gin—downed it, and then dragged her onto the dance floor. "Dance with me, Jay," I said, laying my head against her chest.

And she did. That's the thing about Halloween, about costumes, about playing parts. By the end of the night we were making out in the bushes behind the ballroom, and Maddy was giggling and snapping pictures while Cori applauded and the Wolf of Wall Street, whoever she was, scrambled up, embarrassed, gathering her suit and apologizing for some reason. I yanked the phone out of Maddy's hands and deleted the photos.

"I'm so sorry for my friends. Pictures are gone." I showed the display screen and scrolled backward through the photos to prove it.

Wolf gave me an embarrassed smile. "Whatever. See you

around." She ducked back into the building, and I tossed Maddy the camera and dropped back onto the ground.

"You're so bad." Maddy giggled, collapsing next to me breathlessly and taking a swig from her glittering pink flask.

"*Bad* isn't the word. Mildly scandalous." Cori stretched her long, freckled legs up against the brick side of the building and laid her head in the grass. Cori belongs in *Gatsby*. She's a born aristocrat, a golfer, a coarse and blunt personality with sharp features and a sharper wit. She can be too bristly and opinionated at times and it would be easy to dislike her if she didn't decide immediately to befriend you, but she did decide, so we're solid. "Rest in peace, Spencer."

"Have you even heard from him?" Maddy asked.

I shook my head. "Spencer had his chance."

"How do you just . . ." Maddy sighed and gazed up at the sky. "Make someone like you?"

"I don't." I wished she hadn't used those words. "Liking is one thing. Dancing is another. Just ask."

Cori smirked. "That was more than dancing."

"Then *ask* for more."

She laughed loudly, a hoarse, hearty laugh. Cori's laugh is so distinctive, it drew Tricia and Tai out of the building, Tai carrying her apothecary in her oversize purse and Tricia still dancing. Tai crouched down and opened her bag of refreshments.

"Sounds like time to power up. Chocolate vodka shots?"

"God, no." I turned my head toward her and the stars trailed along. "Give me something that fizzes."

"Prosecco. With notes of grapefruit and honey." She poured me a mini flask, but I gave it back to her and took the bottle.

"Should we begin to wander toward the lake?" Tricia lifted the bottle and took a long drink.

I pulled myself to a sitting position. "Where's Brie?"

"Probably in a dark corner with some other poor loser," Cori said and giggled.

My stomach turned. She wouldn't do that to Justine. And if she did, it would be with me. I would be the one. She would be winding her arms around me, twisting her fingers into my hair, our lips pressed together as we pulled each other close and up and around over the crunching leaves, laughing the cold away. It should be me. It should always have been me. I suddenly felt dark and bothered and like the night had been a waste.

And then she was there, towering above us, breathless, disheveled, her eyes bright and wild with alcohol. "Change of plan. Let's split up now and meet in thirty minutes. Back to our dorms, ditch valuables, do what has to be done, meet at the edge of the green. I have a surprise."

A mischievous grin played on the corner of Tai's lips, but I wasn't in the mood anymore. "What kind of a surprise?"

"It'll be worth it." Brie started running toward the dorms and glanced back over her shoulder. "Thirty minutes."

"Oh yeah," Tricia said. "She's definitely been in a dark corner somewhere."

"Looks like she's off to finish whatever she started," Cori whispered, and the others roared with laughter.

I glared at them. "You guys are like frat boys."

"We're the ones frat guys prey on, Kay." Tai took a long drink and burped into the back of her hand, and the others laughed uncontrollably. "Innocent little us."

I SKIP MY afternoon classes to go for a half-marathon run around the lake and attempt to cool down with a yoga session in one of the private meditation rooms at the athletic center, but I can't slow my pulse or stop my mind from racing. Dinner is no better. Mealtimes have become increasingly surreal since Jessica's death. On the first night, I sat by myself across the cavernous hall from my friends as Tai tried to poison them against me. The next day, Tai was gone and Tricia sat with the rugby team after the memorial. Tonight, there's no sign of Tricia. Cori and Maddy sit at our usual table, and I drag Brie to a deserted corner in the back. I decide to keep Tricia's secret. It's not for me to tell, even to Brie.

"Have you seen Tricia?" Brie asks as I elbow a first-year out of the way to block the table off for ourselves. She gives me

THE HENLEY COLLEGE LIBRARY

a shocked look and Brie shakes her head at me, frowning, and apologizes to the girl, who looks like she's about to cry.

"Sorry," I say, distracted. "I totally didn't see you."

"She's not answering her phone."

"Who?"

"Tricia." Brie feels my forehead. "Are you sick?"

"They suspect me," I say. My whole body feels ice cold. "*Me.*"

"They can't. You have alibis."

"Not for the entire night. Not for that window between the dance and the lake."

Brie places her fork down slowly. "I told you not to tell them about that."

"She cornered me. That woman is like one of those sharks that clamps down and doesn't let go."

Brie closes her eyes and her expression turns serene, but I can tell she's beginning to panic. She gets strangely calm when things are going wrong. "She's going to know we all lied. We could be arrested for obstructing justice."

"Relax. I only told her that I was alone. Not the rest of you. I said I went to my room to change. Which happens to be directly below Jessica's room. Then the detective asked specifically if I was in there, and it seemed like she was implying that she thought I was. No one can prove I didn't kill her and then meet up with you."

"No one can prove you were in her room because you weren't. And you have no motive."

"Jealousy is the oldest motive in the book."

She scoffs. "Over Spencer? If they knew him, they wouldn't even consider it." She takes a bite of spaghetti.

I think for a moment. "You were already wrong once, Brie. The detective said it wasn't a suicide."

Brie frowns. "Yeah. It seems like public opinion is swinging that way, too."

I glance across the dining hall and see Nola gliding out of the kitchen with her tray and I wave her over. She hesitates for a moment and then approaches and sits. "Nola, do you know Brie?"

She rises and curtsies elaborately. Her hair is arranged in a meticulous mass of curls held back by a blue silk ribbon that matches her eyes. "Miss Matthews, I know you by reputation of course."

Brie takes her in and shoots me a wary look. Even in uniform, Brie and Nola are total opposites. Nola is a different dramatic incarnation of herself every day, while Brie is classic and traditional. Nola is makeup and theater and effect. Brie is lip gloss and natural light; she seems to glow from the fact of existing. Nola is always moving; Brie moves with intention. Brie's shirts are pressed and buttoned, casually accessorized with a simple silver chain; Nola wears shirts unbuttoned down to the vest, clunky bracelets, and large rings that overwhelm her tiny hands.

"Nola, maybe you should call off your date with Greg."

She shakes her head and her curls bounce. "No way. We're going to a midnight showing of *Rocky Horror*. I'm dressing as Magenta."

"Okay, but Jessica's death is being investigated as a murder now, and he's almost definitely a suspect. It wouldn't be safe." More to the point, it wouldn't look good if Detective Morgan somehow drew a line between Nola, Greg, and me. She did *not* seem to like the fact that I was in contact with Greg.

Nola raises her eyebrows. "*Intrigant*. Do you think he did it?"

"No," I admit. "But you can't risk that."

"You could," Brie says mildly. She crunches a piece of ice and smiles at Nola sweetly.

"Funny." Nola takes a bite of garlic bread. "I heard you were on the suspect list, Kay. Maybe I shouldn't risk talking to you."

"Who told you that?"

She shrugs. "People talk."

I give Brie a told-you-so look and then turn back to Nola.

"You can do what you want. I'm just trying to look out for you."

She studies me. "Really?"

I nod with effort. My head feels like it weighs a thousand pounds. I need coffee. I feel my phone buzz under the table and

I look down to see a message from Brie.

Third wheel?

She looks at me expectantly, but I shake my head.

All good, I write back.

"Fine. I won't go." Nola texts something into her phone. "He's not my type, anyway. Too decorative. A little ink is okay. Less is more." She looks at me and Brie. "So what are we up to tonight?"

"We study on weeknights," Brie says. She looks at me like she's waiting for me to give my own excuse.

I really should study. But I need to take a look at the next recipe on Jessica's blog, and it should be unlocked by now. I can't mention that to Brie, though. "I have nothing going on."

Nola nods. "My room or yours?"

"Yours, I guess. Mine's a bit of a wreck."

Brie stares at me with a look I don't understand. She rises without another word, gives me a hard kiss on the cheek, and storms out of the dining hall.

8

---

*n*ola's room is nothing like I expect. I thought the walls would be covered in Tim Burton posters, *Vampire Diaries*, goth drawings, that sort of thing. Instead, it's full of light and life. There are plants everywhere. I recognize cacti, aloe, sunflowers, tiger lilies, and amaryllises, but the rest look exotic to me, the kinds of plants you would see in desert and tropical climates. It occurs to me that I don't know anything about Nola, including where she's from.

"You're a gardener?" I ask pointlessly.

"Well, it's not exactly a garden. But I do like plants. These were all cuttings from home. Homes." She tilts a watering can into a cactus pot, and I survey the rest of the room. Her desk is covered in neat stacks of books and vintage writing instruments, jars of ink, reed pens, sharpening stones, pen cutters, and the like. The walls are completely covered with brown butcher paper, with neat columns of calligraphy stretching from floor to ceiling. I stand on tiptoes to reach the top of a column.

"'How happy some o'er other some can be! / Through Athens I am thought as fair as she.'" I turn to her. "Why does that sound so familiar?"

"Because *A Midsummer Night's Dream* is Shakespeare's most-performed play. We read it last year in European Lit, and it was also the spring play. I was Helena."

"Oh." I don't usually bother with the school theater productions. Plays aren't really my thing. I only go to Justine's shows to support her, and I've fallen asleep or texted my way through most of them.

Nola gestures to the wall with a thin hand and then stands by my side. She's a full head shorter than I am. "You think memorizing a few equations for physics is hard. Try cramming all this into your brain."

I turn a slow circle. The entire wall is covered, top to bottom. "There's no way you memorized it all."

"Well, not for one show," she admits. "But I never forget. I could recite *Hamlet* for you right now."

"You didn't play Hamlet."

She looks at me with her freaky globe eyes. "I was the first in Bates's history to play Hamlet. Last winter, as a junior."

I knew the drama club liked to put on Shakespeare

productions, and since we have no male students, they cast girls in the men's roles. But for some reason I never envisioned someone I actually knew playing an iconic theatrical part. Hamlet. The salesman, whatever his name is. I imagine Nola dressed in classic Elizabethan garb with a mustache drawn on with eyeliner and a smile cracks my lips. I can't help it.

Her eyes narrow. "Like hacking away at a soccer ball is such an achievement."

I bite my lip. "I wasn't laughing. It sounds really hard."

"Monkeys can do what you do. They can't do what I do. That's all I'm saying."

I nod. "Agreed. Can we look at the website, please?"

She flounces down on the bed and gazes up at the ceiling. "Have you thought this through, Kay?"

"What do you mean?"

"I mean the website is going after your friends. First Tai, then Tricia. Do you really want to tempt fate?"

"I have to."

She lifts her head and props herself up on her elbows, her hair falling over her shoulders like a dark curtain. "Why?"

Because Jessica knew what I did, and if I don't follow her rules, so will everyone else. "Because I might be next on Jessica's list."

She leans toward me conspiratorially. "What did she have on you?"

I shrug. "Maybe nothing."

"She had something on everyone on the list. Maybe one of them is the killer."

"Or maybe the simplest explanation is the true one. She killed herself and wanted revenge on everyone who wronged her."

"The police don't think so."

"The police don't know about the revenge blog. And they can't find out."

"You told me you needed my help getting into the website because Jessica left a message for you there."

"The website *is* the message. She wanted revenge."

"Why ask you to do it? It's a huge favor to ask someone you never met."

"That's the question."

Nola's eyes cut right through me. "Is there something you did to her? Maybe something you've forgotten? Something you didn't even think twice about? Anything?"

I shake my head and tell what feels like my hundredth lie of the day. "None of us ever spoke to her before she turned up dead. She was a nobody."

Nola shrugs. "Maybe that's what you did. No one wants to be a nobody." She opens her laptop and I sit next to her as she pulls up the website and the software to decode the password for the next recipe.

As she rests on her elbow, her hair falls over one shoulder and her dress slides down a little. I notice a blooming of black ink on her right shoulder blade.

I kneel on the side of her bed. "Do you have a tattoo?"

She glances at me over her shoulder. "No. I draw the same picture on my own back every morning, let it fade over the course of the day, scrub off the remnants in the shower, and painstakingly re-create it ad nauseam. I make a game of it."

"Obviously."

She pulls her dress slightly farther down her shoulder so I can get a better look. It's an intricate drawing of an old clock face with no hands.

"What does it mean?"

"It's art. If I explain it, the point is lost. You don't ask a painter to explain . . . Never mind." She pulls her dress back up hurriedly and her face looks flushed.

"I'm sorry. To hear Ms. Koeppler talk, art always means something."

She smiles and brushes my hair out of my face almost the way Brie would when I say something that reveals my ignorance about something she considers herself an expert on. "It does. But the work of art itself is the artist's statement. The rest is up to the viewer." She drops her hand suddenly, as if remembering that I'm off limits or something. It takes me a moment to remember that I'm technically not. I still feel guilty, though, and check my phone to see if Brie has texted after her stormy exit from the dining hall. Nothing.

The password appears and Nola enters it and clicks on the link for the palate cleanser course.

New Orleans, LA Blood Orange Sorbet
Had an orange, squeezed it pale
Beat it bloody, left no trail
Led it in the woods for lost
Left it in the snow to frost
Thought no one would ever know?
I captured the orange snow.

There are several files attached of what looks like drops of bright-red blood on snow.

Nola's face turns chalk white. "It's me," she whispers. "Jessica was after me, too."

I read the words again. "I don't see it." Then the title hits me. New Orleans, LA. NOLA. "What did you do?"

"She couldn't know. She couldn't." Nola is breathing so hard, she's practically hyperventilating, so I hand her a pillow.

"Hug this. Deep, slow breaths." I read the poem again. "I thought Jessica was only going after my friends."

Nola clutches the pillow to her chest, breathing slower. "Apparently not."

"But it's a revenge blog. Tai and Tricia make sense. Even if they don't remember her, all of my friends have said and done things to other students that we regret. And if we didn't regret it then, we sure as hell do it now." I avoid Nola's eyes. "You don't fit that pattern."

"I might." She looks at me out of the corner of her eye. "I may not have agreed to help you out of pure benevolence. After seeing the first recipe, that is."

"What are you talking about?"

"There *is* one thing that ties me to you, Tai, and Tricia. And Jessica."

I search my memory. I can't think of a single link between the four of us. "I don't think so."

"Do the words *Dear Valentine* ring a bell?"

They hit me like a knockout punch. I take a moment to steady myself. "What do you know about Dear Valentine?"

"I know that my first year I had no friends and I was desperate to make some. So I signed up to be delivery girl. I was assigned to third floor, Henderson. So Jessica was on my delivery list. And on Valentine's Day, she didn't get any flowers. No big deal, she wasn't the only sophomore. I didn't either. But then Tricia tracked me down and begged me to deliver a letter back to Jessica. We're not really allowed to do that. Dear Valentine is a one-day thing. But she was just so nice, and I needed nice so badly . . . So I said okay. Then the next day, same thing. And the next. By the third day, Jessica begged me to stop. But when I tried to tell Tricia no, she told me how awesome I was and how I was everyone's hero. You and Tai and Brie and even the seniors. I'm such an idiot. None of you actually spoke to me. But I guess I imagined all these looks of admiration in class and started showing up at sports games, and oh my God, I was such a loser. Anyway. I don't know what was in those letters Tricia wrote. But every day I could hear Jessica crying when I knocked on her door. And I kept bringing them. For almost two weeks until Tricia finally stopped writing them. Then she went back to pretending I didn't exist. So yeah. I'd say Jessica had a reason to get back at me, too. That's why I really wanted to help you. I've been waiting to see if my name was going to come up. I was just hoping what someone else did to her was worse. Whatever was in those letters was bad. So bad that Jessica's last wish was to ruin the lives of everyone involved in sending them. You were Tricia's friend, and Jessica entrusted you with carrying out her revenge. That means either you were involved, or you were the only one of your friends who wasn't. So I'm asking again. Is there something you did to Jessica?"

I try to speak, but my throat is too dry. Dear Valentine

is a very good reason for Jessica to be upset with me and my friends. And Nola only knows part of the story. Her version just scratches the surface.

She turns the laptop around to show me the poem again and draws a deep, shaky breath. "Do you remember that whole big freak-out a couple of years ago when Dr. Klein's cat went missing? Maybe a week or so after that year's Valentine's Day?"

The memory sends a jolt of electricity down my spine. It was a big deal. Hunter had been a fixture around campus, practically a mascot. He was always trotting across the green, chasing chipmunks, batting leaves around, or basking in the sun. Then he disappeared from inside Dr. Klein's mansion on the fringe of campus. The doors and windows had been closed, but not bolted. She was positive about that. His collar had been left behind. It was ominous as hell. Posters went up everywhere. There were multiple assemblies. The campus police spoke to the student body; the school psychologist had us all come in for interviews. It was huge. But Hunter never turned up. Adorable, fluffy, orange-striped Hunter.

I turn to Nola, dread spreading through me slowly like a fever. "What did you do?"

"It was an accident." She presses her face into her pillow and lets out a muffled shriek, and then lifts it. Her eyes are bright red and watery, and her mascara is smudged. "I didn't take him. I just found him. At least I think it was him. He was in the creek. Alive, but just . . ." She trails off, her eyes overflowing, her nose swollen, lips trembling. Her voice wobbles. "His body was flattened and his fur was matted with blood and in the water it wasn't even red, it was brown and pink, it was so creepy." She chokes and I put my arms around her awkwardly.

"I never saw anything dead before," she goes on, getting more and more worked up. "And everyone was so upset, and I didn't know what to do, and I didn't have any friends, and I was afraid if I said something, everyone would think I did it. Or if they found him, they would say, hey, Nola was out walking by the creek, isn't that a funny coincidence. And she's so weird."

A huge, wrenching guilt rips through me as I remember how nasty we were to her when she showed up with her dyed raven-black hair, black nail polish, and goth makeup. *Necro.* We didn't even give her a chance. We made jokes about her sleeping with corpses and worshipping the devil. Of course it caught on. Everything we do eventually does. No wonder she was terrified. I open my mouth to say I'm sorry, but instead I just say, "No one would have thought you did that."

She looks at me sharply. "Everyone would have thought I did it." She sniffles and slumps into my shoulder. "So I picked him up, and just ran. Through the woods, in the snow, as far as I could. Then I put him down to bury him, but everything was frozen, so I covered him with stones. But the snow all around was covered in blood. For a while, I thought about just sinking into it, and just letting the snow surround me and freezing to death. It sounded like a painless way to die. But I chickened out." She suddenly sits up and blows her nose on her sleeve and then looks at me. "Do you know why?"

I shake my head. "Why?"

She walks across the room and points to one of the columns of writing on the wall. "'For in that sleep of death what dreams may come / When we have shuffled off this mortal coil, / Must give us pause.'"

I squint at her. "Shakespeare saved your life?"

She looks disappointed, almost disdainful. "Hamlet. He couldn't kill himself, because no matter what torments this life holds, the afterlife could be worse. We can't do it if we don't know." She looks so earnest that I nod, although she's dead wrong. Hamlet might not have been able to do it, but some people can. Megan did. I kind of doubt Shakespeare could have saved her, even if all his words covered all her walls.

"What if each of us dies and goes to an individually designed hell filled with our deepest and darkest fears?" Nola says, flopping back onto her bed. "If that's true, you can't possibly allow yourself to die one minute sooner than necessary."

"Sure." I try not to think of death too often since Megan

and Todd passed away, but when I do, I like to frame it in more optimistic terms. "But it's just as likely that the opposite is true. Maybe when we die, we instantly enter our own dreamland. A rerun of all our best memories." A smile crosses my lips, thinking of Todd and me as kids running around the backyard on the Fourth of July, the smell of hot dogs and burgers filling the air, fireflies and sparklers illuminating the twilight, the grass slick under our bare feet. That would be one to add to the reel. I hope he's somewhere like that right now.

"It's probably nothing," Nola says. "But still. It gives us pause." She sighs and looks back at the computer screen. "If Jessica knew I buried Hunter, she knew exactly where his body is. You know what we have to do now."

A sick feeling churns in my stomach. "We?"

"If you want the rest of the passwords, that is." She eyes me challengingly.

I stand, pulling my hair into a tight ponytail, and slip my coat on.

9

It's a clear night, but bitterly cold, with occasional gusts of wind that sweep the breath right out of my lungs. I decide the freezing trek around the lake and into the woods is worth wearing my Todd coat, and if we run into anyone carrying a corpse, I have more to worry about than fashion. The woods are on the far side of the lake beyond the main road, and we make the walk silently, me with my chapped red hands shoved deep into my pockets and Nola swinging her arms occasionally and doing half pirouettes now and then. As we spend more and more time together, I notice these things about her. She dances when she walks. Just little bounces and glides scattered here and there. Her gestures are graceful, and she sometimes stands en pointe, casually, as if without realizing she's doing it. She also speaks lyrically. Her speech pattern falls into a rhythm at times, and she taps her fingers and feet when she sits still for too long. When all is quiet, she begins to hum under her breath, and now I have to shush her once or twice, because if I don't, her voice will gradually rise until she is singing out loud, and eventually we'll be caught traipsing through the woods with a sack full of cat bones, merrily belting out show tunes.

"Are you sure you can find your way back to the spot?" I ask her as we beam our flashlights around the dark wood.

"I think so," she says. "There were landmarks. An old red barn on the right, an abandoned tractor on the left. A boulder with the initials *IKC* carved into it. A pink property-line ribbon and a hiking-trail marker, and three trees down, the stones."

I glance over at her in the dark, my flashlight bobbing low. "Good memory."

"Well, I had to trace my way out again," she says.

I pick my way slowly over the roots and stones, careful not to slip on the slick, frosted leaves. The last thing I need is an injury once I get the season jump-started again. We round a large downed oak tree with enormous, rotting branches sticking up from the ground, and Nola halts.

"Right there," she says, pointing.

I look where she's indicating but can't see anything. She makes her way across a small clearing, her sneakers brushing frost-encrusted leaves aside, and then begins removing stones from a small pile. I hesitate. I don't want to touch it. If there's a rotting corpse underneath, those stones are probably crawling with disease. I hang back and fumble with the zipper of the canvas backpack she decided we would use to transport the body. I shift my weight back and forth from one foot to the other as she rapidly removes the stones and discards them behind her. At any moment the body will appear. It's been there for quite a while and I don't know what to expect. It could be pretty macabre. I haven't seen many dead bodies.

Jessica was freshly dead, cuts and skin preserved by the icy water and the newness of her death. Megan was cremated. Todd was painstakingly made up to look like he hadn't been crushed by Megan's brother's truck. His rib cage was reconstructed under his brand-new navy suit. His hands were painted and powdered and fastened together to lovingly hug a football to his chest. They covered a big laceration on the side of his face and sewed his lips and eyelids to make him look peaceful. And then layers and layers of paint and powder, paint and powder. The most grotesque Halloween costume of all time.

I had begged my mother not to make me go to the wake, not to make me look at Todd's body, but she'd just stood there wordlessly, watching my mouth move. She was on so many pills, she couldn't comprehend a thing I said. It was all too much for her, Aunt Tracy had explained. I would never, ever know the depths of her despair. And yes, I had to go. It was expected. But when I stood there, staring down at the wreck of my brother's body, I thought maybe I understood the depths of my mother's despair a little. Only it didn't feel like sadness, or a pill that emptied my mind, or rage that made me shout things about lawyers or hell or revenge, like my dad did behind doors before I heard his sobs break through the house as loud as laughter. For me, it felt like little pangs, little jolts of impulsivity. Reach into the casket and try to reposition Todd's cold, posed hands. Drain Dad's bottle of special bourbon. What is anyone going to do about it? And later, at Bates. Run against the team captain sophomore year. Make the new girl eat a dead spider or write Coach a love poem or fake a seizure in the middle of chapel. Steal the prettiest clothes from the locker room and wear them around campus, because if you don't hide it and you don't back down, no one is going to call you on it. Jump into the lake after the Skeleton Dance. Whatever pops into my mind. Just to see what happens. Who's going to stop me? What's anyone going to do? Why does any of it even matter?

And then the world started spinning on its axis again. I did become team captain. Mom and Dad latched on. It all became real. Everything started to matter. I don't want to fall back into that wild spinning nothingness again. Because once you're in it, there are no footholds. It takes something extraordinary, a cosmic alignment of divine proportions, to pull you out. Meeting someone like Brie. Finding I do have a place in a school like Bates. A place where I can be sure, beyond the shadow of a doubt, that what is ahead of me is better than what I left behind. But the balance is so fragile.

I pretend to sneeze so I have an excuse to place my fingers over my face and I leave them there, peering out through the cracks. I do not want to see a rotting cat corpse. Nola removes another stone and I fidget in place. "What are we going to do with the body? We didn't even talk about that."

She doesn't look up. She removes another stone and discards it carelessly. "Rebury it."

"Where? How? We don't have shovels and the ground is frozen." I take a step backward into the darkness, so that the grave and the thin beam of flashlight illuminating it are almost blocked by her bent figure. But I can still see a sliver of her pale face curving over the ever-shrinking pile, her expression of concentration, the dirt accumulating under her fingernails.

"Not in the ground. That would be too obvious. It would just turn up again."

I take another uneasy step backward and scream as something touches my shoulder. A tree branch. I've backed into a tree.

Nola turns and glares at me. "You're going to get us caught."

"Sorry," I say meekly.

"You could help, you know."

"I don't think so. I'll stand lookout."

She removes one more stone and peers down. "Toss me the bag."

I throw it to her, unable to force myself to move closer or to back up farther, unable to look away or to make any effort to peer around her. What I see is this: hard-packed earth, tufts of fur, and bones. It's almost more shocking than everything worse my brain was conjuring because it's so simple and staged looking, like a museum exhibit. Fossils. The creepiest thought occurs to me. Nola had said Hunter wasn't dead when she found him. I edge closer and we stare down at the bones wordlessly, and I wonder. I almost ask. But then she carefully scrapes the bones and fur off the ground and into the backpack and wipes her filthy hands in the dirt.

She looks at me with unmasked disdain. "You're gutless, Donovan."

I'm beginning to agree. But it's not going to sway me into touching Hunter's remains. A sudden, paralyzing fear seizes through me that I will answer for his death, one way or another. That by witnessing his bones, I am somehow responsible. And then the fear explodes, and it's not just Hunter, it's Megan and Todd and Jessica. Death is a chain reaction, a butterfly effect. I shiver and begin to scatter the stones back around the clearing with my sneakers. "So what's the plan? We've got the bones."

She slings the backpack over her shoulder and heads down the path toward the main road. "We lay them to rest."

"You said they couldn't go back in the ground."

"Exactly. They're going where they'll never resurface."

The realization makes me shudder. "Don't you think the lake is under enough scrutiny right now?"

She picks up her pace and I try to match it. "Not near where Jessica was found. Near the main road."

I fall into step next to her. "Nola, think this through. If anyone ever finds this, it's way more incriminating than the grave. They can trace the backpack to you."

"How? Have you ever heard of running a DNA test because of a dead animal?"

I fall silent for a while, but I'm uneasy. A lot could go wrong. I pull my cashmere hood over my head as we near the main road and peer down into the darkness in both directions before sprinting across. All is quiet. At the edge of the lake, Nola kneels and unzips the backpack, and I gather stones to weigh it down. Accomplice, a voice in my head screams. Accessory to murder.

I lift a heavy rock, slippery with moss and algae, and slip it into the bag. It crunches the bones and other stones beneath it. "So, I guess after this, we're done."

She pushes her sleeves up and wipes the sweat off her forehead. "Not half. These are pebbles. Give me something to work with."

"With the revenge blog." I pause and begin working on another large stone. "Obviously I can't continue to work on it without the software, but just show me how to use it, and we're cool."

"I didn't say I was done." Her face is a mask of stillness, but her arms are wrapped tightly around her waist, almost protectively.

"Well, I'm saying it."

She lets out a sharp laugh. "You are not firing me."

"I'm not putting you in any more danger. We've destroyed your evidence but your name is still on the list. Just do me one more favor and take your name off the class roster like you did with Tricia. And teach me how to use that stupid password software. I'll take care of the rest."

"Like you have any control over this shit storm?" She smiles up at me in the moonlight. There's always an air of cynicism in her smiles, but for just one moment, with the breeze softly blowing strands of velvety hair around her pale face, her eyes luminous, she looks hopeful.

Then I remember why we're standing here, and the fact that I am directly responsible for her involvement.

Apologize. Do it now. "Fine. You're the foul-mouthed sidekick, though."

"I behave ever like a perfect lady." Nola helps me yank the stone out of the ground and stuff it into the backpack. She zips it up, then stands and attempts unsuccessfully to lift it. "Good sweet holy crap, this is heavy. Give me a hand."

I brace myself against the rail separating the lake from the road and slip one of the straps over my shoulder and lift. Suddenly a white beam of light swings out over us.

"Duck." Nola lets go of the backpack and flattens herself on the ground, leaving me holding it alone.

Like a deer staring into the signals of its own doom, I freeze, equally expecting to look into a pair of headlights and the ghost of Jessica Lane hounding me for disturbing the dead. But it's neither of those. In fact, it's much worse. It's Detective Morgan herself, marching down the lake path brandishing a flashlight.

I drop the backpack and start running.

"You! Stop right there!"

I hear Nola shriek and a pair of footsteps pounding behind me. I have confidence in my ability to outrun Morgan. I am in peak physical fitness, seventeen years old and conditioning daily, at the top of my game. She's probably around thirty-five and may have been an athlete once, but let's face it, there aren't many criminals to chase around here. She doesn't call to me by name, and that gives me hope. I might have a fighting chance to get back without being caught. Nola, on the other hand, is a wild card. Although she's short, she has to be in pretty good shape if she dances regularly. I can't afford to stop and look back, but

I have to hope that she either split off in another direction or stayed hidden. If she gets caught, I'm as good as caught, too, because I have no reason to believe she'd protect me.

I pound my sneakers on the lake path, taking the curves hard, and then cut away from the dorms toward the gym, hoping to outlast them both. Even if Morgan is fast, I'm going to bank on having more stamina. I round the gym and slow down, listening for footsteps behind me. I can't hear anything. My heart hammering, I take my phone out of my pocket and consider texting Nola to see if she made it back. I can't, though. If she's with Detective Morgan right now, and by some miracle didn't rat me out, then texting would implicate me.

I duck into the gym and head into the locker room for a quick shower before I go home. Just in case. When I'm toweling off and slipping into the spare change of clothes I keep in my locker for rainy day practices, I see that Nola's texted.

Close one, she wrote.

My body is still shaking with the adrenaline of the chase and the terror of almost getting caught, but I also feel oddly exhilarated and defiant. It's the Nola effect, I decide.

You owe me, I text back. I grin and head back to the dorm.

10

*b*y the next evening the news is all over campus: The body of a cat was found near the lake.

"It was probably the same person who murdered Jessica," Cori says at dinner. "Apparently, the killer was using cats to whet their appetite for human murder. That's how serial killers start out. Everyone knows that."

Brie kicks me under the table and smirks. Cori was a major player in the original missing-cat story because she was a family friend of Dr. Klein and, as such, had known Hunter from the time he was a kitten. She took his kidnapping very seriously and led student search efforts. As a person who had regularly been in Dr. Klein's mansion, she was also the leading authority on how someone could have gotten in and out without being seen while Dr. and Mr. Klein were having dinner, where Hunter was likely to have been at the time, and other forensic matters. She even started a short-lived true-crime podcast about Hunter's disappearance, but quickly grew bored and dropped it when it became apparent that it was not going to be the next *Serial*.

She unloads her new set of theories to Brie, Maddy, and me in her rapid-fire speech as I pick the mushrooms out of a chicken quesadilla. It's a little bittersweet. Quesadilla night was Tai's and my favorite.

"I thought Jessica committed suicide," Maddy interrupts.

Cori glares at her. "At this point, anyone still clinging to the suicide theory is in denial because they're scared, Notorious. Would there still be crime scene tape on her room if it was a suicide? And why would the detectives still be questioning us?"

I snap my head up. "They questioned you, too?"

Cori eyes me dubiously. "Of course. We were witnesses."

I feel my silverware slipping between my fingers and place it down, wiping my palms on my skirt. "What did you tell her?"

She frowns and tucks a strand of her thick, chin-length brown hair behind her ear. "Him. I talked to the short guy. Lombardi. I told him what we saw. Dead body, very sad, too late to do anything. Now. Back to poor sweet Hunter."

Nola flutters over and sets her tray down next to me and Cori stops talking. Brie smiles tautly and nods a greeting. Cori and Maddy both gaze up at Nola wordlessly. She looks back at them and then at me.

I take a nervous bite of quesadilla. "You guys know Nola Kent?"

"We keep meeting," Brie says. She takes a sip of my soda and it strikes me what a territorial move it is. No way is she jealous. I glance at Nola, who is sipping her own drink and watching Brie, and then at Brie, who hangs on to my glass and swirls the straw around.

Nola turns to Cori. "You're the cat girl."

Cori clears her throat. "Actually, yeah. I knew him personally."

It's not funny at all. What happened to Hunter was sick and vicious and wrong. But the tension at the table is getting to me, and something about the way she says it bubbles a giggle up to my lips. Brie gives me an odd look, and I cough into my hands. Nola flashes me a wicked grin behind her mug of tea.

"What's the matter with you?" Cori snaps at Nola, not entirely fairly. I was the one who laughed. Although Nola did grin.

"So who did it?" I ask Cori, hoping to defuse the situation. "Bottom line."

She takes a bite of avocado and chews thoughtfully. "A student. A junior or a senior. Someone who was here long enough to have a familiarity with Dr. Klein's mansion and Dr. Klein herself, and obviously, someone who's still here." She takes a sip of milk and then goes on, thoroughly enjoying the spotlight. "It was someone who had a reason to resent Dr. Klein. But it wasn't revenge. It was a compulsion."

Maddy's eyes widen. "So you think it's a *serial* killer?"

Cori nods solemnly. "It's textbook."

Brie brushes her foot against mine again, and bounces it back and forth between hers playfully. "Kill any cats lately?" She came to dinner straight from track practice, just slightly breathless, her cheeks still flushed, her hair pushed back from her forehead with a scarlet band. She's always cutest right after practice.

"Funny."

Cori frowns. "What?"

I kick my foot free. "Brie thinks it's hilarious that the detective at the crime scene has a vendetta against me."

Maddy rolls her eyes. "Why was she so mean? She obviously needs a hobby."

"Maybe she's right." All eyes turn to Nola, who looks at us ominously over her mug of tea. I close my eyes in frustration. Why does she have to be so weird? "I mean, Jessica stole her boyfriend. No one else has a motive. Except Jessica's ex, and since Kay's secretly sleeping with Greg, who knows what else they're hiding?" She shrugs, and everyone gapes at me.

"Please tell me you're doing no such thing," Brie demands.

"I'm not!" I turn to Nola, who is grinning wickedly. "She made that up. I'm not dating anyone."

"I didn't say dating," Nola says in a loud stage whisper.

Maddy's mouth drops open and Brie casts me an uncertain glance. I grab my tray and storm away from the table, dumping the remainder of my dinner in the trash. Nola follows me to the door.

"Sorry," she says lightly. "Did I take it too far?"

"What is wrong with you?" I shrug my coat onto my shoulders. "I called Greg because you asked me to set you up. I'm trying to be nice to you, Nola."

She crosses her arms over her chest and juts her pointy, almost elflike chin out. "Yeah? Is it that hard? Is it really so painful?"

I become aware that everyone within earshot is staring at us. "Just . . . be normal."

She shakes her head. "Take a joke, Kay."

"Your jokes aren't funny."

She narrows her eyes. "Yeah? Neither are yours."

I push out the door into a swirl of leaves and stalk back toward my dorm. In a moment, Brie rushes out and falls into step beside me.

"What is going on with you?"

"Nothing. Nola is full of shit."

"Then why are you wasting your time on her?" Her breath clouds out of her mouth, and she bounces up and down as we walk. She's only wearing a sweatshirt and track pants, and I take my jacket off and hand it to her but she pushes it back to me. We play reverse tug-of-war for a second until she finally drapes it over both of our shoulders. "Stubborn."

"She's weird, but she's nice."

"She doesn't seem nice at all. She just made an ass out of you."

"Apparently you don't like anyone anymore."

Brie squints at me. "Why would you say that?"

I shrug. "Maddy."

We stop talking for a moment as we pass through a group of students, who give Brie the customary smiles and greetings, but either I'm imagining it or I get a few weird looks. "Okay, did that anonymously skanky junior just mouth the word *bitch* at me?" I stop dead and glare at her over my shoulder. Her name is Hillary Jenkins; she tried out for soccer two years running and didn't make the cut. And I can make her life a living hell.

Brie steers me away from the wrought-iron lamppost where the juniors have congregated. "Look. With Tai and Tricia gone, people are starting to talk. About you ratting both of them out, getting Hannigan fired—"

"He was fired?"

"Where have you been, and why wasn't I invited? Tai and Tricia are finishing the year at public school, and to them, that's a huge insult."

"Neither of them will answer my texts."

"Well, the word going around is that you made it happen."

"I didn't."

"Of course you didn't. Just like you didn't sleep with Jessica's ex-boyfriend." She purses her lips and raises her eyebrows. "Interesting how these rumors started the second you began hanging out with Nola."

"You're way off." I turn around and glance back at the juniors, contemplating setting the record straight about exactly what went down with Tai and Tricia. But Brie gently pulls me back toward Barton Hall.

"There's one more thing." We've reached the stone steps of Barton and she gazes up at my window. "Somehow it got out that Jessica and Spencer slept together. And people think it's weird that she died right after that. Now, with you turning on all your friends and hanging out with Nola, who has a reputation for necrophilia and devil worship—"

"That's bullshit. We made up that rumor."

"Well, it's coming around to bite you in the ass now. Maybe reconsider hanging around with her until the investigation wraps up."

I kick the grass and stifle a scream of frustration. "This sucks."

"It's going to be okay. We just need to lie low and ride it out."

I study her. "You still think suicide?"

She takes in a deep breath and lets it out slowly. "It's tough to say without seeing the evidence." A lawyer answer. She looks at her watch. "I have a ton of Latin."

"French."

"So, no more Nola?" It's never easy to argue with Brie. First, she phrases requests like statements. Second, her level of self-confidence makes me doubt myself. And third, standing this close, I forget why my side of the argument was important in the first place.

"Come on. Would you stop hanging out with Justine if I asked you to?" I try to say it casually, like it isn't an actual question.

Brie's face clouds over. "Fine. I didn't realize you and Nola were so close." She flings my jacket at me. "Talk soon."

I stomp into the building and up the stairs to my room. I have to get some actual homework done tonight. It takes me until midnight to catch up on my work and I almost fall asleep at my desk, but Nola's jabs are bothering me. Obviously I'm not dating Greg, nor am I interested, but I do need to learn more about Jessica and what she might have known about my past.

Greg is probably the last person I should be speaking to, after what Detective Morgan said. But he also knows Jessica better than anyone else. I brush my teeth, change into my pajamas, climb into bed, and switch off the light before I decide to call him. He doesn't pick up, which makes sense, because by now it's approaching one o'clock. I decide not to leave him a message. He'll see that I called. If he wants to call back, he will.

But by one thirty, I still can't sleep and I somehow end up dialing Spencer's number.

"Katie D. How many lives have you ruined today?" he greets.

"Never mind."

"Don't hang up," he says hastily. I can hear him typing rapidly. "Sorry. I'm in a bad mood because I'm losing. Let me die." For a moment I hear him punching his keyboard violently, and then there's silence. "Sorry. I've missed our Insomniacs Anonymous meetings."

"Can't say the same." I could. But I never would. Both of us are terrible sleepers. We think too much. Night was one thing Brie and I could never really share, because she's an early sleeper, so as much as I love lying next to her for the first hour, it very quickly becomes torturous staring up at a dark ceiling. Spencer and I drove around, made out, talked endlessly about nothing, threw rocks at the moon. Stuff you do when there's nothing else to do. I snuck Spencer into my dorm overnight once—an infraction that could have resulted in expulsion—and we climbed the tower and spent the night watching for shooting stars. I fell asleep eventually, but when I woke, his forehead was still pressed against the window, his eyes trained on the thin halo of light rising over the lake. That was the night I told everyone Spencer and I finally had sex, the night it was supposed to happen. Somehow, though, we ended up just watching, waiting. There was supposed to be a meteor shower. The heavens failed us.

"I love your honesty." I hear him lighting a cigarette and opening his bedroom window. I imagine myself there with him. I've always hated the smell of smoke, except in the freezing cold, tucked under his battered down parka. I can't explain it.

"Then tell me something."

"Ladies' choice."

I want to ask both about Jessica and whether the police have questioned him, but Spencer is impulsive about telling the truth. He's more likely to be forthcoming if he brings it up himself than if I ask him and it's obvious that I care. Because then it's a game. "Are you seeing anyone?" I ask instead.

"Cops aren't exactly my type, you know?"

His other talent is seeing right through me.

"Let's meet up."

"Seriously?"

"Sure. Sleep is becoming a vanishing memory at this point. Meet me at Old Road in fifteen."

He doesn't hesitate. "Bring snacks."

I show up with two Vitaminwaters and a handful of energy

bars. I don't really have anything else. When he pulls up, I climb into his car and am immediately enveloped by the smells of vanilla coffee and cigarette smoke. He gestures to the cup holder and I pick up a coffee cup gratefully.

"I knew you would screw up the snack mission. There are doughnuts in the back."

I reach behind me and pick out a glazed chocolate. "Thanks."

He heads down the winding road through the woods that line the eastern shore of the lake. "What do you want, Kay? You only call when you want something."

"Doesn't sound like me. I just want to talk."

"About?" He flicks his cigarette out his window and rolls it up, and I turn up the heat.

"Nothing. Anything. Coffee and doughnuts."

He pulls the car over and looks at me. "Then let's really talk. About us."

I get the worst sinking feeling. His face has always struck me as angelic and devilish at the same time, depending on the expression he chooses to wear, and right now the hope in his eyes is destroying me. Part of me wants to kiss him and tell him to forget everything both of us have done. Because Brie is never going to want me. Not as her girlfriend. She proved that tonight. And Spencer and I know each other so well. We can call each other on our bullshit, and drive each other wild, talk each other down from the ledge, and turn each other on in seconds. I hate that everything I want is ruined by contradiction. My brain is split, my heart severed. In this moment, right now, I want to unbuckle my seat belt, climb into his lap, and kiss away every memory the past few weeks has scarred into my brain.

But on the razor edge of tomorrow and forever and the second there is air between us again, I can't forgive him for Jessica. At least, I can't forget it. I can't stop picturing. And every time I do, it's the same terrifying way, a waking nightmare. Her dead, cold body wrapped around him.

"Spence," I say quietly, "there's nothing about us left to talk about. We both know it."

"You'd be surprised," he says in a deadly calm voice.

My breath catches in my throat. "What does that mean?"

He starts the car again. "Once," he says, without looking at me. "Jess and I only hooked up one time. Is that what you wanted to know?"

"I didn't ask."

"You didn't need to."

He drives to our meeting place, the dusty dirt road that diverges from the street and loops around the lake and ends between the village and the lake path at the edge of campus.

"Thanks for the coffee."

He clasps his hands and sighs into them. "It wasn't about you."

"Right." I can't help my voice and temper rising. "It had nothing to do with Brie and me."

"*She* hit on *me*."

I stop, the door half open. "Did she say anything about me?"

"She said you were a narcissistic paranoiac who might think people pursue her boyfriends just to make her jealous."

"Whatever, Spence."

He grabs my hand. "Kay." I look back at him. "When she asked if I was seeing anyone, I said no. She called me a dirty little liar. I thought she was being cute, but maybe she did know about us. Looking back, I tend to think she probably did."

I pause. "How did you meet?"

"At a party." He takes a deep breath and then looks at me guiltily. "Brie introduced us."

He's not lying this time. He looks as nauseous as I feel.

I slam the door in his face.

IN THE MORNING, Detective Morgan is waiting for me in the dorm lobby. Barton Hall was constructed in the manner of a grand British estate, a sort of scaled-down version of Downton Abbey, and the common room is all windows, floor to ceiling.

When I can't sleep, I like to curl up in one of the ancient velvety armchairs so I can gaze up at the stars and pretend it's all mine. That's where Detective Morgan decides to question me.

Once again, Dr. Klein is present as my chaperone. I'm still groggy and my muscles are itching for my customary coffee and weekday morning jog around the lake. I'm convinced my blood doesn't flow right otherwise. But Morgan looms in front of the door, standing between me and the crisp morning air, her arms folded, a creepy smile twisting her thin lips, and Dr. Klein hunches in the corner looking smaller and older than usual, dressed in an untucked blouse and drab beige slacks instead of one of her usual bright pantsuits. I attempt a timid smile at her but she just raises a finger toward the common room and I head inside, a cloud of dread settling over me. So. Maybe Morgan recognized me the other night after all.

She has me sit facing the glass wall so the rising sun is in my face and I have to squint to look at her, silhouetted against the spotless glass. Dr. Klein arranges herself on a sofa in the corner, her knees drawn up underneath her, her hand tucked under her chin. It's unsettling seeing her in such a casual pose and it occurs to me that the discovery of Hunter's body has hit her much harder than I anticipated. I didn't think about it much, but I'd assumed that she'd given him up for dead. Maybe she hadn't.

Morgan clears her throat. "Where were you two nights ago?"

"Studying."

"You logged out of the dorm for dinner at five thirty p.m."

"Yes."

"You logged back in around ten thirty."

"That's right." I look at her dark figure. Her face is indistinguishable from the rest of her, backlit by the slowly brightening campus.

"You were studying all that time?"

"I ate first. Then I headed over to my friend Nola's room. We studied, I left, went for a run, came back to my room, and studied again until midnight."

Morgan shifts in her chair, pulls a notebook from her pocket, and jots a few things down. "Let me get this straight. Dinner at five thirty, Nola's at, say, six thirty, you signed out of her dorm at seven thirty-eight, and back into your dorm at ten forty-two, and then you studied until midnight."

I try to swallow the lump rapidly forming in my throat, but my mouth is bone dry. She's already checked the logs and confirmed my exact sign-in and sign-out times. "Sounds right."

She scoots her chair a little closer to me, almost imperceptibly, but her face is still in the dark. "So you were running, alone, unaccounted for, between seven thirty-eight and ten forty-two. That's a hell of a run. You're a Class A athlete, Kay."

"I do okay."

"You look like you're heading out for a run right now."

"I run every day. I have to."

She scoots closer again, the wooden claws of her chair scraping across the floor. "You have to. What happens if you stop?"

"The same thing that happens to everyone if they stop conditioning. Their body weakens. They lose strength, stamina, their heart and muscles suffer, they don't perform to the best of their ability. They die sooner. Do you run every day?" I doubt Morgan has the discipline to even take a five-minute walk every day.

As if reading my mind, she yawns lazily. "No. I walk my dog, though. It clears my head. Beautiful scenery up here. Especially when the leaves turn. I guess you've heard about Dr. Klein's cat."

"I heard they found a cat."

"I did. I found a girl trying to dispose of a body."

"That's horrible." I'm strangely relieved that she only saw one of us.

"It is. It's also unusual, for a number of reasons." Again, she slides the chair forward, just an inch. Now I can see half of her body, up to her waist, but her face remains in the dark. "Typically, when a household pet is mutilated and killed, it isn't buried. It's left on display. The killer is proud of what they did and wants to savor the reaction of the pet's owner."

I am suddenly painfully aware of Dr. Klein hunched in the corner of the room. Although her face isn't visible to me, and although I didn't do anything to actually harm Hunter, I feel a stifling guilt that makes it difficult to breathe. I have a sudden incredible urge to look at her, to blurt out an apology, and my bones itch to jump out of my body and run, get me the hell out of the room before I say something that will ruin my life.

I shift my weight uncomfortably in the chair. I feel like I'm sinking into it, like it will be impossible to rise up out of it without an enormous amount of strength and maneuvering. "That's weird."

"The other thing is how much time has passed. For the killer to wait over a year to suppress the evidence is curious. Why now?"

I shrug slightly, just a tiny gesture.

"Well, there is the other body in the lake," she continues, and she hitches her chair forward again. "Do you see what I'm seeing?" I can see her jutting chin, her sharp nose, but not her eyes. Everything about her is sharp, angles and corners. Maybe she's not as stupid as she comes off. Every time she questions me, she starts the conversation like a kindergarten teacher and ends up giving me mental whiplash.

"Now, I'm thinking maybe the person who killed Jessica also killed Hunter. And when you put two and two together, it looks like the killer is a student at Bates. Possibly with a close group of friends willing to do some covering up. Lying to the police." She finally makes that last nudge forward, and I see her beady eyes fixed on me. "Do you know what we found on Jessica's bed after we secured the crime scene?"

I shake my head, jarred by the sudden change of subject.

"A phone, a photo, a message, no fingerprints. Nod if any of this sounds familiar."

She's speaking so quickly, analyzing every breath I take, every blink, every swallow, every minute eye movement. I'm afraid to breathe.

"A photo of her body floating in the lake, on her phone. And something else. Something of yours." She waits, her eyes sharp and dangerous.

"Do I want to talk to a lawyer or something?" I whisper.

Her thin lips break into a grin. "I'm not questioning you, Kay. We're just chatting. You're a witness. If I *really* had something on you, we'd be down at the station. You'd be in custody, your parents would be here, an officer would've read you your rights, you'd have all the lawyers you want." She pauses. "There's still something that doesn't make sense to me, Kay. You freely told me you had no alibi at the time Jessica was killed. Every single one of your friends contradicted that in their witness statements."

I nod hesitantly.

"They said they were by your side the entire night. If you tell me the truth now, it makes it a lot easier to believe you going forward. Where were you when Jessica Lane was murdered?"

My mind races. The last time she asked me, I told her I was alone and it backfired. I can't risk doing that again. Besides, Greg is the top suspect. I just have to follow Brie's advice and lie low. "With my friends," I finally say.

She looks down and sighs heavily, and then meets my eye coldly. "Lying to the police is a crime, Katie."

"I'm not lying," I whisper.

"We found your shoes behind the ballroom. The ones you claimed to be changing in your room at the time of the murder."

The time of the murder.

When Brie left us outside the party, I *did* mean to go back to my room to change. But everything was ruined and wrong. My head was blurry from the prosecco and my heart felt gigantic and painful in my ribs and I just wanted to bury myself in ice until it all went away. I walked barefoot down the lake path toward Old Road, pressing the cold mouth of the bottle to my lips, dialing Spencer's number, not really expecting him to pick up. And then he did, and he said this horrible, shocking word I will never be able to scrape out of my mind.

He said, "Jess?"

Then he said, "Be there in five."

Now, as Detective Morgan looms in front of me, I've never been more spooked in my life. If I weren't so terrified of my parents' reaction, I would call them immediately. But they would flip. Then suddenly the thought of my parents flicks a little switch inside, and the other Kay, the Kay I've been trying to kill, sparks and ignites. I stand abruptly and look down at Detective Morgan, at her ratty brown hair, the one yellow front tooth that doesn't match the others, her ugly, smug smile with those thin paper lips.

"Is your life actually so pointless that you have nothing better to do than to harass seventeen-year-old girls?"

Her smile fades, and her mouth literally drops open.

"You're delusional if you think you're going to intimidate me into a false confession. How many murders are committed by teenage girls, statistically? How many by pervy old men or jealous ex-boyfriends? Why don't you start looking at some of them and stop stalking me, bitch."

I storm out of the room and head outside. I'm going to be late for my first class, but I don't care. If I don't run this off, I'm going to explode.

11

i avoid Brie all day. I'm not prepared to face her yet after learning that she set Spencer up with Jessica. It's a double gut punch. The fact that she would do that to me is bad enough. But that she acted for weeks like nothing happened makes my brain pulse until I feel like it's going to crack my skull.

Instead, I prepare for our first soccer practice since Jessica's death. I show up early to try to give Nola a bit of last-minute coaching, but she's late. Maddy is just finishing up field hockey practice at the adjoining field, and I wander over to chat while I wait.

She looks surprised to see me. "Kay. I didn't know you were holding practice today."

"Why wouldn't I?"

"I don't know. You've seemed distracted lately." She sprays her face with a water bottle and then rubs it vigorously so her skin turns bright red.

"That doesn't mean I'm not a hundred percent committed to winning."

She grins. "So nothing's changed, really."

I pick up a field hockey stick and swing it. When I was a kid, my parents put me in softball and I sucked. I struck out, threw short, and couldn't catch. The only thing I could do was steal bases, but since I rarely made it to first, it was pretty painful. I hated sports altogether until the day Todd dragged me into the backyard with a soccer ball and challenged me to get it away from him using no hands. It took a while but I was determined, and eventually something clicked.

I smile at Maddy. "Nah. Nothing ever changes."

She looks behind me and her expression freezes. "Oh dear Lord."

Nola has finally shown up, dressed completely inappropriately in a pair of tiny black terry shorts and knee-highs, black Converse, and a white T-shirt with the words I DO SPORTS printed on it in stark lettering.

"Awesome." I jog over to Nola.

Maddy follows and sits on the bench to watch. "This should be fun."

"You're going to freeze," I tell Nola, unzipping my hoodie and handing it to her. I have a long-sleeved T-shirt under my jersey and I'm still going to be shivering until I run a couple of laps. I start to do some stretches and she watches me uncertainly and tries to mimic me, and then gives up and launches into her own stretch routine.

"Revisited the website?" she asks.

"Actually, I've been sidetracked by the murder investigation. The police detective paid me another unfriendly visit." And then it hits me. When Detective Morgan warned me about lying to the police, she called me Katie.

I grab my bag and dig my phone out of it.

Nola performs a practice kick. "Soccer!"

I consider for a moment, and decide that after all we've been through, I can trust Nola with the original Jessica email. "Come here." I show her the email as we start a slow lap to get some distance from Maddy.

Nola hovers over my shoulder and reads out loud. "'At the risk of sounding cliché, talking to the police would not go well for you.' Acknowledging that it's cliché doesn't negate the fact that it's cliché."

I take a moment to choose my wording carefully. "There was an incident where I witnessed a crime, and for whatever reason, the police didn't believe my story. It was the worst. I had to be interviewed over and over and over."

Nola gasps. "Jessica knew about it."

I nod. "Somehow."

"And no one else would know that about you," she says doubtfully. But she stops and looks around the field, as if someone might be watching us right now.

"No one." But it's a lie. One other person knows what I did. The only person who knows that people called me Katie back home. Spencer Morrow.

It's impossible to concentrate during the rest of practice. Nola is horrible. She can't kick, she can't steal, and she can't defend. She can run, but by some ridiculous clause of Murphy's law, she can't run in the same direction as the ball. And she falls. A lot.

By the end of practice, everyone is pissed at me, except Nola, who by some miraculous brand of self-delusion seems to think she did well. Coach pulls me aside and tells me my judgment is sliding; there is no way we are going to make it to states or that I'm going to win a scholarship with Nola so much as wandering within fifty feet from the field. No one will talk to me because they love Holly Gartner, the alternate I had to bench to add Nola to the roster. Holly sat there in tears the entire time as Nola made an ass out of herself and me, and when I tried to approach her after the practice, she stormed off before I could open my mouth.

If I urge Coach to keep Nola around, my chances at being scouted are shot. I have to close a perfect season. Our biggest games are coming up right after Thanksgiving, and once we crush it, I feel confident I can win a scholarship. But I can't do it without Holly. Nola has to go. And I have no idea how to tell her.

Maddy watched the entire practice. I caught her glaring at Nola, but she waved at me sympathetically a few times. I wish there weren't any witnesses to my epic humiliation, but she jogs over afterward and invites me to grab a coffee before dinner. I'm torn. I'm behind on studying and want to open the next revenge-blog clue. But I also want to vent about this disaster of a practice, and it would be a major relief to focus on something mundane for once.

"Sure," I say.

"Yay. Are we going to that cute cat place?"

Maddy shoots an annoyed look over my shoulder. I hadn't seen Nola standing there. I sigh. So much for venting.

WE SIT AWKWARDLY around a small table—Nola with her tea and Maddy and I with coffees—and make small talk until Nola goes to the bathroom.

Maddy bangs her head against the table. "Oh my God, she is so weird."

"We're friends."

Maddy blushes. "Sorry. I figured you were just sleeping together."

"I see." I take a sip of my coffee. "You're not here to dole out sympathy. You're here for gossip."

"No." She sighs into her hand and lowers her eyes. "I wanted to see how you were doing. Everything's been so bizarre lately. First Jessica turning up dead, then Tai and Tricia dropping out. Neither of them will return my texts. But people seem to think—"

"Yeah. Kay ruins the world."

She shakes her head emphatically. "Bates isn't the world, and you didn't ruin it." She plays with the ends of her silky scarf, running it over the smooth tabletop. "Have you talked to Spencer lately?"

I sigh. "Depends on what you mean by talk."

"Are you getting back together?"

"Definitely not."

She chews on a strand of hair for a moment and then smooths it out. "It just seems like you've been having a kind of tough time, and I wanted to let you know, I'm here. If you want to talk."

I eye her suspiciously. "Or I could just tweet it."

She stands up. "Point taken."

"Hey." I grab her hand and pull her back. Her eyes are filled with tears and I'm shocked into silence.

"I just meant, I know how it feels to be shut out."

"When did we ever shut you out?"

She shrugs. "No one ever tells me anything. And it's more

than that. Sometimes you can be in the middle of everything and still be completely alone. I'm just saying, call me if you need to."

I stand and hug her hard. "You call me. I never sleep. Ever. Rest is once upon a time for me. And if you want me to talk to the others about the stupid Notorious R.B.G. thing, consider it done."

Maddy looks startled for a second. "What would you say?"

"I don't know. Maddy's smart, but she's no Ruth Bader Ginsburg?"

She laughs and wipes the tears away. "I'm fine. You call me."

I nod. "Of course."

Her phone vibrates and she looks down at it. "I should run before your girlfriend comes bouncing back."

"She has energy," I manage. "Not so much control."

"Bench her." Maddy twists her scarf back around her neck. "Bring Holly back. If Nola's a friend, she'll understand. She sucks. You don't even have to tell her it's your decision. It's okay to put yourself first. Just don't let her find out."

"I promised her."

"Well, everything breaks. Bones, hearts. Better a promise than an undefeated record." She gives me a meaningful look and then one more hug before disappearing out the door.

When Nola comes back from the bathroom, though, I can't bring myself to say anything. Not yet, anyway. I need her too much.

I MANAGE TO successfully avoid Brie the rest of the week despite a constant barrage of texts, throwing myself into studying and soccer and eating with Nola. I can't get two things out of my head: the fact that Brie set up Spencer and Jessica, and the fact that Detective Morgan might know about my past history with the police.

Honestly, I don't know which one is worse.

After Megan committed suicide in the girls' locker room, officers interviewed every female student in eighth and ninth grade. Then, when they found her video suicide note posted online, they interviewed me again. And again. And again.

Her parents had it removed immediately, before I could see it, and the cops never let me know if or how it referred to me. Maybe it didn't mention me at all. But they kept asking me questions. What did I know about her relationship with my brother? Did she tell me anything about the pictures? Did she show me the pictures? Did Todd show me the pictures?

That was the thing. I never saw the pictures at all.

A bunch of ninth- and tenth-grade boys saw them, and some of the girls. Megan was in ninth grade, and she knew a lot of them. But I didn't. I never saw any of the pictures and I never spoke to anyone who did. I only had that one moment, that shock out of the blue when she told me she had taken them and sent them to him, and he had sent them to everyone, and in that split second between our friendship being everything and nothing, all I could think to say was "I'm sure it was an accident."

I never had a chance to fix things between us because she never spoke to me again.

When I crept into his room later, he looked sick and pale and scared and he said someone stole his phone. Todd, the oldest friend I had. The one who gave me soccer, my saving grace, my ticket out of Hillsdale and into Bates. The kid who got his teeth knocked out standing up for me when Jason Edelman called me a dyke in fourth grade, when I didn't know what that word meant.

What the fuck was I supposed to say in that three-second window?

And that's what I told myself, and the police. Someone stole his phone. Someone stole his phone.

If you say something enough times, it becomes true.

The tricky part is that sometimes you need to fill in details that may not have been there before in order to make the truth real.

Maybe I wasn't with Todd when the pictures were being sent out. Maybe I didn't drive around with him looking for his stolen phone. Maybe I didn't find it with him, hours after the pictures had been sent.

But none of those truths I created were inconsistent with

what I believed. Which were that he *did* lose his phone and drive around looking for it, and he didn't deserve to have his life ruined just because he didn't have an alibi. If Todd took the blame, I could never prove to Megan that what I said to her was okay. That it really was someone else who hurt her. And when I found that person, they would pay in blood.

Only it was Megan who paid.

Then Todd.

And then I was alone.

_n_ ola and I hole up on the top floor of the library on Saturday night to study and unlock the next recipe. It's a long weekend because of Veterans Day, and virtually everyone is taking advantage of the bonus study time. Most of the building is packed with people preparing for midterms, but up here it's quiet as usual. It's slowly become our personal hangout, our refuge from the noise and drama that Bates Academy has evolved into. No one can shut up about the cat or the murder or Dr. Klein's slowly deteriorating physical appearance for five seconds. People have started to whisper and stare at me, and players are showing up late or not at all for practice. I haven't spoken to Cori since our awkward dinner or Maddy since our coffee date, and I've been successful at ducking Brie's calls. Luckily, she's been buried under a pile of books in preparation for the coming midterms, and she usually studies in her room. This weekend is also her and Justine's one-year anniversary. It would have been Spencer's and mine, too. Right now Brie is in New York, probably eating tiny portions of foods I can't pronounce in a restaurant where they serve champagne instead of water and give you massages at your seat. I ate a doughy square of microwave pizza from the athletic center's snack machine as I jogged to the library after practice. It burned the roof of my mouth.

Everything is the worst.

Nola and I settle into the big overstuffed green chair together, and Nola positions her laptop so we can both see the screen.

"I brought snacks." I open a bottle of grapefruit soda, pour it into two paper cups, and break a giant chocolate chip cookie in half. Fuck Spencer. And Brie and Justine and their fancy anniversary weekend. I've got Nola, refined sugars, and revenge from beyond the grave.

"Thanks." She bites into one as she opens the website and password-decoding software, and types into it rapidly. The word *b@ckf1r3* appears. She enters it into the website and clicks on the link to the side dish. The oven opens, revealing the recipe for Prueba Con Coriander, and the timer begins.

Got a tough one? Don't despair!
You only fail if you play fair.
She's the one who knows what's fore

Time to settle up the score

Knock another castle down

Watch the queen fall to the ground.

"Cori would be the obvious target." I read it again. "Isn't *prueba* a proof or test?"

Nola frowns critically. "She plays golf, so she 'knows what's fore.' These puns are getting overbearing. What's the castle and the queen? A chess reference? Castling only works on kings. Does Cori have a secret girlfriend?"

"*Cori* is the castle. Once we knock her out, the queen is left open. Doesn't play fair. Test scores. So, what, she has test answers in her locker?" For some reason, this pisses me off. She's never offered to help *me*, and she knows I struggle. Not that I would cheat. But why wouldn't she offer?

"Sorry. Look, it's not prison worthy. Just talk to her and tell her to ditch the evidence. The others have been pretty incriminating. Drugs, sex scandal, murder."

"I don't know if an animal counts as murder."

Fear flashes in Nola's eyes. "It counts as something. You said yourself they think it's connected to Jessica's murder. The point is, this one isn't actually that bad. Just tell her now before it goes public."

A thought crosses my mind. "Do you think we can stop

that by just removing her name from the class roster? I mean, Tai might have been kicked out, but Tricia *chose* to leave, and you never had to."

"Why is the class roster so important?"

"Maybe one website is linked to the other or something? I don't really understand codes and algorithms and matrices."

Nola holds up a hand. "You're embarrassing yourself. I get what you're saying, though. One might be programmed to detect an alteration to the other."

I show her the email from Jessica again. "It doesn't say the targets have to drop out. But the names have to be removed *and* I have to follow the instructions in the poems."

"Which means you have to 'knock her down.' That sounds like a public callout to me." Nola pauses. "So what did you do?"

The perfect lie is a misplaced truth. "Dear Valentine. Same as everyone else."

We make our way downstairs, where every carrel and table is packed with students poring over books. Nola stops suddenly halfway down the grand wooden staircase that cascades down through the center of the main floor, and grabs me around the waist. She hooks her chin over my shoulder and places her cold hand under my jaw, slowly turning my skull down and to the left. Cori is sitting in a carrel across from Maddy, right in the center of the room, books spread out all around them.

"Do it now and it's over," Nola whispers.

I suddenly wish Brie were here, but she would tell me not to do it, and I don't have a choice. I don't think I could follow through with this if she were watching. I swallow hard and descend the rest of the stairs.

Cori looks up when I reach her side, but she doesn't say anything, nor does she smile. Maddy gives me a little wave, then glances at Cori nervously.

"Can we step outside for five?" I whisper.

"No," Cori says at a normal speaking volume. Several people look up, annoyed.

Holly Gartner glares up at me. "'Ask not for whom the bell tolls,'" she says under her breath.

I look down at her. "I'm sorry, what was that?"

Holly folds her arms over her chest defiantly. "Whose life did you come to ruin today?" The other girls at her table exchange glances.

I'm astounded, not just that she used almost the same words Spencer threw at me casually a few days ago, but because she would normally never dare to speak to me this way. No one would.

Cori turns back to her book. "Tai, Tricia, then Holly. Give me your best shot, Kay."

I throw up my hands. "Fine, Cori. You know what you did."

Holly stands up and gets in my face. "What did *I* do?"

Nola pushes her with her shoulder. "Kay wasn't talking to you."

I pull Nola aside. "Thanks. I've got this." Holly is roughly one and a half times Nola's size. Good intentions will not result in a happy ending if she's in a dramatic mood. I turn to Holly. "Let's talk about this before next practice. Right now I need to straighten something out with my friend."

Cori slams her book shut. "Nope. Not friend. We don't even hang out anymore. You spend all your time with Necro Morticia Manson herself. I don't know whether you're besties with benefits or without, but I hope she's damn good at something. Because she's creepy as hell and she's turning you into a freak."

I glance at Nola, who is just looking at Cori with narrowed eyes and lips pressed tightly together. I feel like she's waiting for me to say something, but I'm so angry, my jaw feels wired shut. I turn back to Cori, my face growing hotter, my eyes burning, aware that everyone has stopped studying and is watching us.

"You embarrassed yourself and your entire team by letting Nola play. You embarrass us by hanging out with her. You never ever went against the group before Nola. Now you ruin lives. Tai. Tricia. You want to try me, be my guest, bitch. Your credibility is gone. Everyone thinks you're crazy. Maddy thinks you've lost it."

Maddy gets up. "Cori, that's not okay."

"Shut up, Notorious."

"I never said that, Kay." She grabs her books and runs out of the room through a stunned crowd.

Cori takes a step toward me and keeps talking in her terrifying, rapid-fire speech. "Even Brie says you're a lost cause. So until you pull your shit together, I am not interested in continuing this paranoid conversation, or any other one." She sits and opens her book again.

I pick her textbook up and drop it to the ground. "Why are you even pretending? You don't need to study if you have the exams in advance. You're a cheater. And you can go crying to Klein to protect you from consequences, but now everyone knows it."

For a moment, the entire room is silent as if muffled by a blanket of snow. Then Cori speaks again, with deadly calm.

"Let's talk about cheating, Kay. You love to play the victim. Poor heartbroken Kay. Torn to pieces by Spencer's betrayal. Except it didn't go down like that, did it? You did it to him first. In his own bed. And your new best friend? I'm sure she'd love to know some of the things you said about her when she first got here. Then there's Jessica Lane. There are only three people in the world who had a motive to kill her. Her ex-boyfriend, the guy she cheated with, and you. And you're unraveling, Kay."

I can't listen to another word or take another pair of eyes on me. I turn around and run.

IT WAS THE first house party of the school year. I had spent the summer at soccer camp and hadn't seen Brie or Spencer since June. We were all drinking, and Justine and Spencer were getting high outside when Brie and I decided it would be funny to switch our clothes. We went into Spencer's room, and the narrow stairs up to his attic bedroom had made me dizzy, so I sat down on the bed.

She lay down next to me to kick her sneakers off.

His ceiling had glow-in-the dark stars on it and there was classic rock music pounding from downstairs—the song "7" by Prince—and Brie started singing in a breathless voice as she struggled with her sneaker.

We had slept side by side so many nights, but there was only this particular moment, in this bed that was the worst possible bed to be in together, with the stars swirling with alcohol, and the shoes that wouldn't come off. And the music and the urgency of Spencer and Justine outside smoking. Before I had a chance to catch my breath, her lips were on mine and we were kissing each other fast and hard, because we knew we were playing with fire. There was an invisible timer running down. Her shirt came off and her bra got stuck, and the clock penalized us. She stopped to laugh at my old-lady underwear when she was pulling my jeans down over my knees.

And that's what the clock didn't forgive.

Because that's the moment Spencer walked in.

Everything had been moving at hyperspeed, and then it skipped and slowed. Spencer closed the door behind him and slid down to the floor against it and just looked at me, his eyes pink and glazed. His cheeks were flushed and his hair was falling in his eyes and I realized I was never going to be allowed to touch him or kiss him again, and suddenly I couldn't breathe. Because that was exactly how Megan's and Todd's deaths finally hit me. I could remember them any damn way I wanted, but they would never be tangible. They could never be proven. I could never touch them again.

I started to hyperventilate, my pulse and mind racing sickeningly fast. Brie pulled my hand into hers and I yanked it away. She looked at me like I'd slapped her in the face and asked me what I wanted and I just kept saying I wanted another chance. She finally got up and left without a word, and Spencer sat down next to me and asked me if I loved him.

I told him the truth, yes, how could I not?

He asked if I still loved Brie.

And I lied, no, it's impossible to love two people.

He held me and stroked my hair until I could breathe again, and he lied, too, and said we would somehow be okay.

13

*t*he next day, I can't bear the thought of facing anyone and escape to the Cat Café to study alone in the corner, armed with an open tab of coffee. It's a little uncomfortable being surrounded by nothing but images and statues of cats now, and it feels almost like they are grinning down like grotesque, mocking Cheshire Cats, taunting me. But this is the place I have always come to unwind, and Hunter's unfortunate demise is not going to change that. It's not like I killed him. I'm very sorry he is dead, and even sorrier for Dr. Klein, but I am not giving up my perfect meeting spot because of it. I force myself to focus on my homework, and I make it until noon until my steady intake of caffeine forces a pee break.

As I'm returning from the bathroom, wiping my hands on my jeans due to the incompetent air dryer, I hear an unwelcome but familiar voice behind me.

"If it isn't Katie Donovan, the femme fatale of Bates Academy."

I turn with dread to see Spencer leaning against the men's room door. He wears his customary grin and his hair is carefully mussed, but he actually looks tired for once. As he stifles a yawn, I notice shadows under his eyes. His cheeks look a little hollow. Maybe the last few weeks have been wearing on him, too. Maybe he's not unbreakable.

I head back to my table and he follows me. "What are you doing on my side of town? Got another date?"

"Probably."

I shake my head. "You're the worst."

"Debatable." He takes one of my empty coffee cups and tips it over his mouth, catching two cold drops.

"Well, this has been fun, but I actually have to study, Spence."

He slaps his phone down on the table and rests his chin on his hands. "You said you wanted to talk."

I blink. "That was ages ago. And it ended with you throwing me out of your car."

"And then you emailed me, and as usual, I come running like an asshole."

I purse my lips. He's messing with me again, and after last night, I am done with people telling me I'm crazy. "I didn't email you."

His cocky smile begins to fade. "You didn't ask me to meet you?"

"No."

He slips his phone out of his pocket, scrolls, and hands it to me. There's an email from kadonovan@batesacademy.edu asking him to meet me here, at the Cat Café, now. It's a little flirtatious, and I blush before shoving the phone back into his hands.

"You know that's not my email," I say. "And you're the only one who calls me Katie."

His face pales. "Why would I do this?"

"To mess with my head. You hate me now. I get it."

He looks at me sharply. "I don't hate you."

"Everyone else does. And they have much less reason."

I feel like crying suddenly. Bates Academy was supposed to be the place where everything turned right side up again. And I've smashed it to pieces.

He scoots around the table and folds me into his arms. "No one hates you."

"My friends do. My teammates. People I barely know."

"Did you maybe do something to piss them off?" He presses his lips together and makes an innocent face.

I push him away. "You wouldn't understand."

"I understand better than anyone."

I look him in the eye. "Have the police questioned you?"

Instead of answering, he kisses me. For a moment, I'm shocked into inaction. His lips fit mine perfectly, because they always have. His smell is comforting, cool mint and Old Spice. He doesn't taste like cigarettes and I wonder if he was hoping for this, but the thought melts away as he pulls me closer, one arm fitting around my waist and the other cradling my head.

I feel heat rising in me and the urge to pull him closer makes me break away and glance around the café. It's empty of customers, though I can hear the sound of running water and dishes clinking in the back.

"Right here, right now?" he says with a wicked grin.

I shake my head and bite my lip. I want to keep kissing him but not here. Not now. He ruins everything. That is, when I don't do it first. "That's not funny. You brought her here."

"Yeah." He pauses. "I did." He takes a deep breath and lets it out shakily. "I should tell you something else."

"First answer me."

He studies my face. "No. Police haven't questioned me."

An icy feeling creeps over me like frost. "You're lying. I can tell."

"Then why did you ask?" He gazes at me with an oddly undisturbed expression. "Why are you always testing me?"

I stand abruptly. "Because the way you lie indiscriminately

makes you sound like a sociopath, Spencer. Did Brie even set you up with Jessica?"

For a moment a spark of hope ignites in my chest.

But he scrolls through his phone and shows me a series of texts from Brie describing Jessica, asking if he's interested, telling him to go for it.

"Now do you believe me?"

Maddy walks in just as I'm storming out, and she freezes in the doorway. "Kay?"

I push past her into the street, ignoring her as she calls my name, sounding more and more upset. I can't take one more second of drama. Last night exceeded my limit.

I KICK MY door open and dump my backpack on the floor. I need to clear my head. I down an entire bottle of water and brush my hair out, counting the strokes, then attempt to do my English reading for Tuesday—more *Othello*, some ravings about a handkerchief. I can't focus.

I set my phone to silent and study straight through dinner. My phone lights up repeatedly and I clock in thirty-seven missed calls and texts from Maddy, Spencer, Brie, and Nola—a new record. Spencer wins with a string of fifteen spanning from six to six thirty, mostly asking where I am; Maddy close behind with seven calls and three texts telling me to call her STAT.

By seven forty-five, my stomach feels like it's digesting itself. There's a knock at my door, and when I open it, Nola sashays in as if last night had never happened. She kicks aside a mound of clothes, places a box of French pastries on my bed, and opens her laptop.

"The timer waits for no one."

I linger by the door, unsure what to say. Last night was horrible. I don't know how she can even face me after I failed to stand up for her. On top of that, my room is a total mess. I've skipped laundry day for two weeks and have been recycling everything but underwear. Even socks.

She looks me up and down. "Get it together, Donovan. It's game time." She kicks off her shoes and removes her coat and hat and begins untangling knots in her damp hair. She wears a pair of leggings and an off-the-shoulder T-shirt with a graphic of a creepy alien in a blazer brandishing a machete over a frightened ingenue's head. ASTROZOMBIES! IN DELUXE COLOR! is printed at the top.

"Cute shirt," I say, trying to sound sincere. Maybe not successfully.

She eyes my dress, a Gucci zip-up with ruffle details and navy and red trim. "Nice dress. Did you sew it together from a pile of old school uniforms?"

I blush. Tricia had rejected the gift from her parents because it resembled our uniform too much. I don't think they look anything alike, and it's a drop-dead dress. But then, I don't get many opportunities to own dresses like this, and I don't turn them down.

"Sorry," Nola says, sighing. "I'm just in a bad mood. It looks good on you. You look like my sister. And she's perfect." She smiles with overtly false enthusiasm.

"I had one of those." I absently pick up a picture of my family from my desk and slide it behind my back.

"A flawless sister?"

"Sibling. A brother." I turn the picture facedown, not wanting to get into the *had* part. "He was the baby who slept through the night and potty trained himself while he was still crawling. According to my parents, I screamed through the night, wet the bed, needed braces, and got into schoolyard fights. You know. He was the easy one."

Nola groans and kicks a pillow. "Why does easy equal good? Everything worth doing is hard. Like, I really struggled out there on the soccer field."

I purse my lips. "Maybe that one isn't worth it."

She blinks. "We have a deal."

"We have so much else going on. You're a dancer, right?"

She curls her legs up under her and casts her eyes down. "Bianca was a dancer. I do theater. I don't even know why I'm trying."

"Bianca's your sister?"

She nods. "Unfortunately."

I notice her lower lip trembling and sit down next to her. "Granted, I haven't seen you perform onstage, but you *are* a dancer. You don't walk to class, you ballet to class. You plié without realizing it. It's obvious how much time you spend practicing."

She laughs, but shakes her head. "It's not enough. My parents need me to *be* Bianca."

That strikes a nerve. I haven't been able to shake the feeling since Todd died that the only way to make things right is to fill every gap his death left, to accomplish everything he would have accomplished. To meet every expectation my parents had of him. In essence, to become him. "Believe me. I know the feeling."

She squeezes my hand tentatively and for a moment there's an awkward silence. Then she sighs and pulls my laptop over and places it half on her lap and half on mine.

"The timer waits for no one," I echo.

She unlocks the password to the revenge blog and the oven opens, bringing up the dessert recipe for Madd Tea Party. There's a nauseous tilting feeling in my stomach. That means the main course is either me or Brie, and one of us is not on the list. Whoever is left is going to be a top suspect. I scan Maddy's poem, feeling slightly dizzy.

Madd Tea Party

Girl in teacup, shoulder deep
Pour the water, start to steep
There's nothing wrong with feeling sad
Or going just a little mad
So pop a pill or maybe twenty
There's room in hell for you, dear, plenty.

I turn to Nola in a panic. "This is bad."

She frowns. "Is it telling us to commit suicide?"

I shake my head. "The clue is about Maddy, not us. What if it's a threat? The killer made Jessica's death look like a suicide, too. Pills, water."

Nola stands shakily. "Jessica was wrists and water. But this would mean—"

"That Jessica didn't write the blog. The killer did." I grab my phone and coat, dialing as I head out the door. "We need to find Maddy."

My head spins as we race down the stairs. There's another fear I didn't mention to Nola. The fear that it might be real. My last conversation with Maddy rushes back to me. I thought she was trying to be there for me, but what if she was asking me to be there for her? She asked me to call her. She told me she felt shut out, completely alone even when she was surrounded by people. Why didn't I reach out to her after that conversation we had? I should have known after Megan. After Mom. I should be an expert. But I made so many mistakes in the aftermath of Todd's death, it became my policy to shut up. When my mother overdosed on the sedatives that were supposed to help her navigate the depths of her grief, Dad said mental health is private. No one is supposed to know anything about anyone else's pain.

Mom spent three months in a hospital in New Jersey. Dad and Aunt Tracy and I drove four hours every weekend to visit her, during which I would listen to music and pretend to sleep and Dad and Aunt Tracy would talk about her wedding plans. At the hospital, we would talk at Mom about all kinds of stupid things she didn't care about. She would never look up at us, and she would never say anything back. Until the Christmas morning when Aunt Tracy's fiancé showed up drunk and called her a whore, and Mom suddenly stood from her chair by the window and broke his nose with one clean swing.

Everything shattered back to normal after that. The doctors could see that she wasn't a danger to herself or others. Just that asshole if he came near Aunt Tracy again. It's funny how violence to protect a loved one's honor is so deeply ingrained in our culture, how accepted it is. Also ironic, considering why Mom was in the hospital in the first place. She was suddenly eager to hear about all the soccer games she missed. And school and every stupid detail of my life that even I didn't particularly care about. And then my parents hatched the perfect solution to all of our problems: sending me away to boarding school.

Outside, the temperature has dropped even further, and light, feathery flakes fall as we hurry along the winding path across the green toward the lake. The seven missed calls from Maddy this afternoon are making me feel sick. I continue trying to reach her as I sign into Henderson and shuffle up the stairs, scraping the icy moisture off my shoes on the carpet as I go. Maddy's room is on the third floor, and since she's a junior, she has a roommate, Harriet Nash.

I pause outside their room and rap my knuckles on the door. There's only silence from within.

Nola tries again as I dial Maddy's number and hold the phone to my ear. Faintly, as if muffled by sheets or piles of clothing, I hear her ringtone coming from inside the room. An odd feeling creeps over me. Maddy's ringtone is very distinctive. The pulsing beat and bouncy synth sound distorted and far away.

I pound on the door, louder. "Maddy!"

She doesn't answer, and the call goes to voice mail. I dial again, and the creepy muffled sound starts up again. The hairs stand up on the back of my neck.

Nola places her hand lightly on the door with a puzzled expression. "She's not home, Kay. It doesn't mean anything." She doesn't sound convinced.

I try the door one more time and then punch it, frustrated.

"Excuse me?"

I turn around. Kelli Reyes, a sophomore who almost made the team, peeks her head out from her room. She has a retainer protruding from her mouth and a matte layer of green skin cream spread evenly over her face. Her eyes seem to pop out from the ghoulish mask, and my heart gallops in my chest at the sight. "Jesus, Kelli."

"Are you looking for Harriet or Maddy? Harriet is visiting her family for the weekend." She looks me up and down and I can tell she was in the library last night.

"Maddy," I say. "Sorry for banging so loudly."

"Oh *no!*" she says, her voice dripping with sarcasm. "Not at all. I was just studying for my Latin midterm. Bang away."

"If you see her, can you ask her to call me right away?"

Kelli points down the hall. "She's in the private bath."

I follow Kelli's gaze. Every dorm has one group bathroom with six shower stalls on each floor, plus one private bath with a tub. Every weekend or holiday in particular there's a scramble for the private bath. We're allowed such indulgences as scrubs, salts, bubbles, oils, and creams as long as we then clean the entire bathroom. It's not a bad deal. With a couple of battery-operated candles and the right music, you can practically create a mini spa retreat. I thank Kelli and head down the hallway, wondering if Kelli fought Maddy for private bath privileges. It looks like Kelli was going for a DIY spa, too.

When I get to the door, I notice a halo of soapy water bleeding out from around the bottom of the door. Soft music is playing inside, the kind they play in spas, soothing harp music with water trickling in the background. Or is that a faucet running? I look down at my sneakers sinking into the soaked carpet and a flicker of dread sparks deep within me.

"Girl in teacup," Nola whispers.

I nod. A teacup is an awful lot like a porcelain bathtub. I knock softly on the door. "Maddy?"

There's no reply.

I knock louder. "Maddy?"

My heart slams. Panic is rising in me like a flood. I try to visualize my walls of ice but they are fractured with a thousand spidery cracks as the room fills up with water. I run through the hallway, down the stairs, jumping the last four of each flight, shouting for help. The world begins to tilt when I reach the bottom floor and arrive at the apartment of Mrs. Bream, the housemother. I tear the skeleton key from her hand and make it back up to the top floor before she does, before she calls 911, before the RA has even poked her head out of her room.

Nola stands aside helplessly as I fail three times to turn the key in the lock, and then she closes her hand around mine and we open it together. She gasps and falls back as I finally wrench the bathroom door open.

The first thing I see is the slightly fogged, oval-shaped mirror hanging over the sink, which Maddy had lined with various oils and lotions. On the misty surface is a message written in lipstick, in large capital letters, bold, as if the tube had been pressed hard and carefully run several times along each line. It reads:

NOTORIOUS
RE
BOUND
GIRL

I tear my eyes away to the source of the flood, and silence cuts off my access to sound and speech and movement. My ears, my tongue, my fingers feel numb.

The tub is overflowing, spilling cascades of water over the gleaming white-tiled floor. Maddy's golden hair floats like a halo above her at the surface of the tub. The rest of her fully clothed body is folded below.

14

*t*hat bumps my dead-body count to four. Is there some rule of three? Because when I saw Todd's body, there was that soft little click, that flicking-on of the switch in the previously unilluminated section of the Kay Donovan complex. The part that knows the depths of my mother's despair. The part that allows me to do the things I do, because no one can stop me, and nothing really, actually, eventually matters. When I saw Jessica's body, a tiny, urgent anxiety began to flare up in my chest, a feeling that, until routine resumed, control of my life would not be restored. When I saw Hunter's poor little pile of bones and fur, raw fear spiked through me, terror that I would be held accountable. Not just for his death, but for all death, for the fact that death and the aftermath of death exist. For Dr. Klein's sloping posture and ugly little blouse-and-slacks ensembles, for Mom's lingering pill dependency, for the fact that I will never ever be able to quit soccer or my family would disintegrate into a horror of screaming, twisting madness.

That was when I had a body count of three.

When I see sweet Maddy's head suspended below the overflowing, rushing water, angelic in the eerie harp music—Maddy, who never had an original mean thought, who only followed me and Tai and Tricia—I crumble onto the thin layer of water on the tile and sob. I press my face against the floor and scream into it, slamming my palms against the tile until I feel a set of arms hook under my shoulders.

Nola hauls me to my feet and drags me into the hallway, past where Mrs. Bream is performing CPR on Maddy's limp, pale body. Why didn't the EMTs perform CPR on Jessica? How were they so sure? The thoughts are wild and disjointed, too fast and fragmented for me to vocalize. Nola attempts to get me into the common room, but I wrestle myself out of her grasp and stumble down the stairway. I need Brie, but Brie is gone. I make it to the front door when a pair of paramedics rush through, pushing me back into the lobby, and two police officers trail close behind, followed by Detective Morgan. I try to push past her, but she grabs my arm.

"Since you're in a hurry," she says, guiding me into the first-floor common room.

I sit on a wooden chair across from her, blank and broken.

If she asked me to confess right now, I might. I have no fight left in me. I would say anything to go home and crawl into bed. To just disappear.

"What happened?" Her voice is a little softer than usual, and it catches me off guard.

"Maddy is dead."

"Maddy was one of your friends? One of the girls who found Jessica."

I nod.

"Okay." She writes it down. "How do you know?"

"I saw her."

"You didn't make the call."

"No. I ran."

"Okay. Calm down."

I didn't realize it, but I'm shivering my words out, and I take a couple of deep breaths. "I found her in a bathtub with her head underwater and the floor was flooded. The water had been running a very long time. She was definitely dead."

"Okay." She writes more. "Anything else you want to tell me?"

My face crumbles. "She told me to call her and I didn't. And I ignored her calls. And I keep letting people die, and I keep letting people die."

Her mouth drops open. "Kay, I'm going to call your parents and have them come down to the station."

"No." I shake my head. "That's not what I meant."

She looks at me sharply. "You better explain what the hell you meant."

I don't stop crying. "She asked me to call her and I didn't do it." I press my fists into my face and suck in a gulp of air. "Before I moved here, my best friend committed suicide. Because I abandoned her."

"Kay. No one is out to get you. I have a job. A girl was murdered. Maybe two. You need to tell us everything you know. Or I can't help you. You say things like you keep letting people die, and all of a sudden, I may have probable cause." She shifts in her seat, moves closer. "Now, I can't question you as a suspect without your parents."

"No. You can't call them."

She holds her hands up. "I wouldn't have to if I had a better suspect. I want to believe there is one. So I'm giving you another chance. What can you tell me?"

The tears streaming down my face make it almost impossible to see. A better suspect. "Greg and Jessica had a huge fight the night she died," I finally whisper. "About their breakup."

She looks disappointed. "We already know that. I need something new."

Then something rushes back to me from our first conversation. "He told me she was afraid of blades."

"Okay." She notes this down, yawning.

"No. The night after Jessica was found. Before he was questioned. None of the newspapers mentioned how she died, but he told me there was no way she committed suicide because she was afraid of blades. How did he know she was cut?"

She gives me a twisted smile. "You're a toughie. I've seen your record. I know why you did it. Kids lie. You even thought you were doing the right thing. I hope you learned that you didn't protect anyone. Who knows? If your brother had been in jail, maybe he wouldn't have ended up dead."

The words dissolve on my tongue. She shouldn't have access to my brother's case.

"I know, I'm a cold-hearted bitch. There are worse things to be. I see right through you, Katie. I know you. My partner worked on Todd's case. But I'll follow through on your lead. We help each other out; we're cool." She pauses at the door. "Although, how could *you* know she was cut by a blade?"

I look up at her. "I was at the crime scene."

"But the murder weapon wasn't visible. All kinds of objects can inflict wounds like the ones you saw. Scrap metal, sharp edge of hard plastic, broken bottle." She watches me, but I don't have the energy to respond. Not now. She shakes her head briskly. "Anyway. I'm sorry for your loss. Losses."

I FEEL SECTIONS of my hair crunch almost instantly when I step outside, and my clothes are like pure ice on my skin. I run against a wall of cold to Brie's dorm, bypass the front desk, and throw my entire body against her door before I remember that she's still away for the long weekend. I bang my fists against it anyway, irrationally, before kicking it with all of my might. Then I pull my phone out of my only pocket that wasn't drenched from my collapse on the bathroom floor, but I can't text her. My body is still convulsing too hard from the cold, and I can't hold my fingers steady. I grab the marker attached to the dry-erase board with a silky green ribbon, and with childlike handwriting, I scrawl the dark message pulsing in the pit of my heart: *You might as well be dead, too, Brie. <3 K*

Then I go the only other place I can think to go, Nola's room. I only have half a hope that she'll be home, and the cold has frozen my clothes and rattled me so severely that I can't run anymore, so I walk across campus stiffly, like a creature from a horror movie. I can't sign myself in at the front desk because my fingers are not only still shaking, they're now frozen into a stiff red little claw. I croak out my name to the security guard through chattering teeth, and she writes it down, giving me a pointed side-eye.

I don't feel like I have an ounce of energy left for the stairs, but I can't separate my fingers to push the button for the elevator, so I manage the stairs by pressing my back against the wall and pushing myself up one step at a time, with minimal bending of knees. When I get to her door, I lean against it and take a moment to catch my breath and then tap my forehead against it three times.

Nola opens the door and I let my muscles rest, sliding to the floor.

"Kay?" She sounds alarmed.

I gaze up at her from the floor and my eyes focus, unfocus, refocus. She's dressed in a silky black nightgown with a retro velvet robe and her makeup is scrubbed off. She hurriedly shuts the door. "I was so worried. Did you get my texts? The cops forced me to go home. Do you want me to call student health?"

I shake my head. "Frozen."

"Take your clothes off," she orders. She flutters around the room, and in a moment, hot water is bubbling in a forbidden electric teapot, and I am stripped down to my soaked bra and underwear, staring down at a tiny black long-sleeved shirt and matching pajama pants. At best, they will graze the top of my ankles. The top is printed with the words O GOD, I COULD BE BOUNDED IN A NUTSHELL AND COUNT MYSELF A KING OF INFINITE SPACE, WERE IT NOT THAT I HAVE BAD DREAMS. I hold the T-shirt up against me and cringe.

"Those are the biggest clothes I have," she says.

I reluctantly begin to pull the T-shirt on but she interrupts me.

"You can't leave your soaking wet bra and underwear on. I'll turn around if you're a prude."

"Please do, and I'm not." I resent the name-calling. But I don't feel comfortable with her staring at me.

She rolls her eyes and turns around, and I quickly shimmy out of my underthings and into the pajamas. They are skintight and the pants reach only mid-calf. The shirt exposes an inch of my abs and pulls at the shoulders. But it's dry. She tosses me a black fleece blanket, and I sit on her bed and cocoon myself in it gratefully.

"Are you okay?" Her tone softens as she pours the steaming water into two mugs and drops a bag of chamomile into each. I don't particularly care for tea but am grateful for something warm to drink and hold in my hands.

"Thanks." I take the mug and relish the feeling of the scalding ceramic. "Yes. I guess. No. Maddy is dead. Are you okay?" I suddenly look down at my teacup and feel sick to my stomach. I push it away.

Nola sighs and presses her lips against her cup. When she removes them, they are bright pink. "I'm not great, but I barely knew her."

"It wasn't suicide. It's too big of a coincidence. The blog

described her death. That means Jessica didn't write it. Either she never wrote any of it, or someone hacked in and added Maddy's poem."

Nola shudders. "Those rhymes are all written in the same style. Same voice."

"Why would someone pretend to be Jessica, use me to get back at her enemies, and then kill Maddy?"

"Because you're at the center of it, Kay. You're a top suspect, you were the one Fake Jessica chose to carry out her supposed revenge, and you've decided to solve her murder. To the police, you probably look like a textbook serial killer inserting herself into the investigation."

I falter. Textbook. Why does everyone know these things except me? "We don't know that the blogger killed Jessica. Just Maddy. To all outward appearances, the blogger wants to avenge Jessica. It just doesn't make sense that he would kill her. All we know about Fake Jessica is that he wrote the blog and either killed Maddy or knew about her death as soon as it happened. It's like he knows everything that goes on at Bates the second it happens. Everyone's secrets, every move we make." They even knew about Maddy's nickname. Not Ruth Bader Ginsburg. Rebound Girl. I hadn't even known she was dating anyone.

She takes a contemplative sip. "You keep saying he."

"Do I?"

"What did you tell the cops?"

"That it was suicide. And that Greg probably killed Jessica."

Nola nods, but she doesn't look convinced. She looks like she's humoring a child. I feel my heart double its rhythm and my face grow hot.

"They had that huge fight right before she died. He has the best motive."

She places her mug down and crosses her room to retrieve the laptop from her backpack. "When that was your motive, it was the worst motive. Right?"

"Can we not talk about this for one night?"

"Of course." She settles down next to me and puts her head on my shoulder. "We can watch the walls peel." She points to a corner of the ceiling where the paper she's taped up is beginning to curl down. For some reason this makes me giggle, and she does, too.

"Or a movie or something?"

She pulls up her Netflix account and we watch a mindless romantic comedy. I usually like sci-fi and action, and all of Nola's recent shows are classics and noir, but I can't take any more suspense than wondering whether the adorable female lead will fall for the unattractive and stalkery male lead before or after he destroys her business venture.

My phone buzzes halfway through and I look down to see Brie calling. I silence it. I can't think of what to say, and one more ounce of pressure will split me in half right now. Nola glances at me curiously and I shrug it off. But I'm pretty sure she can guess.

"Nola." She looks at me. "What would you do if you found out I killed Jessica?"

She looks stunned and a little suspicious, as if she's trying to figure out what trap I've set for her. "Call you a liar?"

"Play along."

She studies my face. "Ask you why."

I shake my head. "Not allowed to ask. Just react."

She laughs nervously. "What new devilry is this?"

"I don't know who to trust anymore. Everything is strategy. School, soccer, relationships, the police. What do you say, how do you say it, when do you say it to get what you want. I'm worse than anyone. Greg trusted me and I told the police to look at him. Brie was my best friend and she stabbed me in the back. And I think Spencer tried to get back together with me today and that is the opposite of what needs to happen."

Nola raises her head with interest. "Perfect Brie is a back-stabber?"

I pick up an amaryllis plant and stroke the silky petals. It's the first time I'm saying this out loud and I can't bear to see

Nola's reaction. "She set Spencer up with Jessica. I have no idea why she did it."

Nola slips her hand into mine. "I'm sorry."

I swallow the lump in my throat and finally look up. Her expression is soft and sympathetic. "Let's make a pact. Our friendship is strategy-free. No bullshit. I need that right now." My lips feel wobbly and I tighten them. I thought I had that with Brie. I was wrong.

Nola reaches behind her and grabs a pair of hair scissors and slices a small cut in her index finger and then offers it to me. "Blood promise," she says eagerly. "It's tradition."

I look distastefully at the reddened tip of the scissor. "Do you have anything to disinfect it?"

"Just use the other blade," she urges.

I hesitate. "Sorry, I have a germ thing."

She spins the scissors around her finger skeptically. "The whole point of a blood promise is sharing blood."

"We unburied and reburied a cat together," I remind her. "That's a bone promise. Way more hard-core."

She wipes her finger on a tissue, seeming satisfied. "Fair enough. But we have to seal it with something."

"I know a kick-ass handshake," I offer.

But Nola crawls toward me, and before I can respond, she presses her lips against mine. They are delicate, waxy with

Chapstick, and her breath is sweet like honey and chamomile. The smell of baby powder deodorant mixes with her citrusy perfume as she scoots closer and presses her body against mine, softly and seductively. Not like the way we usually touch, not even like the way Brie and I touch. It might feel nice except for the terrible guilt, the dark feeling that drops like a panic from my chest down to my gut and floods me with memories, the sounds of Tai and Tricia screaming with laughter, the sound of *my* laughter, of Nola's glossy eyes, of words, words, words. *Necro.* She touches my face with her cold hand, and I spring back from her, feeling like I can't breathe.

"Sealed," she murmurs, brushing her lips once more against mine.

"Nola?"

She looks at me, something like fear flashing in her eyes.

"Let's not do that again."

She shrugs. "Fine by me."

She switches the light off, and I curl into a corner of the bed. She faces the other way and we lie back to back silently. I feel her pull her robe off and toss it onto the floor and then curl her body up into a little ball, and the guilt washes over me again. It's now or never.

I clear my throat. "I'm sorry we were such bitches to you when you first came to Bates."

She is silent for a long moment. "How so?"

"You know." I grope for the right words. "What Cori said. Sometimes jokes are funny for the person telling it, not so funny for the person it's about."

"You're not that funny, Kay. None of your friends were funny, either."

I pause. "I agree. I was just trying to apologize."

"I appreciate it."

My entire body relaxes. But it's hard to get those images out of my head now that they've been revived. And they're mashed up now with the scent of Nola and the feeling of her lips on mine. And that awful image that keeps revisiting me of Spencer and Jessica together. The longing I feel to see him mixed up with the pain that results every time I do. My last memory of Megan, slamming her door in my face, and of Todd, a coffin closing on his. A dozen envelopes, sealed and labeled Dear Valentine, that would set this nightmare in motion. And Brie. Brie when she was so close, I could never imagine her being lost. The shock and pain of her betrayal. But I'm grateful for all of it. Because it pushes Maddy out of my mind. In the morning, I'll have to face her death again.

15

When I wake up, Nola is seated at her desk, staring gravely at her computer screen.

I sit up groggily, and she brings me a mug of chamomile tea. "Stay sitting," she says.

"What's going on?" I wipe my eyes, trying to orient myself. I don't remember right away that I fell asleep in Nola's room, and then last night rains down on me in fragments like shards of broken glass. Maddy, Spencer, Greg, that awful note I left Brie, the kiss, my conversation with Detective Morgan, every horrible emotion I had. My head is pounding painfully, and my nose is stuffed and itchy. I sneeze violently, and Nola hands me a box of tissues. I blow my nose and look instinctively at the Matisse calendar hanging on her wall. I'm sick, the murder investigation is still on, and there are only a few scheduled games left before the end of the season. They won't start up again until the investigation ends. I need to keep running, keep my speed up.

Nola hands me her laptop, opened to a local news website. "First of all, you were right about Maddy. The police are investigating it as a homicide. Possibly linked to Jessica's."

I pull the comforter around me, shivering. "The police think it's the same killer?"

"Same place, same pattern. Maddy overdosed, but she died by drowning. No note, no indication that she wanted to die. Jessica didn't leave a note either. That's today's breaking news. If the same person killed Jessica and Maddy, that proves that the killer wrote the revenge website. F. J. has been masterminding this whole thing and manipulating every move we've made."

"F. J. is?"

"Fake Jessica. The blogger." There are dark shadows under her eyes, and I wonder whether she slept at all last night. She's no longer wearing the silky nightgown. Instead she's dressed in a conservative black button-down shirt with a white Peter Pan collar and a knee-length wool skirt and knee socks. I'm embarrassed about the short-circuited kiss from last night, but it's suffocated by the shock and numbness I feel about Maddy's death and guilt about the message I left Brie.

"We can't just assume Maddy and Jessica were killed by the same person." I try to keep my voice steady. "They're two very different people. They had nothing in common. And what about Greg? He has no connection to Maddy."

"Well, maybe Greg didn't do it," Nola says quietly.

I take Nola's laptop without a word and open the revenge website. We unlock the password and click on the link to the main course. It goes dark and the oven opens, revealing the final recipe poem.

Oh Kay Dead Meat Pie
Chop her, mince her, grind her up
Call the cops to drink and sup
The recipes are writ and posted
Hope you've liked the meal I've hosted
Two things left—to book and cuff
Katie can't suffer enough.

I suddenly notice the kitchen timer flying at breakneck speed. "What's going on?"

She clicks on it a few times but it keeps moving. "Hold on." She types something into the password box, but nothing happens. "Um."

Fifteen seconds. I grab the laptop from her. "What happens at zero?" I shriek.

"How am I supposed to know?"

I watch helplessly as the timer ticks to zero, and then the website disappears and the words *Server not found* appear on the screen. "What just happened?" I ask, a panic rising in my stomach.

She stares at the computer incredulously. "The site's been taken down. It must have been set to expire a certain amount of time after the password was unlocked. It's gone. For good."

I sink back against the wall. "I'm being set up. And that was the only evidence."

Nola takes a deep breath. "I think I have an idea who F. J. might be."

I close my eyes and cover my face with my hands. "It's *not* Spencer."

She gapes at me. "How did you know?"

"He's the only one who calls me Katie. He knows every person on the revenge blog. Plus Jessica. Intimately. He even has a reason to want to hurt me."

"The incident Cori mentioned, I presume."

"Obviously. But if Spencer wanted to get back at me, he could have just killed *me*. And he had no reason to hurt Maddy."

Nola rolls her eyes. "You're a revenge amateur." She tosses me her phone. "And Spencer had every reason to hurt Maddy. To shut her up. Funny how she dropped dead hours after he tried to get back together with you."

I look down at an unfamiliar Instagram account showing pictures of Spencer and Maddy cuddling and making out at a party, dated shortly after our breakup. And then everything makes sense. Maddy being so nice to me. Constantly asking if I'd spoken to Spencer. Brie acting cold toward her all of a sudden, and Tai and the others giving her that new nickname, Notorious R.B.G. Rebound girl. Maddy and Spencer. This doesn't just strengthen Spencer's motive, though. It pretty much doubles mine. And when you consider that Spencer and I met alone the day she was found dead, it's absolutely damning. But I know I didn't do it, and the fact is, Spencer might have.

I am suddenly hit with a vivid memory of the night we met, the moment that cemented our friendship. I had finally relented to his suggestion that we find an unoccupied bedroom, and we really did stay there all night drinking and playing I Never, no funny business, at least much less funny than our public display for Brie's benefit. The game had started so blandly and rapidly escalated until the final three.

"I never broke a person's heart." Neither of us drank.

"Liar," I said, watching the ceiling spin in circles as I hugged a flannel pillow to my chest.

"Appearances can be deceiving. No tears shed over me, Katie."

I already regretted telling him my nickname from back home earlier in the game. I Never had a nickname.

The next one slid off my tongue before my waltzing mind had time to process it.

"I never committed a felony." I crawled over to him on my elbows and took a swig of his gin and tonic before the better part of me, the smarter part of me, had time to shut it down, to scream at me to stop and go home. He stared down at me, took the drink out of my hand, and drained half the glass.

"I obstructed a police investigation," I said dizzily, nestling my head into his lap. It felt so good to say, and I was so sure I would never ever see this boy again. It was the perfect confession. He was warm and fun and irresistible, and it was so easy to talk to him. Tomorrow I would go back to Brie and she would have forgotten about that bitch she was ignoring me for. Brie would never go for a theater girl. Too much drama.

"I framed my father for grand theft auto."

I opened my eyes and gazed up at him, his face gently rotating with the rest of the room. "That's impressive."

"He was a shithead. He put my brother in the hospital and forced my mom to run to a shelter twice. So I stole a car and made it look like he did it. We're all much better off." He sucked in a lungful of air and puffed it out. "That feels really good to say. I've never said that out loud. Do you want to go to IHOP?"

"I don't think we can drive. Also, don't steal any more cars."

He grinned. "I got *his* car when he went to prison." He started laughing. He had a perfect smile, more perfect when an edge of darkness crept into his eyes. "It sucks in a way because he definitely loves me, and I'm, like, the only one he didn't beat, so, like. Fuck him."

I climbed up onto my knees with the world spinning and leaned against his chest. "Everything about me is a lie and I'm terrified everyone will find out."

"They won't," he said simply, looking deep into my eyes. "Don't tell them and they won't. I got your back, Katie."

And then I whispered the last challenge of the game. "I never killed a person."

We both drank at the same time.

"You first," he said.

I closed my eyes. "When I was a kid, I was really close to my older brother. He would hang out with me and my best friend all the time, reading comic books, playing video games, all the nerdy stuff his cool friends weren't into. Then the summer after seventh grade they started flirting and it got weird and eventually they started hanging out without me. So, school starts again, and Megan suddenly texts me that she wants me to hang out again, and when I get to her house, I'm still just hurt and pissed at both of them and I'm all ready for this huge blowout fight, but instead, she pulls me into her room and locks the door. I see she's been crying for a long time. And she tells me that she had texted Todd photos of herself naked. Like, a lot of them, throughout the summer. And that day, apparently, they broke up and he sent them around to everyone at the entire school."

"Shit," Spencer said.

I opened my eyes and looked up at him. His glass was raised to his lips, but it was empty. I took it from him and pressed it to my hot forehead. "I didn't know what to say. She'd ignored me all summer and I had more or less refused to speak to Todd in all that time. But it seemed so unlikely that he could have done that deliberately. I knew him so well . . . forever. She was looking at me like the next thing out of my mouth would either fix everything or destroy everyone's life. It was like *Romeo and Juliet* or something. Like, why was I chosen as the fatal messenger? I wasn't included in Acts One through Four."

I started to laugh. I couldn't help it. It was that or cry, and I had worked very hard up until that point not to let tears win. The glass slid onto the bed and Spencer picked it up and set it on the counter.

"Game over." Spencer helped me sit up. "You didn't kill anyone."

"I did. They both died. I told Megan I thought it was probably a mistake, and she screamed at me to leave and never spoke to me again. Then when I asked Todd what happened, he told me someone stole his phone that day and must have sent the pictures out. I believed it. But no one was with him at the time, so I lied to the police and said I was. It made sense at the time. But those pictures just kept getting posted on websites and people commented and said the worst things about Megan. I wanted to call, but I was afraid. And then one day school was canceled. And we found out she killed herself."

"God, Katie. You don't need to tell me all of this."

"I want to. And you can never ever mention it again. To anyone else, or to me."

"Okay." He folded his hands in front of his crossed knees, almost prayerlike.

"So. I never killed someone." I took the empty glass off the table and drank a sip of air.

"Do you . . . ," he began hesitantly. "Do you still think your brother was telling the truth?"

I shrugged. "Too late to ask him now. Megan's brother murdered him after she killed herself."

"But what do *you* think?"

I look him in the eye. "I don't think I'd blame myself if I was one hundred percent sure he was innocent. Do you?"

"It's not your fault," he said, taking my hand. "You believed him at the time. You can't go back and change things based on what you know now."

"Oh yeah? Who did you kill?"

"I didn't. I was just finishing my drink."

I LOOK AROUND Nola's room for the clothes I was wearing last night and note with regret that they are still lying soaking wet exactly where I stripped them off. I look down at myself. I can't make a walk of shame across campus to my dorm wearing this ridiculous ensemble. Not in this weather. The wind is keening relentlessly outside, and I'm genuinely worried that if I don't take care of myself, I could get pneumonia. I'm helpless. And that's my least favorite feeling in the world.

I hear my ringtone from within the wet pile of rags and dive for it. Nola watches me, chewing on her thumbnail, with something like jealousy in her eyes. Or maybe I'm delirious. It's Brie. "Hello?" I rasp.

"Oh my God. Are you okay?"

In one instant, all of my anger evaporates and I want her to be home again. I'm sick and falling to pieces and I just want to be close to her.

"I'm sick."

"I mean, did you hear?"

"I found her."

A shocked silence follows, and then her voice tightens. "I'm so sorry I'm not there, sweetie."

An icy chill runs down my spine. That means she hasn't seen the horrible, bitchy, heartless note I left on her door. "Don't be," I say queasily. I stand up, but the room swirls around me and I need to cling to the bedpost to keep from face-planting on the floor.

"I'm coming home right after breakfast."

"Don't." Brie and Justine had been planning the New York trip for months. They even had *Hamilton* tickets. It was no small thing. I was a Class A narcissist to blame her for wanting to spend her anniversary with her girlfriend.

"Maddy's dead."

The words fall out of the phone like bricks from a crumbling building, and I don't know how to respond. Maddy is dead. It sounds new every time I think it or hear it. It sounds like funeral bells. There is no way to keep the world going forward anymore. Not by myself. Brie has to find out, just like Mom did, like Jessica's family will, and Dr. Klein, like everybody does, that death is just a skip in the record. After Megan and Todd died, I became convinced for a very short time that I had a heart defect and was dying, but was reassured in the emergency room that I was very healthy and experiencing something called PVCs brought on by anxiety, trauma, and extreme stress. A PVC is a premature ventricular contraction.

It feels like your heart isn't beating anymore, like it's skipping, but really it's just that the rhythm's been thrown for a loop, and it almost always jumps right back into routine immediately afterward. No matter how convinced you are that everything is falling apart, it's actually working exactly as it should. I briefly saw a behavioral psychologist for my anxiety disorder, and she put it to me this way: "You go to sleep at night, and you wake up in the morning, and all that time you've relinquished control of your body *to* your body, and it does everything it's supposed to."

I walked out of her office and stepped on a dead bird that had not been dead long enough to attract scavengers or to look very dead, and it occurred to me: Death is the PVC. It feels like the end of all that has been done and known. It seemed like the street should be quiet without the bird, but there were plenty of birds singing and chipmunks chattering to each other. I somehow thought the school would board up the locker room after Megan died in it, but they just cleaned out her locker, and I started changing in the bathroom down the hall. It felt like the football team should have stopped playing after Todd died, but . . . playoffs. Mom went off to the hospital, but Dad kept going to work. I went to school, and at first I got away with not doing any work, but then I failed a test. My best friend was gone and my brother was gone. Some girl wrote on my locker, "I heart perverts." Some other girl crossed that out and wrote, "I heart dead perverts." I got high and hooked up with Trevor McGrew behind the school and started having PVCs. And things just kept going and going and going.

"You still there?" Brie sounds far away. My brain feels cloudy and I'm having a hard time making myself focus.

"Yeah. I'm in Nola's room. I slept over."

There's a pause. "Why?"

"Because I was alone and fucking scared, Brie."

Nola raises her eyebrows at me and mouths, *Should I leave?* I shake my head.

"Call me when you get back, okay?"

"Okay." She draws the word out, sounds like she wants to ask me something else. "Do you want me to pick anything up on my way back to campus?"

"Nyquil. And orange juice."

"I'm sorry I wasn't there," she repeats in a softer voice.

"You didn't know. None of us did."

"Don't die, Kay."

I smile and blow a kiss into the phone. Nola isn't smiling when I look up.

"Can we focus, please?"

My nose is stuffed, my head aches, and my throat feels like there are razors scraping up and down when I speak. The only thing I want to do is rest.

I lie back on the bed and close my eyes. "On what?"

"Spencer."

"The eminently unfaithful."

"The eminently homicidal." She shows me the pictures of Spencer and Maddy again.

I throw her phone back at her, my eyes stinging. "Maddy is dead. I have some kind of plague, and my head feels like it's stuffed with explosives. I can't talk about this anymore."

She bites her lip. "Fine. But someone killed Maddy, and Jessica, too. Your best bet at clearing your name is recording a confession." She produces a small recording device from her desk, seals it in a ziplock bag, and places it in my jacket pocket. "I use this when I'm rehearsing for plays. It's ancient, but it works. We'll need a better one to record an actual conversation in a public place with background noises, but this is better than nothing."

"I'm not using that on Spencer."

"Think about it. Now that there are two bodies and your motive applies to both of them, the clock is ticking." Nola pushes the hair back from my forehead. "You are on fire, Kay." She digs through her desk drawers and retrieves a bottle of aspirin. "Take one."

"I'll think about it," I tell her.

16

i wake up soaked in sweat but shaking with chills. I must have drifted off still lying in Nola's bed, dressed in her pajamas. I sit up and blow my nose while my eyes slowly adjust to the light. My phone is glowing on the floor next to me and when I pick it up, I see that it's already early afternoon and I have three missed calls from Brie and one text consisting of a picture of the god-awful message I left on her door. I rub my forehead with my palm. A migraine is gathering force. There's also a missed call from Spencer but no voice mail. I tap his name, but as soon as the phone rings, I end the call and dial Brie's number.

"Where are you?" she says by way of greeting.

"I'm still in Nola's room." My wrecked vocal cords and stuffed nose combined with congestion in my ears make my voice sound like a maniacal troll's, and it startles me so badly, I nearly drop the phone.

"Be right there." She hangs up, and I sit there uncomfortably, feeling like a child waiting in the principal's office for her parents to arrive so that the punishment phase can begin. It's even worse that I'm dressed like a character in a whimsical movie where a child's wish to be a grown-up suddenly comes true with hilarious consequences. I reach for the clothes I was wearing last night, still in a pile on the floor, but to my dismay, they are still damp and cold. I grit my teeth distastefully and text Brie, bring clothes please?

I look around Nola's room. It's an odd feeling being in someone's room without them. The first time I was alone in Spencer's room, I tore every inch of it apart. I looked for evidence of prescription drugs, ex-girlfriends, embarrassing childhood photographs, a retainer, anything I might not already know about him. Nothing particularly scandalous turned up. There were a couple of mildly pornographic sketches in the back pages of his math notebook, some girl's pink fuzzy sweater stuffed in the back of his closet, and an Altoids box in his underwear drawer containing a handful of assorted pills I identified as three Adderall, four Klonopin, four oxycodone, and seventeen actual Altoids.

I was a little curious about the sweater, a new-looking cashmere cardigan, but it was so buried back there between soccer jerseys and winter coats that it didn't particularly worry me. And the tiny stash of pills was like candy compared to some of the crap Spencer's friends messed around with. Altogether it was a disappointing expedition, and I never mentioned my findings. I wonder about the sweater now, though. This was months before the incident that broke us up, but it clearly belonged to *someone*, and Spencer may have had her in his room before the night he walked in on me and Brie.

I stand, my head fuzzy and legs wobbly, and make my way over to Nola's desk. It's meticulously well organized, with stacks of books on one side, electronic devices on the other, and rows of knickknacks lining the edge. She has a wooden box that looks like it's been carved out of driftwood, an old-fashioned inkwell, and an array of writing instruments, including several antique fountain pens and a feather with long, dusty plumes. There is a replica of a human skull mounted on a polished mahogany stand with a brass plate engraved with the words ALAS, POOR YORICK. Even I recognize the quote from *Hamlet*. She has stacks of suede- and leather-bound journals and scripts, some of them Shakespearean and some by playwrights I've never heard of: Nicky Silver, Wendy MacLeod, John Guare.

I pick up one of the journals and flip through. It's filled with beautifully calligraphied journal entries in violet ink. The first one I turn to is dated three years ago and describes a breakfast in excruciatingly boring detail—we're talking oatmeal with milk and honey, a cup of tea, and a glass of orange juice. The entry describes the consistency of the oatmeal, the acidity and amount of pulp in the juice, the cracks in the ceiling. It must have been a writing exercise or something. I start to flip ahead in the journal, but a sudden knock at the door sends a wave of guilt through me. I replace the book and open the door to find Brie standing in the doorway, unsmiling, holding a stack of clothes. She's even more difficult to read than usual with a pair of aviator sunglasses and a hood partially obscuring her face. Her skin looks ashen and her usually glossy lips are dry and cracked.

"Hi." I sniffle.

She shoves the clothes at me and slips into the room, closing the door behind her. "Get dressed," she orders. "We're going."

I obey meekly as she removes her sunglasses and eyes the room distastefully. She scoops up my clothes and places them in her backpack. "So, what, you're like Nola Kent's bitch now?"

I squeeze myself out of Nola's tiny T-shirt and glare at her. "What's that supposed to mean?"

Brie lifts the T-shirt off the floor with one finger like it's contaminated with bedbugs. "First, you're dressing like a little clone. And FYI, you look ridiculous in this."

"I know that." I pull the warm fleece Brie brought me over my head and instantly feel comforted by both the familiar feel and smell of it. It smells like Brie, like *our* cranberry-pomegranate shampoo and *our* mint-basil deodorant. I feel a little bit like myself for the first time in days.

"And that bullshit message you left on my door." Her eyes well up, and it feels like a knife twisting in my chest. "That's not you."

"It is." Now my eyes feel hot and prickly. "It's not her fault. She wasn't even there."

"What the hell is going on with you, then?"

I slide the skintight pajama pants off and pull on the track pants Brie brought me. I shake my head, unable to offer an answer, and reach for my coat, but it's still wet. Brie shrugs her own coat off and hands it to me, and that's the thing that breaks me. I sit down on Nola's bed and shove my face into my hands. "I don't know," I choke.

I swipe at my face with a handful of tissues, but I'm awful with crying. It takes me forever to stop once I've started, and sometimes it escalates until I lose control of my entire body in spasms of bursting, pulsing sorrow—grief that runs through me like shock waves. It's the most terrifying feeling in the world. That's why I decided to never do it again, why I designed the room with the thick ice walls. To keep me from losing myself inside myself.

"Let's not talk about this here," Brie says. "I got you Nyquil and orange juice. Can you make it back to my room?"

I nod. I don't want Nola to see me cry again, anyway, and I still feel weird about last night. I walk back to Brie's room with my head cast down so that my hair completely covers my face. There's no need for it, I know. People expect me to be crying, and Brie, too. One of ours is dead. I wish I could call Tai and Tricia. Even Cori. We should be together right now. But I can't be the one to make the call. I have to be the one to answer it. I really hope I get a chance to.

When we get to her room, she takes her coat back and hangs it up neatly, and puts my wet clothes on her radiator to dry. Then she pours me a cup of orange juice and dosing cup of Nyquil.

"Are you sleeping over?" she asks.

"Are you going to abandon me while I'm sleeping?"

She gives me a horrifically disappointed look. "Really?"

"I'm sorry. My brain is scrambled. I'll go if you want me to."

"I'd rather keep an eye on you, to be honest."

That stings worse than anything else. I take the Nyquil and wash the nasty taste down with the juice. "I'm sorry. For the note and everything else. I haven't been myself."

"That's a cop-out thing to say," she scolds. She sits down next to me and looks me in the eye. "Are you and Nola sleeping together?"

I feel guilty for some reason, which is completely irrational. "Why would it matter?"

"Because I'll be pissed off if I'm not the first to know. And because I don't like her."

"No, we're not. But she did kiss me."

Her eyes widen. "Bad idea, Kay."

"I forgot. I'm Soccer Spice. You're Gay Spice."

She looks hurt. "That's not what I meant, and you know it. You've completely blown me off since I told you what I think of her."

I stand. "Do you really think I've been avoiding you because of Nola?"

"Why else?"

"Because I found out what you did," I snap.

"What did I do?"

"You threw her at him."

Brie freezes, her body statuesque. She is so still that the sound of my own breathing begins to make me feel uncomfortable. "Kay, I have no idea what you're talking about."

"The eminently unfaithful," I say. "He chose to cheat. That's on him. But you wanted it to happen. You helped."

Brie reanimates and her face turns red. "Kay, you're freaking me out. You're not making sense."

"Unbelievable." I grab my clothes off the radiator and she stands in front of the door, her arms crossed, her face crumbling.

"You can't just mess with people's hearts, Kay."

I feel like the world is spinning in the wrong direction. I don't know anything or anyone anymore. Brie is the one who didn't want me. It was the first time I recognized having feelings for a girl, and they knocked me out like a tidal wave. She was this amazing person, the best friend I was lucky to have, breathlessly gorgeous. Everything about her was warm and I wanted to be near her so feverishly badly—when we sat next to each other, my skin went electric and I buzzed with life. I loved being close to Spencer, but Brie was next level. Compare a magnet to a collapsed supernova. It was amazing and terrifying and I could only stand it because I was so sure it was mutual. There was so much flirting, so much teasing, I didn't have the humility to doubt there would be a kiss at the end.

But then there was the Elizabeth Stone incident. Elizabeth wanted on the tennis team and started following Tai around everywhere for weeks and it was unfortunate, but pathetic. When I called Tai out for letting Elizabeth drool all over her, she said I was worse, hanging all over Brie like a rejected lesbian rescue puppy. I said if anyone's a lesbian in this scenario, it's Stone, because she has the haircut, the man hands, and smells like a volleyball team.

It was a horrible thing to say and at least once a day it

pops into my head at some point just to remind me what an irredeemable person I am.

But everyone laughed. Almost everyone. Brie looked at me like I was a stranger she didn't want to meet. I hadn't thought before I'd spoken. She hadn't come out yet, but I knew how I felt. But when I finally got up the courage to slip her a note (so pathetic, so pathetic) asking if she wanted to go to that year's Skeleton Dance *with* with me, she wrote back no. Just *no*. And we never talked about it again. She took, of all people, Elizabeth Stone. They dressed as Roxie Hart and Velma Kelly and they were hot and amazing. I borrowed Tai's Tinker Bell costume from the previous year with zombie makeup and went as a death wish.

I never made a joke like that again. And I cried so hard that night after our lake ritual.

I DON'T KNOW what I'm supposed to think now, as Brie watches me through wet eyes. Those feelings aren't totally gone, but they're not the same, not in that aching way. It would hurt too much to be around her if I allowed myself to completely open that door again. I wouldn't be able to look her in the eye, and I can't stand to shut her out of my life. I know she loves Justine. I know she regrets kissing me. But we're always so close. I can't not feel it. It burns.

I close my eyes and open them again, my lashes damp. "I never messed with your heart."

"The second you met Spencer at that party, you dropped me like I was some stupid plaything you were bored of."

"That's not what happened. You abandoned me for Justine. And this is after you spent a year rejecting me. Skeleton Dance, Valentine's Day, Spring Gala."

"I was *talking* to her. In less than five minutes you were all over him."

That's not how I remember it. "If you and Justine were just talking, why did you go home with her? Why are you still with her?"

Brie sinks back against the wall and looks at me wearily. "You had another chance to choose me, Kay. In Spencer's room. When he walked in, I took your hand and you shoved me away."

"What did you expect me to do? After two years of you pulling me toward you and pushing me away over and over until I have no idea what you want?"

"I don't trust you, Kay." Her lips tremble. "I don't trust you not to hurt me."

"Brie, if I could take everything back . . ." I pause. "I don't even know where I would start. There's too much to undo."

"You were with Jessica and Maddy seconds after they died."

"You were with Jessica, too."

"What did you do?"

My voice quavers. "I've done a lot of things. I'm not a very good person, okay?"

"Then just be honest with me, Kay."

"I am honest with you." I can't stand the way she's looking at me. Not after what Cori said. Lost cause. "Okay, you want to know what you've missed?" I pull up the email from Jessica on my phone and flash it at her. "Correspondence from corpses. That final project? A website blackmailing me into carrying out a dead girl's revenge against my best friends. And it's all on me. Tai, Tricia, Cori, Maddy, Jessica. I'm screwed. And you're mad because I didn't invite you along. You should be thanking Nola for bumping you out of the passenger seat. What else would you like to know, Brie?"

"What website?"

"It doesn't exist anymore."

She bites her lower lip. Her eyes are full and her voice is thick when she speaks again. "It just disappeared into thin air?"

The realization breaks over me like an icy wave. "You do think I'm crazy."

Her gaze wavers. "This is a bad idea. This is stupid."

"What?"

"I'm done."

I stand, alarmed. "Brie, stop it. You're not giving up on me.

This is just a fight. You're my best friend."

She looks me in the eye. "Did you kill Jessica?"

"No!"

"Hunter?"

"What? No."

"Maddy?"

It's like one slap in the face after the next, but I deserve them, so I stand there and take them. "No. Is that all?"

She tears her coat off and rips her shirt up to reveal a voice-recording instrument. "Done. I'm so done."

17

i call Nola as soon as I get outside, but the call goes to voice mail over and over. I try Spencer next.

"You told me about Jessica. Why did you hide Maddy from me?" I say as soon as he picks up.

"I tried. When we met at Cat Café, I tried to tell you. We weren't exactly speaking before then. Then I was going to tell you at dinner but you never showed." He sounds like he's been crying, too.

"We didn't have plans."

"Jesus Christ." He pauses. "I have a text from you telling me to meet you."

"Right. Someone faked my number just like they faked my email. Is that even possible?"

"Yes, but it's pretty damn convoluted. You could just say you blew me off."

"But I didn't, Spencer. And you flooded my inbox with texts. You have to be cool."

"Really? Is that how I have to be? How many lies have you told the police this week?"

"Have many lies have you told me? Like, you forgive me for Brie? What's it going to take? Will you have to sleep with the entire student body before we're even? Maybe throw in a couple of professors?"

"It's not about getting even."

I feel like running and never stopping, but I'm weak and the constant urge to cough makes it hard to pace my breathing. I head for the lake and walk briskly around the path toward Old Road, our meeting point. I don't know what my plan is. To ask him to meet me, to keep on going through the village and never look back, to make an endless circuit or plunge into the water and scream into the icy darkness. "I never, *never* tried to hurt you."

"By hooking up with Brie in my bed?"

"It was a mistake, it wasn't about you, and I regret it. You can't possibly say the same."

"I did regret it. The second I woke up, reality hit and I wanted them gone."

The words knock me breathless. I look up suddenly, and stop cold. His car is parked at the curve of the path. "Where are you?"

"Driving in circles."

I turn around slowly, but I'm completely alone. I've come far enough along the path that the thorny hedges and thick border of trees now separate me from the campus buildings. That's definitely his car, the battered, ancient Volvo with a dented hood and smashed left headlight. I begin to back down the path toward campus, keeping my eye on his car. "Where?"

"Near campus. Want me to come get you?"

"Why are you here?"

"Because—"

"Why are you always here?"

I hear footsteps behind me and turn to see him walking down the path, and I break into a run. I hear him follow, and I sprint toward his car. There's no other option. The thornbushes are too thick; they'll only ensnare me, and the lake will similarly suspend me. He calls after me to stop, and I shout that I'll stop if he does. I finally slow when I reach his car and hear him halt behind me. I turn around to see him a good ten yards back. We're at the edge of the village now, and since it's the middle of the day, people are strolling from shop to shop. I beckon him toward me cautiously.

"What did I do, Katie?"

"*Don't* call me Katie. Especially not now."

He closes the last few steps between us and looks down at me, the liveliness gone from his eyes, his face a wreck. He smells like cigarettes and coffee and he hasn't shaved in a couple of days. "I don't know what you want from me anymore."

"I want to know how far you'd go to hurt me."

He closes his eyes and a ghostly cloud of breath escapes his lips. "I didn't sleep with Maddy to hurt you. It just happened."

"Jessica?"

"Maybe." He opens his eyes. They are the same pale blue I fell almost in love with, but the angelic-demonic paradox is gone. They are blank and broken and empty. "Did it work?"

"Did you kill Maddy to hurt me?" The words sting my mouth, but I have to say them. It will hurt worse if I don't. I can't stand uncertainty anymore, not even the shadow of it.

He takes my hands in his and turns them over, examining my palms. Then he traces a line and looks up at me, one last spark igniting in his eyes with a twisted smile. "You see this line? Everyone focuses on the life line and the love line. This is the killer line. You're a killer, Kay. You look so innocent, but you shatter everything you touch." He pauses, and then presses my hand to his lips.

"That's not fair," I whisper.

His eyes fill and he closes them. "No. Not everything. Just everyone who loves you."

He drops my hand and walks back to his car, leaving me standing frozen and speechless.

Then something inside me hardens. "Well, everyone you fuck is dead, Spence."

A disquieting calm falls between us, and for a moment the rest of the world goes silent. The image of him with Jessica, dead, flashes in my head once more. "That's one hell of a coincidence."

He eases back onto the hood of his car and places his hands over his mouth. "Do *you* think I killed Maddy?"

"I don't know who did it." I flick my eyes over to the village. There's no one passing by just now. Just Spencer and his car in front of me, a barrier of thorns to one side, and to my other, the lake where Jessica was murdered.

Spencer hops off the car and I take a defensive step back, but he turns away from me and yanks the door open.

"Good-bye, Katie."

Then he's gone.

I TRY NOLA again, and finally dial Greg's number, even though he has no reason to speak to me again after what I did to him.

He answers on the first ring. "Ms. Kay Donovan," he says in a pleasant voice. Clearly, he doesn't know what I did. On the plus side, it doesn't sound like it did too much damage.

"Are you busy?"

His voice sobers. "Are you crying?"

"I just need to talk to someone."

"I'm not busy. Are you okay?"

"The polar opposite."

"Want me to come get you?"

"Can you meet me at Cat Café?"

"Sure. Do you need anything?"

"Just be there." I hang up. My nerves are too raw to design my answers with wit or grace.

I barely recognize myself in my reflection in the glass door of the café. The cold and the crying fit have puffed my face out to twice its size. My eyes look swollen and bruised, and my lips are dry and pale. I haven't showered in over a day, and my hair is matted and frizzy, escaping from its ponytail in wild bursts. I order a decaf tea, load it with lemon wedges and sugar, and blow my nose into a wad of napkins. Then I settle myself into a corner table far from where icy air is leaking into the room through the front door.

A freezing gust of wind sweeps in with Greg. He jumps over a table and sits down across from me.

"What happened?"

"My best friend tried to secretly record me confessing to killing Jessica, a cat, and one of my other best friends."

He slides his hand across the table and takes mine in his. It's rough and soft at the same time.

"The good news is that I don't think you're much of a suspect anymore," I say.

"That's funny." He pulls his wool hat off and shakes his hair to unflatten it. "Because after Madison Farrell died, they came around again. I don't think I've seen the last of them."

"Do you always tell them the truth, the whole truth, and nothing but the truth?"

"The truth isn't always enough," he admits.

"I'll drink to that." I raise my cup and he bumps his fist against it.

He sighs. "I didn't know Madison. Why are they asking me about her?"

I can't think of a reason. Unless they really, really want to draw a connection and I've been underestimating how much the police have been focusing on Greg all along. God, did I play a part in that? "Wish I could tell you." I pause. "They asked me about you."

"Ah. So that's where the blade line of questioning originated."

I feel my face turn bright red. He doesn't look the slightest bit disturbed. "You mentioned the blades. The police didn't release that information."

"Oh my God, Kay, I must have killed my girlfriend," he says in a mocking voice.

I wait. "I know if you were confessing you would be crying or something. Because you loved her."

"Justine told me how you and Brie found Jessica. We both cried. Is that satisfactory?"

I feel stupid. "I'm sorry."

"This is real *Game of Thrones* shit. I mean clearly you're Cersei."

"What? No. The wildling with the red hair."

His face splits into a grin. "Ygritte. She has a name. She dies."

"Don't they all?"

"Some of them get to avenge first. I like to consider myself—"

"Jon Snow. Your hair gives you away. But don't even think about it."

Greg leans back in his chair. "I like that we can be tactical adversaries and still converse like friends. Is this what it's like to live in a comic book?"

I shake my head. He puts me in a good mood. He reminds me so much of Todd before Todd was ruined. It hurts and feels good at the same time.

"Why don't you suspect me?" I ask him. "Even my best friends think I'm capable of murder."

He pops a piece of gum into his mouth and chews thoughtfully, and then looks straight into my eyes. "Because you don't have the face of a killer."

"That's the dumbest thing I ever heard."

"Oh? Why are you so sure I didn't do it?"

"Well, I did talk to the cops about the whole blade thing," I admit. "But it's true. You don't seem like you could have hurt Jessica."

"What do the neighbors always say in the interviews? Quiet guy, kept to himself. I never thought he would be capable of something like this."

"My neighbors think I'm definitely capable of something like this."

"Well, my classmates whisper." He taps his fingertips on the table rapidly like he's playing a silent piano concerto. "Let's not feel sorry for ourselves. We get to live."

I try to smile but something misfires. "Do you think we'll still feel that way after twenty years in prison?"

"Do you know what I really thought when I first saw you?" he asks, his eyes clear as a still pool.

"Get out of my coffee line, you stuck-up bitch."

He grins and brushes his wavy hair out of his face. "Who is this girl who ruined my play?"

I shrug, uncomprehending.

"I directed the fall student showcase production last year. I had this narcissistic habit of watching the audience, because by opening night, I'd done everything I could with the actors, and I just wanted to see how people reacted to our work. And in the fourth row, six seats from the left aisle, there was this girl who had texted and whispered through half of the show. As did half of the audience. The only ones with their eyes really glued to the stage were parents of the actors." He rolls his eyes and smiles into the palm of his hand. "But toward the end, people stopped texting. Because almost everyone starts paying attention at the end of *Our Town*."

I place a hand over my mouth, remembering. That was the show Brie and I went to the night we met Spencer and Justine.

"And during Justine's farewell speech, this girl who had been texting and whispering and smirking this whole time just got this beautiful, haunted still look on her face. And because of exactly where she was sitting in relation to the stage, a pale beam of light fell onto her, like a spotlight. And silent tears started running down her face, just at the moment I had been desperately begging Justine to start crying."

I remember that speech. Justine's character had died and returned to her life to say a final good-bye to everything she would miss. Every single word had stabbed me like a pin in a separate and distinct section of my heart.

"And I thought, girl in the audience, you are ruining my play, because you *are* the ghost. The hairs on the back of my neck stood on end, because I had dreamed you without knowing you. I felt like I had somehow picked this play unconsciously just to meet you. Then you suddenly got up and ran out of the theater. And then later at the cast party, before I got up the nerve to speak to you, I saw Spencer Morrow slobbering all over you, and then you insulted my play pretty harshly and called me a six-foot-tall Gollum, and my second impression superseded my first."

I feel like I've been holding my breath for a thousand years and if I don't let it out, I will burst. "What's your point, Greg?" I manage.

"I trusted you before we met. My gut says you're good. I know we haven't known each other that long, but if you ever need to talk, you can talk to me. Suspect to suspect." He rolls his sleeves up, exposing his intricately tattooed forearms. "So. Are we finally going to trust each other?"

I wrap my fingers around my mug and consider my options once again. Brie and Spencer are gone. I have Nola, but things are weird now. Time is running out. With the police putting a wire on Brie, for all I know, they're moving in to make an arrest, although it sounds like things aren't going well for Greg either. At the very least, they may be considering calling my parents to come so they can formally question me, and I need to avoid that at all costs.

"*Trust* is a strong word."

"Fair enough. We'll keep things casual with a side of

paranoia. Let's talk alternative suspects. I like you, but I do see how perhaps your neighbors may view you as potentially evil. That six-foot Gollum comment didn't exactly make me feel warm and fuzzy."

"It wasn't personal," I say quickly. "I don't even remember saying it. I say stupid crap like that all the time. Used to. I'm . . . rethinking some character choices."

He looks at me dubiously. "You're not an actor? You talk like one."

"Nola. Everything is dance and theater. She's rubbing off on me."

"Well, do you think your prior choices may have earned you some enemies?"

"I'd say that's a definite."

"Every motive in the book can be boiled down to pride. You insult someone, you potentially make an enemy for life. Maybe a deadly one." He whips a notebook and pencil out of his pocket. "So, let's profile our killer. Maybe she's a Bates student after all. Someone with access to Jess, the lake, and the party."

"You've eliminated Spencer?"

"No connection to Madison."

"I see." I let him continue.

"It could be a student with a grudge against Jess, or you if you're being framed. A frenemy. A rival. Or a victim of bullying. Not to demonize victims, but revenge is a strong motivator."

"So, basically the entire student body."

He shoots me a reproachful look. "Everyone?"

"You're implying that I've never been bullied, right?"

"I didn't say—"

"No one gets away unscathed, Greg. People like you think you're so morally superior. There's someone lower on the social ladder that you laughed at or made fun of, or didn't invite, or picked last."

"I don't think I'm superior at all," he says. "Just because I'm nice to you doesn't mean I don't have, like, a stadium full of regrets."

"*Regret* is too polite a word."

"For?"

I feel so tired, I make a cradle of my arms and rest my head on them. He scoots closer. "Tai and I—my ex-friend, I guess—used to say the bitchiest shit, but people thought we were funny, so we'd get away with it."

"Okay."

"You can get away with murder if you're lucky. You don't even have to be smart. Just have a social or political one up on everyone else. People look the other way if they want to. Everybody knows it."

"That's true sometimes."

"I don't want to get away with it anymore."

He is very quiet for a long moment, and then his voice comes out in a whispery rasp. "Was that a confession, Kay?"

"No. Forget it." I squeeze my eyes shut tight to minimize the risk of crying. Of everything that has happened in the past few weeks, the worst has been Brie slipping away, and it didn't happen in an instant. By the time she agreed to try to trap me, I'd already lost her. Did I start losing her years ago, when I made that unforgiveable joke? Because I was so afraid to apologize, because that would mean admitting I did something awful?

"How do you ask forgiveness for something that can't be undone?"

"If you're sorry, forgiveness isn't the point, is it?" he says. "It's not about feeling better, it's about doing better." He grins. "Totally plagiarized from Pastor Heather." He pauses. "But it makes me feel better. Having something to *do*."

"I'm not the same person I was," I say. "I'm not."

He squeezes my hand. "I believe you. I never thought you were evil. But, Kay. I'm not just here for group hugs. We're murder suspects. We have shit to figure out. Have I convinced you that the killer was a student?"

I sigh. "Do you have one in mind?"

"Actually, I do. There's someone out there who had the same means and opportunity as you."

"Motive?"

"A long-standing grudge."

"Really?" I try to look at his notepad but he holds it out of my reach. "Do the police know about this?"

"She's been lying to the police. You've been helping her lie."

"What?"

"The only missing piece is an encounter on the night of the murder. If Jess fought with someone that night, I think that's enough evidence to arrest."

"She did fight with someone. You."

"Or maybe Brie."

18

i'm so shocked I laugh. "Brie didn't kill Jessica. She's not even capable of yelling."

"So maybe she did it quietly."

"I can't believe you're serious."

"Dead serious." He shows me his phone, and I see a picture of Jessica and Brie wearing Bates Academy orientation T-shirts, arms linked, grinning into the camera.

I cover my mouth with my hand. "Brie barely knew Jessica."

Greg shakes his head. "They were best friends for the first month of school, and then they had an epic falling-out."

"You didn't know her then." But I didn't know Brie then, either.

"That's how bad it was. This thing saturated Bates for Jess. That's why she was never there. She sent me this picture when we started dating and told me, 'This is Brie Matthews. She comes to cast parties. Never speak to her.'"

"What happened?"

He shakes his head. "They got really close really fast. Told each other all their deepest, darkest secrets, swore to be best friends for life. I think Jess may have had feelings for Brie but I kind of got the sense that it maybe wasn't reciprocal."

I nod, trying to ignore the weird hot sensation that creeps up the back of my neck. "Not outside the realm of the imagination."

"Then Brie started hanging out with some other girls, and I guess Jess maybe wasn't cool enough for them or something. The next year, Brie apparently pulled some unspeakably mean shit that Jess wouldn't go into detail about."

"I don't believe it."

"People never believe someone they love could do something cruel."

I'm glad I didn't tell Greg about Todd. But the way he's looking at me, it almost seems like he knows.

"Jess was really upset, so she went to Brie's room and found the door unlocked, and her computer unprotected, and she forwarded a bunch of Brie's emails to her parents. I don't know who they were to, or what was in them. But, suffice it to say, there was resulting animosity between Jess and Brie."

"There's no way," I say simply. "I would trust Brie with my life. Even if she decided never to speak to me again, I'd take the fall for her."

"You would, wouldn't you?"

"Because I know beyond the shadow of a doubt that she's innocent."

He smiles sadly. "It's things like that, Kay. It makes it hard to believe you're a killer."

I stand. "I'm sorry I can't get on board with your theory."

"She made my girlfriend miserable and now Jess is dead. There's no one else I think could have done it."

"Maybe your girlfriend lied."

He shoots me a warning look.

"Sorry." I stare into my cup, afraid to look him in the eye. "Whatever Brie might have done to hurt Jessica's feelings, what I did was worse."

He looks at me blankly. "What did you do?"

I tell him the truth about Dear Valentine, the one thing that connects me and everyone on the revenge blog to Jessica.

Dear Valentine was supposed to be a fund-raiser where students could purchase a flower to be delivered to another student during classes and the money would go toward the Spring Gala. But it usually served as something of a popularity contest. Tai, Tricia, Brie, and I always ended up with enormous bouquets of roses, while the majority of students generally got two or three flowers from their besties.

Two years ago, I got a really beautiful, expensive white

orchid plant from an anonymous sender with a note that said *Be mine*. It had been months since the Elizabeth Stone incident, and Brie had been acting cutesy and flirty again, so of course I assumed it was from her and humiliated myself by thanking her with a badly written (rhyming) poem. But she swore up and down that it wasn't her in front of the entire dining hall. It wasn't any of the rest of our friends either. I had been so sure it was Brie, and that this was finally going to be our big cinematic love-story moment, that I just kind of started hating those flowers. They sat on my desk in the generic glass vase from the village flower shop, taunting me with their presence every night while I tried to sleep. And they were there in the morning, still stubbornly alive, pale and perfect and undying.

Because they were sent anonymously, I couldn't figure out who they came from, but I hated the sender, too. How cruel did you have to be to send flowers with an unsigned note that says *Be mine* to a person who is so obviously head over heels in love with someone else? Of course I'd assumed they were from Brie. And of course I was crushed when they weren't. I thought the sender was taunting me for some random bitchy thing I said or did to them. Let's be honest. There were too many to narrow it down.

I was sure it was done out of malice by someone who watched me repeatedly break my own heart with Brie and wanted to torture me. So I decided to torture them.

With Tricia's financial backing, I bribed the students running Dear Valentine to deliver a set of gifts back to the sender. They wouldn't reveal her identity. But they were happy to arrange a series of deliveries. One for every bloom on the orchid she sent me. The twelve days of valentines, Tai called it. She and Tricia helped me brainstorm, and Tricia alone dealt with the messenger. The first day was a simple note—*I'm yours*—with one of the orchid blooms enclosed.

The second, a lock of my hair, again, with one of the blooms.

The third, a smear of blood on an index card. With every note, we sent another orchid bloom.

On the fourth day we sent a carefully scrubbed rib bone from the dining hall with the note *All of me*.

That night, Tricia said the Dear Valentine delivery girl showed up at her door, looking nervous. She said the sender was pretty upset and asked us to please stop delivering the notes. But by then we had so many ideas, Tricia happily bankrolled the rest of the project, and the delivery girl agreed to take the money, no questions asked. I guess now I know that's not the whole truth. Nola was the delivery girl, and Tricia didn't pay her in money. She paid her in promises and lies. It was just as cruel as the actual prank.

We'd had so much fun on the Dear Valentine project, hunting for "body parts" online, in village shops, even in the woods.

Only Brie wouldn't be a part of it. She completely dropped off the radar during that whole period. On the day I burst into her room with a weirdly realistic candy brain we'd ordered off the internet, she looked at me and just pointed to the door without saying a word.

That just made me throw myself into the project with more determination. If Brie didn't get it, Tai and Tricia did. It was a *joke*.

At the end, the orchid plant was just two skeletal stems wired to fake plastic twigs, and I felt a little better. I tossed the stems, scrubbed the vase, and filled it with chocolate kisses, which Brie *had* given me a bag of, with no card and no real kiss. It served Dear Valentine girl right. *She* was mocking me with her gift, and if she had anything to say to me, she could say it to my face.

I thought that was the end of it.

But when I texted Brie asking her to the Spring Gala, she turned me down again, with no explanation. I wrote back with my heart pounding, *Someone else?* And she wrote, *Dear Valentine Girl.* She didn't show up at the dance at all.

We never talked about it again.

That was my first and last prank. Initiation and hazing, yes. But nothing like Dear Valentine.

I finally look up at Greg. "I did that to Jessica. My friends, too. She probably thought Brie was involved, but Brie refused.

That's probably the unspeakably mean thing Jessica was referring to."

"Jesus, Kay, it didn't even occur to you that she might
have actually liked you?"

"You tell me. I was hanging out with Brie at the time. *All*
the time. They weren't mean; I just took them that way."

He sighs heavily. "She never told me, so there's no way to
know. She still retaliated against Brie, so Brie had a motive to
get back at her."

"She didn't do it. She wouldn't even send a shitty valentine."

"It all depends on what happened afterward," Greg says.
"Did they or did they not run into each other the night of the
murder? Is it possible?"

I think back to the night of the murder. I had drained half
the bottle of prosecco when the headlights swept over the dark
water. The details of my thinking were fuzzy, like scribbles on
torn notepaper, but the *ideas* were bold and urgent and strong.
I didn't stand up when Spencer got out of his car and slammed
the door, because I knew I might sway and crash, and I needed
him to understand how serious this was.

He looked down at me, shocked. "Katie?"

"Who the fuck is Jess?"

He checked his phone. "Oh shit. I'm so sorry. I got two
calls in a row. I just assumed."

"You said everything was going to be okay."

"I wanted it to be. I still do."

"After what you did?"

"I don't know what to do anymore." He took a sip from my bottle and made a face. "God, Katie."

"Make it okay." I pulled him close and kissed him. I was still sweaty from the dance and cold from the chilled night air and the combination made me shiver against his warm skin.

"I don't know how anymore," he whispered into my mouth.

"End it. Whoever she is, get rid of her. I don't want to hear her name again. I never want to see her face." I edged back into the shadows, pulling him by the hand.

"Will I still hear Brie's name?"

"She's gone." I kissed him again, slower, dancing my body against his, guiding his hand around my waist, the other on my shoulder, his fingers entwined in the strap of my dress. "Get rid of this girl."

NOW GREG LOOKS at me expectantly. "Is it possible Brie could have fought with Jessica that night?"

I shake my head. "I doubt it."

19

When I get back to my room, I find a piece of masking tape over my nameplate with the word KILLER printed on it in thick red letters. The door is plastered with messages scrawled in black and red permanent markers, along with a few newspaper clippings about the recent murders. Someone has drawn a grotesque cartoon of a hangman with a cat's body dangling from the gallows with the letters K-A-Y in the blanks. The phrase *You might as well be dead, too* is repeated several times in a variety of colors and handwriting. There are subtle references to at least a dozen girls I've pissed off over the past three and a half years, funneled into a general hostility and summed up by the cartoon of the hanging cat, the corpse I handled, but whose death I played no part in.

I hear a muffled laugh behind me and whirl around so fast, I almost lose my balance. The congestion from the cold has given me vertigo and sudden movements yank the earth out from under me. But a door slams across the hall before I have time to see who's behind it, and I'm so disoriented that I can't tell which one it was. The one straight across, or two down, or even echoing all the way from the end? Maybe it's good that I'm still a person of interest in a murder. At least they're too afraid to say all of this to my face.

I escape into my room and crawl under the covers still dressed, shivering from fever and cold and being completely alone. I don't want to call Nola. I can't help feeling like this is partly her fault, even though I asked her to be a part of it. I bribed her to unlock that first password.

I roll over in bed, kick my shoes off, and then blow my nose until the skin around my nostrils is tender. My instinct, as always, is to call Brie, but there's nothing to say. I can't apologize and I can't demand an apology. What she did was unforgivable and it also put me on notice that *I'm* not forgiven. I check my email to find a slew of last-minute reminders about the pre-Thanksgiving exams coming up this week. One good thing about Bates is that they break up the first semester midterms and give you half of them before Thanksgiving break and the other half just before winter break, so you don't have to spend the entire week ignoring your family and studying.

Of course, I don't spend Thanksgiving with my family. The year Todd died, we spent it in Mom's hospital, which was sad and gross and gave me slimy-turkey-and-cranberry-flavored-hoof-treat-related food poisoning. I stayed with Aunt Tracy for the rest of the weekend while Mom and Dad did intensive couples grief therapy. We watched *Days of Our Lives* while drinking pumpkin spice coffee and eating low-calorie vanilla ice cream in quantities sufficient to cancel out the benefit of the calorie count.

Since I enrolled at Bates, I have spent every Thanksgiving with Brie's family in their Cape Cod mansion pretending to be an equally perfect, beloved second daughter. They do things like yearly family football matches on the enormous back lawn overlooking the ocean as the sun melts down into the evening sky, ghost stories next to a fireplace that takes up an entire gigantic wall, and family movie nights with stove-popped cara-mel corn and homemade hot chocolate. For dinner the cook prepares enormous fresh-caught lobsters swimming in butter, roasted chestnuts, acorn squash with a hard little crust of burnt sugar like crème brûlée, almond asparagus, and garlic smashed potatoes. It's the same every year, and it's delicious.

Being there makes me feel better than I am. More impor-tant, more worthy. They are a *real* family. I feel separate from my parents when I sit on the sofa between Brie and her mother under the enormous cathedral ceiling watching classic com-edies. At home, even if my parents were around, we would be eating something like cold turkey sandwiches in the darkened living room in front of a football game none of us cared about. I would be texting or pretending to text so that it wouldn't be too awkward not to talk to them. Dad would be asleep or pretending to sleep for the same reason, and Mom would be digging through her purse for a sedative, because that game on the television that none of us cared about? It would be Todd's favorite team. And they'd probably be losing.

This will be the first year I won't be invited to Brie's. I don't want to know what she's going to tell them. For some reason, I feel ashamed, like I've let her family down. Like they took a chance on me, they took the abandoned puppy in, the dangerous breed everyone knows is predisposed to attack babies and harmless old ladies, and I repaid them by biting their daughter.

I decide not to tell my parents at all. It's too late to tell the school I have nowhere to go, but I'll figure something out. I scroll past the exam notifications and see that I have an email from Justine. I open it reluctantly.

Stay away from my girlfriend, bitch.

Lovely.

I forward it to Brie, with the following message:

Let your girlfriend know I have no intention of speaking to her girlfriend ever again.

I click send.

Then I can't help adding an addendum.

Thanks for the décor.

I snap the light off and slide under the covers and open my Facebook page. I have forty-three notifications. My wall has been plastered with notes and my inbox is full of messages similar to the ones scrawled on my door. At least these aren't anonymous. My eyes mist and I blink hard as I read every word, study every name and face, and mentally add them to the growing list of people who may have wanted to screw me over. This was much simpler when it was just a question of who might have wanted to hurt Jessica. There are so many names here. Tai. Tricia. Cori. Justine. Holly. Elizabeth. Brie's name isn't there. Thank God for that. I see that most of the comments have several likes and strings of their own comments, and, cringing, I click on one of them to reveal the threads. My throat closes up.

Justine wrote, "Watch your back, bitch."

Under it, Nola replied, "Got it. Who's got yours?"

I click on the others. Nola has responded to nearly every single one, jumping to my defense.

I check my phone. She hasn't sent me a text or called. She's just quietly run damage control on each of these comments as they've been posted. As I'm reviewing the page, a new comment pops up at the bottom from Kelli, and Nola replies within seconds. I turn my phone off, sighing. I'm going to have to take a break from people—online, in person, and even in my memory—if I'm going to pass my exams.

I BURY MYSELF in bottles of Nyquil, boxes of tissues, and stacks of textbooks for the next week and a half. I have an exam in every class except French before Thanksgiving break, and with my congested and (legitimately) doped-up brain moving at a snail's pace, it takes every spare moment I have to catch up on my readings and prepare for the tests. The messages don't stop coming, via email, Facebook, my door, which is so covered in graffiti I can barely see the wood anymore, and now, phone. I tried to make an appointment with my dorm housemother to talk about it, but she was very distant and said she was all booked up until after the break. I even put a phone call through to good old Officer Jenny Biggs at campus police, but she blew me off.

"I'm being harassed," I told her. "Can I file a report or something?"

She paused for a long time. "To be honest, Kay, there have been so many harassment reports against you over the years, I don't know that I want to do anything about it."

She hung up on me.

Nola and I make outlines and flash cards and take turns quizzing each other and using Pavlovian conditioning to try to force information into our brains. When she gets an answer correct, she gets a Skittle. When I get an answer correct, I get a cough drop. I unhook my campus phone and put my cell phone on silent. No one calls me anyway, except with vague threats. My weekly calls home have become even more torturous than usual. They begin with an interrogation on whether games have resumed yet and devolve into ranting (Dad) about the unfairness on the part of the administration of taking sports away from grieving children and fretting (Mom) over how distant and unresponsive I've become. I end up shouting that I can't do anything about the administration, Dad yells that I could start a petition or write an editorial in the newspaper or something, and Mom says she doesn't know me anymore and when did I become so angry and aggressive? Then I hang up and try to put my phone on silent before I receive a threatening phone call from some random townie promising to kick my ass (yes, the townies are at it, too, now). I will not be spending Thanksgiving with my family, Brie or no Brie.

So it's an automatic yes please when Nola unexpectedly asks if I'm interested in going to her family's place in Maine.

She looks surprised when I say yes. "Oh. Really?"

"My family doesn't do Thanksgiving. I was planning on hiding under my bed and eating pretzels and applesauce."

She pauses. "Well, we don't usually do anything fancy, but it's a step up from pretzels and applesauce."

"Deal."

Nola has not only been the sole person to stand by me through all of this, she has also been fiercely protective. I wouldn't have had it in me to defend myself. Maybe if I didn't deserve at least some of the hate being thrown at me, I could. But I know people are using the murder as an excuse to vent pent-up anger because of things I did or said to them, maybe years ago. Little things that didn't seem to matter at the time. It's impossible to disentangle that. It makes it so hard to fight back. I don't know what I'd do without Nola. I was pretty horrible to her and she forgave me, proof that I'm not beyond saving. A part of me keeps hoping people will notice this and think, "Oh, look! Kay was a total bitch to Nola and now they're like BFFs. I should follow her example and forgive Kay, too. How glorious the high road is! Come back to us, repentant Kay! All is forgiven!"

I guess redemption doesn't work that way.

20

---

*W*e leave for Nola's on Sunday evening. The train to
her house cuts across the same landscape Brie and
I used to take to the coast and then juts up north along the
rocky shore where we used to hop on a bus to head south to the
Cape. I have always adored the New England shore. My parents
used to take me and Todd to the beach in New Jersey every
year. The New Jersey beach is *down* the shore. The sand is a
burning golden blanket, and the water is a warm, murky green.
I loved our summers down the shore, digging for sand crabs
in the frothy surf, chasing the ice cream truck down the hot
pavement, and spending hours boiling in the water, forgetting
to reapply sunscreen, and emerging at the end of every day
burned bright red and untouchably tender.

After he died, though, it was unthinkable to return.

New England beaches are nothing, nothing like any of that.
You don't go down the shore, you go up the coast. The sand is

large and prickly and granular and sticks uncomfortably to the bottom of your feet, and the cold, translucent water rinses up over pebbles. If you stay in too long, you start going numb. The colors are gray and bone and a muted medley of sea glass; the only golden you come across at the Cape are the purebreds trotting around the dog parks or at beaches that allow them to frolic in the surf. At least, that's Brie's Cape. There are always parts you don't get to know when you become acquainted with a place through the lens of a specific person. But when we travel up the coast, or bus south to the Cape, that's all we see. That pastel palette of bone and sea glass, shark-eye gray and ghostly white.

That's mostly what I see heading up toward Nola's house, too, only the coast is rockier, and the sea seems angrier, slapping against the sides of cliffs. The sun sinks down into the watery horizon too quickly to put on much more of a show than a couple of brilliant tangerine ribbons, and then we're left with a sliver of moonlight and the occasional lighthouse sweeping its thin beam back and forth over the water.

Nola is curled up in a ball with a satin, lace-trimmed eye mask over her face, her coat pulled over her like a blanket, earbuds blocking out the sounds of the train and our fellow passengers. I try to close my eyes, but the overhead light is too bright and the sound of a woman crying into her phone behind me is too distracting.

I look over at Nola and wonder how far we are from her stop. It can't possibly be that much farther. The whole trip was only a few hours. I touch my forehead to the window, trying to see past my own reflection. We're slowing down, about to enter a station. I kick Nola's feet and she growls and removes her mask, squinting at me with one eye.

"Are we there yet?"

She glances out the window, one eye still squeezed shut, giving her an odd pirate look, especially with the mask still half on and her hair gathered into a loose, messy braid. "Unfortunately, yes." She yawns, heaving her bag onto her shoulder as the train grinds to a halt and the conductor announces the station name. "Prepare."

I follow her out into the dark parking lot, a little nervous to meet whatever bizarre humans spawned Nola Kent, but as she walks under the bright parking-lot lights, her Mary Janes clicking on the slick pavement, an energetic gray-haired man bounds toward her and attempts to lift her into a bear hug. "She returns!" He beams.

She wriggles away and gestures to me politely. "This is Katherine Donovan. Katherine, this is my father."

He looks surprised and very pleased. "Well, that's wonderful." He reaches a hand out to me at a wide angle, so I'm not sure whether he's going for a shake or hug.

I go for the shake. "Kay is fine. I'm sorry, Mr. Kent, I thought you were expecting me." I cast Nola an uncertain glance.

She shakes her head vigorously. "It's fine."

"It's more than fine. And call me Bernie," Mr. Kent booms. He ushers us into the backseat of a gleaming Jaguar and jumps into the front seat. "Next stop, Tranquility."

"Dad," Nola says through gritted teeth.

I look at her questioningly.

She just shakes her head.

When we get to the house, I understand.

Her house is not a house. It's a mansion. Next to it, Brie's family lives in a shack, and next to that, I live in a shoe box. Nola's house makes mine look like a diorama. It's one of those traditional pastel seaside manors with dozens of rooms that you couldn't possibly do anything with except decorate and hire someone to constantly clean while you wait for guests, possibly guests who never come. In Nola's case, I suspect I might be the first, although for all I know her parents are avid entertainers. They're definitely talkers. Tranquility is the name of the house. It's posted on a charming little white sign with red-and-white-rope trim at the mailbox and again inside the foyer, which is the size of my living and dining room combined. There, a framed, calligraphied sign WELCOME TO OUR HOME hangs over a leather-bound guestbook, a feather quill and inkwell set next to it. I run my fingers over the rows of names in the open page of the guestbook, wondering if Nola made the sign. The handwriting is much neater than the practiced script I remember from her notebook and the lines of verse on her dorm walls. The ink on this page is fresh and there are plenty of names, all of them pairs. Couples, no singles or families.

Nola shuts the book on my finger and I step back guiltily, feeling like I've been caught snooping in someone's underwear drawer. "It's not for us; it's for them," she says dismissively. She waves me down the hall.

The floor is polished hardwood and the walls are lemon cream. Enormous bay windows beside the front door reveal a front yard enclosed by a wrought-iron security gate and bordered by balsam firs. Through gaping arches on either side of the foyer are curved hallways leading on one side to a cavernous library where walnut shelves stretch from floor to ceiling. At the end of the other hallway is a glass solarium filled with an array of exotic-looking plants.

A woman even shorter than Nola with her same dreamy eyes and elfin features floats down a spiral staircase in a silk nightgown. Her hair is dyed bright red and tied in a tight bun on top of her head, and either she's had some masterful work done on her face or the gift of eternal youth has been bestowed upon her. "Sweetheart," she says in a breathy southern accent, "you are wasting away."

"I am exactly the same weight as I was September first," Nola says, standing politely still as her mother pecks the air beside each of her cheeks.

She turns her glittering eyes on me. "Who's this?"

"This is Katherine."

Once again, my teeth sort of itch at the sound of my full name. I don't go by Katherine. Nola knows I don't go by Katherine. It's starting to annoy me. "Kay," I say, pressing my lips into a smile.

"Will you be joining us for the weekend?"

I look to Nola.

"Mother, the weekend's over. She's staying with us for the week."

Mrs. Kent blinks. "Well, that's just perfect! There's room for everyone. I want to hear all about your classes, sweetheart, but if I don't take my migraine pills and lie in bed with a washcloth over my eyes right now, I will be out of sorts for the duration." She kisses the air again. "There's leftovers in the kitchen. Marla made quiche and potatoes au gratin, and there's always the usual small dishes if you want some nibbles." She nods toward me. "It's nice to meet you, Katherine."

Bernie winks at me. "The crab quiche is not to be missed," he says. Then he kisses Nola on the cheek and follows his wife up the stairs. Beyond the staircase is the kitchen, at the back of which is a pair of glass doors leading to a thin sandy strip and a border of rocks, and beyond that, a sudden drop to the sea.

I wait until they're gone and then turn to Nola curiously. "Room for everyone?" I want to ask about her mother's bizarre question about the weekend, but I wonder if the answer isn't as simple as "alcohol."

She shrugs. "It wouldn't be Tranquility if it weren't teeming with obnoxious well-wishers and rando acquaintances leeching off you, would it?"

I follow Nola into the kitchen. I feel self-conscious walking on the spotless white tile floor and I slip my boots off and dangle the laces over my fingers.

She eyes me almost with contempt. "It's just a floor. It's used to being walked all over."

"I can't help it. It's cleaner than the dining hall dishes."

"Because Bates's kitchen staff is lazy."

I'm actually a little appalled at this blatant display of elitism. Nola doesn't say things like that at school. I guess everyone acts differently at home. I'm as guilty of that as anyone else. But no one's even around to see it. She piles a plate with seafood salad and cold potatoes and grabs a Diet Coke, then leaves me alone with the enormous refrigerator. It's difficult to know what to do with it. It's two feet taller than I am and about as wide as my arm span, and every inch is packed, probably in anticipation of the coming holiday feast. I don't know what's off limits, so I follow Bernie's suggestion and make myself a plate of quiche and potatoes. When I turn around, I see Nola calmly pouring two generous servings of rum into quaint little glasses shaped like mason jars.

I glance reflexively toward the staircase. "Is that a good idea?"

"They don't care." She loads the drinks and plates onto a tray and heaves her bag onto her shoulders, and I follow her up the stairs, down a long hallway, and up a second, smaller spiral staircase to her room.

Nola's bedroom is a little tower perched atop the rest of the house. It overlooks the sea from one side and the village on the other, and the view is breathtaking even with just the sliver of moonlight. We sit on her bed in the darkness, watching the silent water crumple and crash against the rocks outside, and a foreign sense of calm settles over me. I decide I'm going to stay here. I'll live in the crawl space or the servants' quarters or something. I'll become a dishwasher. Not lazy like the kitchen staff at Bates. The real deal. I'll get in with Marla, plead my case to her first thing in the morning. I'm not sure about Mrs. Kent, but Bernie seemed like a decent guy. Good plan. Or I could just declare myself an indefinite guest and become one of those Tranquility leeches Nola spoke of with such disdain. I turn to Nola to crack a joke about it, to find her hovering with her face just inches from mine. I startle so suddenly I nearly fall off the bed.

"What the hell?"

"I drank my rum and Coke too fast and now I have to pee."

I stare at her glowing eyes in the darkness. "Then pee."

"Okay." She rises unsteadily. "You didn't drink yours," she points out.

"Because I don't like diet soda or rum. Together they taste like synthetically sweetened liquid butterscotch candy."

"Okay." She takes my glass with her and leaves, presumably to go to the bathroom. I dig into my overnight bag and change into a pair of sweats and a long-sleeved Bates T-shirt, then brush my hair out and weave it into a braid. I'm relieved to see that there are two twin beds in this room, each with a frosting-pink comforter and cream-colored canopy and dust ruffle. It looks like the room was decorated when Nola was five and hasn't been altered since. I settle my things under one of the beds and am about to peel back the covers when Nola emerges from the bathroom with an empty glass in her hand, walking a little unsteadily, wearing nothing but a bathing suit and striped knee socks.

"You've got to be kidding," I say.

"Night swim," she says. "It's tradition."

21

i 'm getting over a monster cold and it's barely above freezing out," I remind her.

"So? People swim in the Arctic in the dead of winter. You don't stay in for long. It's about the ritual, not leisure," she says, tugging at my arm.

"I'm not going out there without a coat and hat," I say firmly.

She shrugs. "Fine. Hold my towel."

I tiptoe down the stairs after her, feeling trapped. If we get caught, I'm going to be the bad influence, the one who got the Kents' precious daughter drunk and flung her into the icy sea. But if I try to stop Nola, I'm the loser who doesn't like rum and doesn't jump into freezing, turbulent waters in late November. When did I become this?

Oh yeah. Halloween, just after midnight.

Nola leads me along a narrow, winding path that cuts steeply down the side of the cliff behind the house until ending abruptly, some twenty feet above the water. She turns to me, shivering. It's freezing even huddled inside my Todd coat, my hat pulled down over my ears. I cling to the side of the cliff for balance and bend forward, peering down. The drop is clean and steep, but the water lashes roughly against the side. Unfortunately, my gloves are cashmere, and my fingers are now soaked. I press my back against the cliff wall and shove my hands into my pockets.

"Don't tell me you're going to jump."

Her teeth chatter. "That's the tradition, Kay. You don't know this spot. I've lived here my whole life. There's plenty of clearance."

"What about the current? Your bones will be smashed. And I'm not jumping after you."

She looks hurt.

"Two smashed bodies are not better than one, Nola! Who came up with this grand tradition? Where are they now?"

"My grandfather. He's dead. He's been jumping this cliff to kick off Thanksgiving week since he was our age."

Oh. "Okay . . . Was he the only one to engage in this tradition?"

She shakes her head, her body shuddering so violently that her voice comes out in almost unintelligible bursts. "But when he died and we moved into the house, my family mostly stopped talking to each other, so my cousins didn't come anymore. So it's just me now. Well, and my sister. But Bianca's not coming this year. Meeting her fiancé's family is more important."

I take off my coat and put it around her shoulders, but she shoves it at me angrily. I grab for it, but a strong gust of wind rips it out of my hand and hurls it over the edge. I watch helplessly as it flaps down like a large, doomed bird to the sea below and lands lifeless against the rocks before being dragged under the surf. Then I snap.

"What the hell is wrong with you?"

She cringes, but it's not in a really dismayed or apologetic way. It's in an oops-my-bad-moving-on kind of way.

"Go ahead, Nola, jump. Do it now. It's tradition, right? Get down there and bring my coat back. Get it back, or I will never forgive you."

She looks at me uncertainly, but I just point down to the madly churning sea. I tell myself that I'm not in the wrong. She has full agency, and this was her idea. She's been insisting, pushing, and it is not my responsibility to talk her out of it. And now she's lost my coat, Todd's coat, my piece of him that no one can take away. She's taken it and hurled it into the sea.

"I've never actually jumped alone," she says finally.

"Then I will." I pull my shirt off and push it into her arms.

"You can't do that." An edge of panic has crept into her voice.

"Of course I can. I have to. It's tradition." The rocky cliff face digs into my back as I lean into it for support, removing my sneakers one at a time.

"Kay, you don't know how. The water's too rough tonight. We'll come back and look in the morning."

I slide my sweatpants off and hand them to her and creep to the very edge of the cliff, unsteady on my aching feet.

"You'll die, Kay," she finally says in a trembling voice.

I look down at the dark water. She could be right. And even if I didn't, I still might not be able to find Todd's coat. I think I see a piece of it caught on a rock, but I don't know. "Forget it."

I grab my clothes and begin hiking back up to the house in silence. I can hear her sobbing behind me, but there's just nothing I can say to her. It was an accident, but she was still responsible. She had no intention of jumping, not really. So why did she drag me out there? It should probably just bounce off me after every other piece of hell that's been thrown at me this semester, these past few years; but instead, it feels like a fresh splinter in my heart. I want my coat back. I want the worn collar and loose buttons and imaginary Todd smell, the too-long sleeves and the inner pocket I never open—the one that has to remain closed—because if I look at the picture inside, I will fall apart. The picture of Todd and me the day he died, just before the game, him hugging me and giving the camera a cheesy thumbs-up with Mom attempting to spike a football in the background, and me glaring into the camera. I need that picture. I want the coat back, and everything that goes with it. I want to curl up in it tonight and cry over all of the wonderful and terrible things in my life I've lost.

WHEN I WAKE in the morning, the floor is heaped with dozens of winter coats. Nola is sitting on her bed wearing a navy-and-white-striped polo shirt and a pair of khaki pants, no makeup, her hair swept back into a ponytail. She looks like she just walked out of the pages of a J.Crew ad. Family Nola Kent is so different from School Nola Kent, it gives me the creeps.

"I got up at sunrise and searched the water and it's gone," she says simply, a matter-of-fact expression on her face. "This is every coat every visitor has ever left at this house. We keep them so people can claim them when they come back. But almost no one ever does. Take whichever one you want. Some of them are pretty schmancy."

"Of course it was gone," I croak in a morning voice. "The ocean was dragging it all night." I wade through the mountain of winter coats. "I don't want your crappy hand-me-downs."

"Are you sure? Some of these abandoned items were once the property of British royalty." She holds up a shabby camel-colored peacoat with tortoiseshell buttons that looks like it was scavenged from a homeless shelter. "Perhaps this is to your liking?"

I shake my head and dig through my bag for my toothbrush. "No thanks."

She searches through the pile. "Her majesty does have odd taste. May I suggest this mint-condition Burberry wool navy coat? It's not that different from your old one, just a slightly different shape. And way better quality, to be perfectly frank."

I glare at her. "You can't replace my coat. That was my brother's coat. He's dead. There won't be another one."

She pauses, then throws the Burberry coat on my bed. "I'm really sorry, Kay. It was an accident. You still need a coat. That other thing you traipse around campus in is barely a sweater." She sits down next to me. "You've never mentioned your brother was dead. You talk about him like he's still alive."

"You've never mentioned your grandfather was dead."

She rolls her eyes. "Everyone has dead grandparents."

"I've got four. None of mine started a family civil war."

She smirks darkly. "Oh, that. Well, when there are spoils to be had, there's always war."

I sit and place the coat on my lap. It's a peace gesture. I should try to be gracious about it. "Were you close to your cousins?"

"They were basically my only friends. Before we lived here, we moved every three or four years for my father's work. And my sister lives in her own perfect little galaxy. So my cousins were my only constant friends. But when the will dispute went down, things got ugly really fast. Actually, that started even before Grandfather died, because as soon as he was diagnosed with Alzheimer's, Uncle Walt accused my father of convincing my grandfather to change his will. And then Uncle Edward's lawyer said that none of the cousins should speak to each other until the dispute was settled, so that side of the family wasn't allowed to have any contact with the rest of us. Edward's daughter, Julianne, had been my best friend. And when I called her to say how stupid all of it was, she accused me of trying to sabotage their family's legal claim and said I was selfish and greedy just like my Jew mother. So, that was the end of that friendship. We don't speak to any of them now."

"Wow. She went right for the swastika."

"Yeah. Turns out my family aren't nice people." She pauses. "It's not like you and your friends were so much nicer, though, were you?"

Slap in the face that I deserve. "I hope you're joking."

"Totally." But her face is expressionless and her voice softly singsong, and I get the feeling she might be mocking me. It's the first appearance of School Nola since we arrived at Tranquility. Then she smiles reassuringly. "Don't give yourself too much credit, Kay. Your whole operation is small-time."

I suddenly feel a little lucky to have my grief-stricken

mother and pushy father, completely disconnected from me, irreparable as it sometimes seems. Even Aunt Tracy. She was there for us when we needed her, even if her idea of comfort and nourishment is soap operas and ice cream. That is comfort and nourishment for some people. Maybe some wallowing is healthy. It's healthier than anti-Semitism and alienation.

"What about your brother?" Nola tries on a luxurious fur coat and settles herself at my feet.

"He was murdered."

She slides the coat off. "Well. Now my family drama feels trivial. I'm so sorry. I can't believe you never mentioned that."

I kick at the pile of coats. "It's not my favorite memory."

"Can I ask?"

"What happened?" I trace a line on my palm absently. "He was dating my best friend. Ex–best friend. They both kind of ditched me for each other. Then they broke up and all these nude photos she'd sent him mysteriously got sent out to his friends."

"And by 'mysteriously,' you mean he sent them."

I sigh. "He said someone stole his phone."

She chews her lip. "Not to speak ill of the obviously beloved dead, but stole it *and* cracked the password *and* knew exactly who to send the pics to?"

"I know." I pause. "But that wasn't my thought process at

the time. So I told the police I was with him at the time and that he didn't do it."

Nola nods.

"Megan—my friend—never spoke to me again. Soon after that, she committed suicide."

"Oh no." Nola puts an arm around me.

"It looked like Todd wasn't going to be punished, and Megan's brother decided that couldn't happen. So he murdered him."

She squeezes me tightly. "That's *Romeo and Juliet*–level vengeance."

"Except Romeo never broke up with Juliet and showed Benvolio and Mercutio nude sketches of her."

She looks at me oddly. "You do know some Shakespeare."

"Only that play. It struck a chord." Not the love-story part. The vengeance killings. The families who cannot forgive. The part where Romeo tries to make peace and ends up causing his best friend's death.

"You're missing out big-time."

I don't think so, though. There's enough drama in my life. Love, loss, revenge.

And fatal errors.

I wish I could ever know what to think about the brother I loved so much, who defended me when anyone put me down. Who did one bad thing. One unspeakable thing.

Does someone who does one bad thing, even one really bad thing, deserve bad things to happen to them? Deserve to be murdered or framed for murder?

I can't wrap my head around whether I'm still allowed to remember Todd the way I want to, as the brother I adored, or whether the shadow of what he did has to darken and twist that forever. I think that shadow might be darkening and twisting me, too. Because I can't stop loving or missing him. Maybe my brain is broken, or my heart is rotten. I want to be a good person who only says and does good things and loves good people, but I don't and I'm not. I wish I could call Brie right now. I feel like I'm disappearing.

22

We spend the morning in the game room, a bright, sunlit room in the northeast corner of the house that overlooks the sea. Its centerpiece is a full-size pool table, and the walls are lined with relics from carnivals, like antique Skee-Ball games, pinball machines, and one of those creepy fortune-tellers with glowing eyes where, for a penny, you can ask a question and it spits the answer out of its mouth on a slip of paper. I'd like to remain indefinitely at the pinball machine, which is crowned by a rather smug-looking clown grinning demonically down at me. But after an hour or so, Nola seems to grow bored of throwing perfect Skee-Ball games. She glances outside. "Do you want to hit a few golf balls into the ocean?"

"What?" I don't look up from the evil clown. "Who am I, Cori?"

"She doesn't own golf," Nola mutters. She plants herself

on a carousel horse and produces a notebook and pencil from her pocket. "Fine. Who do you like more, Spencer or Greg?" she says.

I turn from the pinball machine reluctantly, one hand still on the flipper. "Seriously? After everything that's gone down, I'm probably going to lay off dating for a while."

She laughs. "I meant who do you like more as a suspect." She bites the end of the pencil. "Spencer has a weird creepy obsession. He kills Jessica and frames you to get back at you for hurting him. Then he kills Maddy when she stands in the way of getting you back. But Greg has a pure jealousy motive. It's cleaner. No connection to Maddy, though."

I hesitate. "I can't see either of them killing Maddy."

"Can you see either of them killing Jessica?"

"No more than you or me or Dr. Klein." I slide down to the floor. "What's the worst thing you ever did?"

She chews on the end of the pencil for a long moment. "I broke Bianca up with her boyfriend. We look almost like twins, and when we were little, we used to switch clothes, friends, boyfriends, just to see how long we could go before we got in trouble."

"So you were close at one point."

"It stopped being fun when I realized how much more people liked me when I was her. So I broke up with her first boyfriend while I was 'playing' her. I told him he smelled like a dead hamster. I mean, she forgave me for it. I was only eight."

"Well, you're probably not going to hell for that," I say, sighing.

"If you believe my father, you can be forgiven for anything," she says.

"He sounds like my dad." My father before Todd died. He stopped being Catholic after the funeral, because it was outrageously unacceptable that a person could kill and ask for forgiveness and be absolved. No, Megan's brother would burn in hell. That was Dad's new religion. The religion of righteous burning in hell. Of seeking no earthly revenge, because you just can't. That's just not what we do. But the bastard will burn. That's the faith that will keep the Donovans going.

"He absolutely did manipulate my grandfather," she says with a faint smile, leaning her head against the horse's pink-painted mane. "My father."

"To get the house?"

"Wouldn't you?"

I look around. It's beautiful but eerily empty now that I know it used to be bursting with family. It doesn't surprise me anymore that they have so many visitors. Otherwise, you might just disappear in it. "He could have shared it, right?"

She seems disappointed with my answer. "Not as a

permanent residence. You wouldn't get it. You've probably lived in the same place your whole life. You're so normal, Kay. It's enchanting." She smiles and pats my head, and I duck away.

"What if Spencer's guilty?" I sit down on the floor and support my head with my hands.

She slides down next to me. "Then you breathe a sigh of relief because it's over and life goes on. If Greg did it, life goes on. This nightmare ends one way or another." She turns my face gently toward hers. "You are resilient as hell, Donovan."

I try to smile, but my face is plaster. *Resilient* is the wrong word for someone who attracts tragedy like a magnet but survives to watch her loved ones die.

LATER, AFTER A warm soak in an enormous claw-footed tub with rose-scented sea salts, I feel much calmer. Nola and I sit together in the library on a leather settee, watching the hypnotic flames of a gas fire leap and dance.

I gaze into the rings of fire, blue melting into yellow and gold. "We don't have the full picture."

Nola glances at me wordlessly.

"Our suspect list is clouded by what we know about people," I say. "What we think about them. And ultimately, what we want to happen to them. We have no physical evidence. The cops have such an overwhelming advantage. That's how you can be so wrong about someone you think you know."

"But we also know about things they don't. Like the revenge blog."

"That's true. But my point is, we need to go deeper. Brie tried to record a confession because she thought she could get one out of me. Not because she *had* any evidence. Because she thought if she said the right things, she'd lead me to it."

"And you think you can do that?"

I nod slowly. "I think I have a shot. Spencer definitely. Greg maybe. He leaves himself wide-open."

"Then do it."

An image materializes in my head of Spencer pushing Maddy underwater, and it sucks the air out of my lungs. I cross my arms over my stomach and lean forward, trying to mask my inability to breathe. Slow inhale. Long exhale. "Unless Maddy and Jessica were killed by different people."

Nola shakes her head. "They weren't. The revenge blog proves it."

"Anyone could have written the blog. Any seven people could have written the blog." I'm talking too fast. But she doesn't seem to notice. I keep counting my inhales and exhales.

"God, Kay, who are you trying to protect?"

I freeze for a moment, and then realize it's a rhetorical question. "No one. I just think we need to keep an open mind."

She sighs and rests her head on my shoulder. "Spencer has a stronger motive. But it's up to you who to question first."

I tap my fingers on my knees. "Greg thinks it's a student and it all comes down to whether Jessica got into a fight on the night of the murder." I don't mention who the student is.

"That would be convenient for him. But all signs point to him or Spencer." She squeezes my hand. "You can do this."

I wonder. "One problem. I may not get a confession from either of them."

Nola clears her throat. "You were framed."

"So?"

She looks me in the eye. "So all bets are off. If you become absolutely positive that you know who's framing you, I say frame them back. There's nothing shady about framing someone for something they actually did. It's not really framing. It's just planting evidence to make sure they get caught for it. To lead the police toward him and away from you."

"You're serious."

"You lied to the police for Todd. Why not to save yourself? Playing nice isn't working, Kay. The bad guys can't win this time."

For a moment we stare at each other, and the silence is thick and painful. Then the air between us vanishes, and Nola's lips are on mine. This time I kiss back, and even though I don't feel that magnetic pull I felt with Brie and Spencer, I am warm and happy, and it feels good to relax and smile into her mouth. She caresses the back of my neck and slides closer, slipping her arm around my back and wrapping one leg around me.

I glance around, but she squeezes my shoulder reassuringly. "Don't worry, my parents are off tennising or teaing or something that involves leaving the house. The empty, empty house they fought so hard for."

I kiss her again, trying to push our conversation out of my head.

She bites my lower lip and slides down to the floor, pulling me on top of her. She runs her hands up and down my sides and for a moment every bad feeling that's held me captive in the past month floats away. She kisses my neck and then my shoulders and then stretches my bra strap aside.

I sigh and roll over onto my back, and she brushes her lips against mine. Another kiss and my head swims. She pulls my arms over my head and kisses me deeply. I feel safe. Safe and sweet and delicious. But with every passing second, I feel a rising anxiety in the pit of my stomach, like I did the first time we kissed. It doesn't feel the same as those quick, crucial moments when Brie and I swirled together in Spencer's room, or the thousand times he and I flung ourselves at each other.

"Are you happy?" she murmurs, and tastes my lips.

I look up at her, unsure what to say, and then push up slightly on my elbows.

"Do you wish I was Brie?"

My body suddenly feels like ice water has been poured over it. Nola stiffens suddenly and rolls away. I look up, and Mrs. Kent is standing in the doorway, a tennis racket in her hand, a strange expression on her face.

"Sandwiches and lemonade in the solarium," she says, and then disappears up the staircase.

Nola straightens her shirt and pants and smooths her hair. "You have a choice to make," she says primly, as if the kiss had never happened. "Spencer or Greg."

23

*t*he next day, Nola tries to convince me to accompany her into town to buy a better microphone to record the confessions, but I fake cramps and stay behind for a nap. I really just need a break from the investigation. I thought that was what this week was supposed to be. I also need time to clear my head after yesterday's kiss and Nola's bizarrely timed question about Brie. I watch from her window as she gets into her mother's car, backs out of the driveway and through the security gate, and disappears down the long winding road that lines the cliff side. Both of her parents have left again and Marla has the day off, so the house is empty and silent.

I head downstairs, grab a grapefruit-flavored soda, and wander into the game room, but I halt when the sun catches me straight on through the glass walls, reflecting my image back at me. I almost don't recognize myself. I've lost weight and muscle tone in the past month. Since the night Maddy died and

I got sick, I haven't even been running. I'm pale as a ghost—and that's to be expected this time of year—but the dark gray shadows under my eyes make me look gaunt. I look ill, not just cold-and-flu ill, but the way my mother looked that year when she was helpless to do anything but hang on to life and not let go. For me. I look like I've been worn down to a wisp.

I step slowly toward the window, but as I draw near, the sun becomes blinding and I disappear. It's chilling, like the moment in a ghost story when the ghost realizes they've been dead from the very beginning. But I'm not. I'm just unrecognizable, with hair that's become a ratty tangle of unspooled yarn, skin I haven't taken care of, a body I haven't been conditioning. I back up a few steps until my reflection comes back into focus again and shake my hair out. That's one thing I can change. Right now. And not have to deal with for a long while. I walk purposefully to the kitchen and rummage through the drawers until I find a pair of scissors, which I take up to Nola's bathroom.

I wet my hair and comb out all the snarls until it hangs in waves down over my face and shoulders. Then I pull a handful tightly down between my middle and forefinger and close the scissors with a satisfying snip. I cut off six inches around at first, giddy at the sudden lightness of my skull, and then a nauseous wave of nervousness hits when I realize how difficult it is to cut it evenly all the way around. I have to rewet it several times and use a variety of handheld mirrors, and the kitchen scissors do not cut very easily.

There are some useful tools in Nola's bathroom hutch, including several sets of salon scissors and buzzers, which I experiment with. I end up pulling the top layer of my hair on top of my head in a bun and shaving the lower layer about a half inch short, something I saw once on a pro soccer player I admire, then cutting the top layer short in the back and long in the front. It looks a little different on me because my hair is so wavy, but it's still pretty cool. I think my waves actually hide the fact that I can't quite manage to cut it perfectly straight. Just as I'm finishing up the last few snips, I hear the front door open and slam shut downstairs. I hurriedly sweep all of the evidence up into the trash can and rinse the scissors and combs, then towel dry my hair and change into a shirt that isn't covered in damp hair cuttings.

I jump on the bed and grab one of Nola's books, assuming a poker face. I want an honest reaction.

Nola flings the door open and flicks the light on. "I had the best idea. When you call Spencer—" She stops. "What did you do?"

I jump up. "Ta-da!"

"You look like a circus freak."

I cross my arms over my chest, feeling less confident but also annoyed. "No I don't. I look like Mara Kacoyanis. She's, like, my personal hero."

Nola approaches, cringing, and turns me around in a circle. "Why didn't you ask me first?"

I gape at her. "For permission?"

She rolls her eyes. "For my opinion. Not to brag, but I know a bit about couture."

"Not here you don't."

She pauses. "Do you have a problem with the way I dress around my parents?"

"Do you have a problem with the way I wear my hair around them? Or my name, for that matter? I never go by Katherine."

She sits and sighs into her hand. "My grandmother's nickname was Kay, and she is revered as something of a beloved ghost that's never mentioned."

I shift my weight back and forth. "Is there some Freudian reason why you befriended me?"

"No. It's just one of those family things. Kay is sacred. It's taken. You can't be Kay. She got dibs."

"And my hair?"

"That's just ugly." Her expression softens. "I'm sorry. It's not ugly. It's just not what I would choose." She pauses. "Let me fix it for you."

I take a step back from her, stung by the sudden change from yesterday. "No. I like it."

She bites her lower lip and looks like she's struggling not to say something. "Fine."

"Why do you care?"

"I liked you the way you were," she bursts out.

I touch the soft new ends of my sharp curls. "I am the way I was."

She paces a bit and chews on her nails. "I just like things a certain way. Forget it. What's important is what Spencer likes."

"Oh my God." I push her away and sit down on the bed. "He doesn't care what I look like."

Nola flinches at that. "Isn't he the enlightened one." She throws a plastic bag at my feet. I open it to find a body microphone and recording unit, tiny and sleek and very expensive looking. The receipt falls out at my feet, and when I bend to pick it up, the total catches my eye and I gasp.

"I cannot possibly accept this, Nola."

She pushes the bag into my hand. "You have to. I won't let you refuse." She takes my hand in hers and looks into my eyes. "Kay, I am not watching you go to prison because of someone else's crimes. This has been a nightmare. One last push. Then life begins again, and everything goes back to the way it was."

The words churn in my head. Nothing is going to go back

to the way it was. But if there are two paths in front of me, and one leads to prison and one still holds the possibility of scholarships and college, I don't have a choice. I take the plastic bag and stuff it into my overnight bag.

"Thank you," I say, swallowing hard. Failure is not an option.

AT DINNER, BOTH Mrs. Kent and Bernie compliment me on my new haircut. Bernie calls it "winning" and Mrs. Kent says I look like a young Dolores Mason. I'm not sure who that is, and I don't want to sound ignorant, so I don't ask. Since Marla has the night off, dinner is Chinese takeout. It takes me back to the months after Todd died and Mom was absent. Dad and I had a rigidly planned weekly menu. On weekends we visited Mom, but every other night was a set schedule. Monday was my turn to cook: mac and cheese from the box. Tuesday was Dad's night: spaghetti and sauce from the jar. On Wednesday night, we ordered pizza. The first half of the week was admittedly carb heavy. Thursday night was Chinese.

"This is the best Chinese north of Chinatown," Bernie jokes, and Mrs. Kent laughs, but Nola rolls her eyes and mouths at me, *Every time.*

"I'm sure it's better than what I'm used to. I practically ate it daily back home."

I take a sip of the Pinot Noir Bernie has set in front of me.

It's much drier than any wine I've ever tasted, and has an odd cardboard aftertaste. I wonder if this is what people mean when they say oaky.

Bernie and Mrs. Kent both shoot me a sympathetic glance.

I eye my shrimp lo mein. I've avoided Chinese food since that dark period. Oversaturation, for one thing, but also, it brings back that feeling of isolation, of sitting in the living room silently, eating in front of *Pardon the Interruption* and wondering how long I had to sit there before I could escape and go for a run without feeling like I was abandoning Dad. Or if he would, like, kill himself if I left him alone for too long or if I got hit by a car or something terrible happened to me. This isn't very good lo mein, anyway. The place at home was better. These noodles are greasy and there's too much garlic in the sauce. I nibble on a piece of shrimp, which at least is plump and, I'm sure, very fresh.

Mrs. Kent suddenly turns to me with a coy smile. "So, Miss Katherine. Can you tell us anything about Bianca's mysterious new gentleman?"

I dart my eyes to Nola, who purses her lips and gives me what is probably meant to be a very meaningful and communicative look. But I have no idea what she's trying to get me to say.

"I'm as curious as you are," I say, trying to return the coy expression.

Mrs. Kent looks dissatisfied. "Well, I hope it's worth lying about."

It takes me a moment to absorb the sting of her words. I lie fairly openly and unapologetically. Everyone does it, though maybe not as often as I do. But never once has an adult called me on it so casually. It makes me feel insignificant, like she's putting me on notice that I'm way out of my depth.

"No one is lying, Mother. I just don't see why we should talk about him until we're sure things are serious."

I wonder how much more serious things can get than an engagement, but then Nola does seem to have a crappy relationship with Bianca, so maybe there's a jealousy thing going on.

"Like the last one, mmm?" Bernie says darkly.

Nola glares at him.

"It's too bad Bianca couldn't make it," I offer.

Nola kicks me under the table.

Mrs. Kent holds up a finger as she coughs into her napkin. "Too bad Bianca couldn't make what?"

I twist my napkin into knots under the table. Nola's family is terrifying. "Dinner, I guess?"

Mrs. Kent places her fork down and studies Nola sternly. "Well."

I decide the direction the conversation has taken is mostly

my fault, and it's on me to change it. "Who cares about dinner when there's a wedding to plan, right?"

Everyone looks at me with irritation, even Nola.

"For Bianca." I take a sip of wine and wish I could disappear.

Bernie folds his hands on the table, all trace of his friendly, breezy personality evaporated. "*Nola.*"

"For God's sake," Mrs. Kent breathes into her wineglass, fogging up the sides.

"*Bernie.*" Nola downs the rest of her glass and sets it down a little too firmly.

"Why are you discussing our family with strangers?" Bernie taps his pinkie finger against his plate, and for some reason the sound makes me want to scream.

"Katherine is not a stranger," she insists. She casts me a desperate look, but there's nothing I can possibly do to save the situation.

"So I noticed," Mrs. Kent says drily.

"She didn't tell me anything," I attempt weakly. And I thought my friends were secretive. Who forbids their daughters to discuss each other outside of the family? "I saw a picture of Bianca with a guy and I asked who he was. Nola said they were getting married." That's when I really start kicking myself. Because the key to a good lie is vagueness.

"Which picture was that?" Mrs. Kent asks icily.

"Katherine, please excuse yourself," Bernie says in a dangerously calm voice.

"You don't have to go," Nola says, her voice rising in volume and pitch.

"This is my house," Bernie growls.

Nola stands, slamming her fists on the table. "No it isn't. It's not supposed to be. You lied to get the house. You're a hypocrite."

There's a long moment of silence, and then Bernie turns to me calmly. "Katherine, we'd be pleased to have you another time, but I'm afraid this week just won't work. If you pack your things, I'll happily pay for your ticket home and drive you back to the train station right away."

I flee up the stairs as Nola screams at her parents and they shout back at her. There are all sorts of ugly phrases bouncing back and forth, mostly with the tags "my" and "mine" attached. "My guest" and "my house." "My sister" and "my friend." And from Mrs. Kent, "you promised" and "last chance," though I can't tell whether that's directed at Nola or her father.

I wait outside in the biting cold until Bernie comes out to drive me to the train station. Nola doesn't come outside to say good-bye, though I see the light go on in her room upstairs and watch her fling herself down on her bed. I wonder what's up with Bianca's fiancé, and whether Nola's parents are as shitty as her cousins. Her mother definitely didn't look pleased when she walked in on us. Maybe that was the deal with Bianca, too. Nola never actually said the fiancé was a guy—but I did, at the dinner table. Now that I've seen more of them, I'm not sure I want Nola's family to like me.

I sit quietly in the backseat as Bernie drives me to the station.

He clears his throat. "I'm very sorry about that," he apologizes awkwardly. "You really are welcome to return another time." Yeah. I'll be on the next train. "It's a complicated issue. My life coach has been adamant that I deal with family conflicts directly and right away, and I just don't think we're able to do that with guests."

I wonder about the life coach (code for shrink, maybe) but also about how much progress you can possibly expect to make when you only see your daughter a few times a year.

"Sure," I say.

When we arrive at the station, he walks around the car and opens the door for me. "Thank you for being understanding," he says. "And for being a friend to Nola. And for not mentioning this unfortunate incident to any of the other girls at school," he adds with a meaningful look, and presses an envelope into my hand. "Happy holidays, Katherine. Buy yourself a ticket to visit your folks." I'm too stunned to react as he gives me a hug and then disappears into his car, waving as he drives away. I sit on the bench waiting for the next train, the lone figure in an empty station, and peer into the envelope. It's stuffed with fifty-dollar bills.

MY FIRST IMPULSE is to call Brie, but even if I hadn't sworn not to, I don't think she would pick up. So I follow Bernie's advice. I go home. It's well after midnight when I arrive, and I take a cab to the darkened house.

It's the last one on a dead-end street lined with skeletal shrubs, leafless trees, and yards littered with rusty bikes, frozen kiddie pools, and broken cars in an endless state of refurbishment. Ours is the smallest, a two-bedroom with a combination kitchen-laundry room, a living room that has just enough space for our ancient TV set and a battered couch, and an attic loft my father converted to my room when I was ten.

The last time my parents and I spoke, we fought, and I'm not even sure they'll be here now. We haven't had Thanksgiving at home since before Todd died. I don't bother to knock; I just let myself in, creep up the stairs, and then look for evidence that they're here. Mom's purse on the kitchen table, Dad's wallet on the counter. Tiptoeing around the kitchen, I'm pleasantly surprised to see how well things look. The room is tidy, no dishes or stacks of bills piled up. I peer into the refrigerator, and tears actually well up in my eyes when I see signs of a partially prepared Thanksgiving dinner. There are peeled potatoes in a big bowl covered in plastic wrap, cartons of cider and eggnog, oranges and packages of cranberries, even a small, half-frozen turkey. I blink and the tears spill down my face. I wouldn't have guessed it in a million years before actually getting here, but I'm glad I came home. Even if I regret it tomorrow, even if Mom is a raging bitch and Dad won't shut up about getting the soccer team going again, just for this amazing sight of food prepped for Thanksgiving dinner, I am so grateful that I got kicked out of Tranquility and sent home in disgrace. Hallelujah.

24

*t*he first thing Mom does when she sees me in the morning is scream like she's seen a ghost. Then she hugs me and cries. Dad hugs me, then asks about soccer. He says I look just like Mara Kacoyanis. I can tell they're both extremely pleased to see me, and neither asks about Brie.

I take on the task of dicing potatoes without asking. We don't do mashed potatoes on Thanksgiving; we do potato salad. It's an ancient Donovan tradition. Dad chops cranberries and Mom tries to boil the turkey in an attempt to finish defrosting it.

She sees me watching her and shoots me a defensive look. "It doesn't have to be edible until tomorrow, Katie."

"Is this the first time you've tried to cook one?" I say as she stirs it awkwardly in a giant pot.

"Since Grandma died," she answers, avoiding the more precise date. Dad doesn't look up from his cutting board but clears his throat loudly, as if to warn me away from this line of questioning. He looks like he's gained weight since summer, and Mom has more color. Her silver-streaked auburn hair is swept up into a loose bun at the nape of her neck, and she's wearing a denim dress that she's had since before I was born. I'm convinced it's the softest item of clothing in the world, though I've begged her repeatedly over the past seventeen years to burn it.

I wonder what they've been doing. We only talk about me when they call, and even then it's just questions about school and soccer. Occasionally what's Brie up to, or how is Spencer. I realize that they don't even know we've broken up.

"What have you guys been doing the past few Thanksgivings?" I ask, and Dad clears his throat again, this time with a warning look.

Mom just turns up the dial on the gas stove, and the flame flares up underneath it. "Chinese," she says. "Cooking is such a headache."

"What's the special occasion this year?"

"Well," she says, placing the wooden spoon down on the counter. "This year we have something to celebrate."

Dad stops chopping. "Karen, maybe this isn't the time."

Mom sits next to me at the table and takes my hand in hers. "Katie, we need to talk to you about something."

"You're pregnant," I blurt out. No, that doesn't make sense. They're too old. Aunt Tracy's pregnant.

"Actually, yes," Mom admits, her eyes bright and cheeks flushed. "But it's very early, and at my age a lot of things can go wrong, so we're not telling anyone, even Aunt Tracy. We weren't even going to tell you until Christmas, but . . . well, here you are."

I study her. Is this a replacement baby? Then it dawns on me that there are certain expected reactions in these situations, and I give her a big hug and say, "That's amazing!"

"You don't have to pretend you're not shocked," Dad says, and I swear I see the first smile crack across his face since Todd died. "We realize how ancient you think we are."

"I wouldn't say ancient," I protest. Well, not to their faces.

"The house is empty without you, Katie. We just felt ready." Mom squeezes my shoulder and I force myself to smile. I manage to freeze my face into that idiotic grin until the rest of the potatoes are diced, and then I walk as casually as I can to the stairs and up to my loft before collapsing onto my mattress and sobbing into my pillow. They made me go to Bates. It was the solution to all of their problems. Those were her exact words. That's why the goddamn house is empty. Todd's death and my exile.

Mom calls up after a little while to ask if I'm all right and I use my standby excuse, cramps. Then I tiptoe into Todd's room to find a new comfort item to replace the coat Nola hurled into the sea, something new I can cry into, but to my shock, the room that had been preserved into a museum exhibit for four years is empty. No furniture, no trophies, no posters or photos on the walls, no cardboard boxes of his things, even. The closet is empty, and the walls have been scrubbed and painted a creamy white. The hardwood floor has been covered with a thick fuzzy carpet, and the window blinds have been removed in favor of gauzy yellow drapes. I close the door and walk back downstairs.

"What happened to Todd's room?"

Dad casts me another warning look. "It's going to be the baby's room."

"What about all his things?"

"We needed to let them go," Mom says in a calm, measured tone, as if repeating something told to her, something that had to be said over and over until it finally made sense.

"Why didn't you tell me?"

"Because it wasn't up to you," Dad says, dumping the contents of his cutting board into a bowl.

"It should be. I'm part of the family, too."

"Not the part that makes decisions," he says, handing the bowl to Mom and retreating into the family room, where a football game is blaring.

Mom holds the bowl helplessly. "Brad," she calls after

him. "Katie, what would you have wanted us to tell you? You have enough to worry about with your grades and your soccer."

I laugh. I almost tell her right there about the things I actually have to worry about. But the fallout just wouldn't be worth it. "What if I wanted to keep something to remember Todd?"

Mom starts crying.

Dad bounds back into the room. "This is why you can't be here, Katie. You won't let the past go. Hasn't your mother gone through enough?"

"It's not her fault, Brad."

"What exactly did I do?" I can't keep my voice from trembling, but I stand my ground. "Apart from not saving Todd, what did I do to get kicked out of the house?"

Mom reaches for me, but I yank myself out of her grasp. "You were never kicked out of the house."

"Yes, I was, and now you're making a new person to live in it. What did I do?"

"Katie, no one blames you." Mom takes my hand tentatively and strokes it. "Bates was never a punishment. Being here was painful for all of us. You were miserable. Those kids were awful to you. All the things they wrote on your locker, the names they called you. The girls that followed you around and made your life a living hell? After everything that happened, we wanted to get you out because you deserved better." She chokes up and that makes me start crying. "We're trying so hard, Katie. We're not going to let everything that's happened break us. We're looking at a fresh start. You have four years of a premier school behind you, and four years of a college education in front of you."

I look to my father. "Dad?"

"No one blames you for anything." His voice is a perfect echo of my mother's.

I don't believe him. I can't. I've been pushing myself too hard for too long, past the limits of what I can reasonably accomplish to make up for Todd's loss so they can forgive me for letting him die.

But Mom refuses to see this and goes on. "You have your soccer, your friends, Brie and Spencer. We're so proud of you. We just don't want you to slip away from us." She tries again to hug me and I let her. "We love you, Katie."

I wrap my arms around her tightly. I wish there was some way to rewind, to go back to the place where I had a choice about slipping away. I miss my mother. I miss my whole family. But there's no way to explain everything. It's just too much. "What would you do if something bad happened to me?" I ask.

She squeezes me harder. "Please talk to us. Whatever it is."

"That came out wrong. I'm just afraid I'm going to let you down." I straighten up and look at both of them. "I might not be cut out to be a soccer star. I might not get a scholarship. I might fail at school and life and everything. Spencer and I broke up. Brie and I aren't even talking."

They both wait as if I'm leading up to a big revelation. I could do it. I could tell them right now.

Instead, I just say, "I don't want to make things any worse."

Mom shakes her head. "Don't shut us out and you won't," she says.

Easier said than done.

I WAIT UNTIL the next day to visit Todd's grave. I always get massive amounts of anxiety about these visits because I'm afraid the headstone is going to be covered with graffiti like my locker was, but it isn't. It looks just like all the other headstones, indistinguishable but for the name and dates. Thanksgiving must be a popular day to visit the dead, because the cemetery is filled with flocks of extended families. I recognize some people I knew way back in the day. I hope none of them recognize me. I really don't keep up any ties with my past in this town. It wasn't a happy time in my life, not after Todd and Megan died, or really after the Todd-Megan scandal. That was the turning point. There was soccer after that, and some partying, but I couldn't call that happy. Just busy. Throwing myself into the act of being alive.

The earth is dry and cracked and the grass matted and yellow, and it crunches under me when I sit. I run my hands over the face of Todd's headstone, tracing the words with my fingertips. I can't help thinking about Hunter's body when we dug him up, about that pile of bones and tufts of fur. It's been much longer since we buried Todd, although (and it grosses me out so much to think about it) he was pumped full of preserving chemicals before he went into the ground. Despite that, I still would guess he would mostly be a pile of bones by now. I am literally sitting on the earth above my brother's bones. I think when I die, I will insist on one of those environmentally friendly burials where instead of a casket they bury you in a biodegradable sack and mark your grave with a tree. I like the idea of my earthly essence being absorbed into a tree to go through the seasonal cycle of life year after year, budding green and blooming wildly, and then bursting into autumn flame and dying all over again just to be reborn. Better than spending eternity as a box of bones.

I remember my last unspoken promise to Megan, that I would find the person who stole Todd's phone and make him pay in blood. Todd had vowed to help me. But the morning Megan was found dead, Todd and I both sat in his room on the floor crying, and there was nothing left to fix. Nothing would make it right. Mom hovered over us, trying to force us to eat, and threatened to take us to the doctor. I threw up after choking down a piece of toast. Todd wouldn't even look at food, wouldn't leave his room for days. He was inconsolable. It wouldn't be okay.

The fact is, he did lie to me. He sent the pictures to his four best friends: Connor Dash, Wes Lehman, Isaac Bohr, and Trey Eisen. Collectively, the four of them sent the pictures to twenty-seven more students, including Julie Hale, who sent them back to Megan. It didn't stop there. No one is sure who posted them on the Rate My Girlfriend website. Or who wrote the hundreds of degrading comments.

I know this because, six weeks after Megan's death, her brother, Rob, pulled his truck up beside my bike on the way to school and forced me inside. I was terrified I was about to be kidnapped or murdered, but instead he just silently handed me a folder of evidence from the civil case they'd been building against Todd before Megan died. He stared straight ahead, his fingers tightly gripping the wheel, as I read page after page proving everything Todd and I told the police to be false. Then there were pages and pages of little notes, scraps of torn, wrinkled paper with ugly words written on them. *Slut. Skank. Whore.* No one ever wrote on Megan's locker. They just slipped anonymous notes inside. I never knew. At the end of the folder was a list of names on a legal pad. Todd. Connor. Wes. Isaac. Trey. A chain of people who destroyed Megan. And off to the side, one name with a circle around it, connected to Todd's with a thick red line. Katie.

I don't think Todd shared those pictures to hurt her. It was like them being broken up meant it was some random girl now and not his girlfriend. It was creepy and messed up. I think he thought they would stay between him and his crew and she'd never know. No one would. And not until they were forwarded did it really hit him that they weren't going to stay between them. Nothing stays between friends. If any of this had occurred to me, in time, I would have told the police. Todd would have been arrested. And he wouldn't be dead.

His headstone isn't as smooth as it should be. Graves should always look new. Nola had said I talk about Todd like he's not dead and maybe that's because it still feels so recent. But it isn't. He's falling further into the past.

I kiss my fingers and press them to the cold granite and then stand, dusting myself off.

Good-bye again, Todd.

25

*m*om asks me to stay the rest of the weekend, but I tell her I need to get back to study for my remaining exams. I do need to study, but I also need to put an end to this investigation once and for all. As I'm standing on the train platform, my phone rings and I glance down at it. Greg Yeun. I pick up cautiously.

"Hello?"

"You missed a lot."

"Like?"

"Thanksgiving in a holding cell."

A train passes and I can't hear what he's saying. "Hold on!" I shout, running down the platform to try to find a quiet spot. "Are you calling me from jail?" Just at that exact moment, the train passes and everyone on the platform turns and gawks at me. I flash a sarcastic smile and wave.

"What? Like I would waste my one phone call on you. I'm out, obviously. I'm calling to warn you."

"About what? So, wait, you're in the clear?"

"Apparently, for now. They held me overnight and asked a shitload of questions. They wanted to know about fragments of a broken bottle they found by the lake. They think they have the murder weapon."

My blood runs cold. "What kind of bottle?"

"Some kind of wine bottle. They're running a DNA test, but it takes a couple of days and it's probably been contaminated by now. You may have twenty-four, forty-eight hours. Depends on how contaminated."

"Shit. Why did they arrest you?"

"They found something of mine in the lake, too. A bottle with a label they traced back to my father's credit card. Problem is, no fingerprints, no traces of blood. I don't even drink. I think someone was trying to frame me, and I think the police may have finally, definitively excluded me."

"So why are you warning me?"

"Because I saw the evidence board, and you are on it. With only one other person. Spencer Morrow."

I grit my teeth. "That blows your Brie theory."

"I've been wrong before. Kay, stay away from him. And get a lawyer. And when they ask you about—" As my train approaches, his words are drowned out.

Shit.

I MAKE A LIST of everything I know so far on the train ride back to Bates.

> *The location of the body, and the time we found it.*
> *Estimated time of death, time and content of the*
> > *conversation between Jessica and Greg.*
> *Description of the body:*
> > *The marks on the wrists, position of the body.*
> > *Full clothes, eyes and mouth open.*
> > *Wristband from the dance, in costume.*
> *Relationships: Greg, Spencer, family, teachers,*
> > *unknown volunteers, community members.*

I sigh. If the police have access to all of these people and are still only focusing on Spencer and me, that's not good.

> *The revenge blog*
> *Connected people: Tai, Tricia, Nola, Cori, Maddy, me.*

I pause, and then add *Hunter*.

By the time I switch to the westbound train, my notebook is a spiderweb of information. I am about to nod off into my hand when someone stops in the aisle next to me and places a Hershey's Kiss on my pad. I look up to see Brie gazing down at me nervously.

"Hi," I say doubtfully.

"Everyone missed you," she says.

"That's it?"

"And I'm sorry. For everything. Things have gotten really out of hand."

"How did you find me?"

"Called your mom."

"Did she tell you to go back to school, switch trains, and travel *away* from civilization for a couple of hours?"

"She gave me your train number and departure time. I hope you don't mind. I wanted to see you." She pauses. "I like your hair. You look like that soccer pro everyone hates."

"They hate her because she's the greatest."

She smiles a little and sits in the seat next to me. "I know. I'm really sorry, Kay." She sheds her coat and snow-colored scarf and smooths her dress, soft gray wool with a white collar. "I shouldn't have recorded you—I should have just talked to you. But I'm allowed to have my doubts. Doubt is the cornerstone of faith."

I try not to smile, not because there's anything funny about any of this, but because that statement is so essentially Brie. "How profound," I say, in mock awe.

"It's true. Blind faith is meaningless. And it doesn't last."

I give her a pointed look, and she slides a folded piece of paper on top of my notebook. "I do still have faith in you. Don't open that yet."

"I thought you were 'so done' with me."

"You've hurt me, Kay," she says sharply. "What you wrote on my door was just the last straw. You've done some shitty things in the past and I've looked the other way because that's what we do. Tai says shitty things. Tricia. Cori. I don't like it, but I like you. So I suck it up. But I've spent a lot of time pretending to laugh with you guys over the past few years. And that's on me, I chose that. I chose you."

"You chose Justine."

"I love you both. But she's the one I'm with. And you've changed. You stopped returning my calls and started hanging out with Nola Kent all the time. And after Maddy died, I thought about it. The scratches on your arms. The window of time when you disappeared. The Spencer thing. When you add all those things up. Maddy and Hunter—Detective Morgan told me she found you dumping his body in the lake. Is that true?"

I open my mouth to deny it but I'm determined not to lie anymore. Not to Brie. "It's extremely complicated."

"I bet I can guess." She sighs and lays her head on my shoulder. "Then you show up in my room accusing me of making Spencer cheat on you or something and talking about a revenge website that didn't exist. You just stopped making sense at some point."

I think about it for a minute. "First of all, the website did exist. It was taken down. As for you setting up Spencer with Jessica, there's been either a lot of hacking into cell phones or a lot of lying about hacking into cell phones lately."

"Sounds like Spencer, either way."

"Says his biggest fan." I straighten up. "I'm sorry. Everything that's happened in the past month has been kind of larger than life."

"Fair enough." Brie looks across the aisle at a train rushing by in the opposite direction, a faint blur of colors and faces behind frosted windows. It's early afternoon, but the sky is so overcast that it appears much later. "I'm sorry I didn't say anything about Maddy and Spencer. Justine told me and I didn't want it to be true. And if it was, I didn't want you to find out. It was just once, right after you and Spencer broke up, but I knew how hard it would hit you. Then Tai made it worse with that stupid Notorious R.B.G. thing and I was sure you were going to figure it out. She's obviously been in love with him forever."

"Consider me clueless."

"I always have." She tries at a smile. "And you kept asking why I was acting weird around her and I lied. I'm sorry. She was sweet. I'd feel so horrible if she thought I hated her." Her eyes brim, and I lean in and press my face against hers.

"She would've known exactly why. She wouldn't have blamed you. She had me to do that." I poke my shoulder into hers, and she rubs her face against it and sighs.

"No more. No more killing. No more lies."

I hesitate. "There *was* one more thing. Greg told me you and Jess used to be friends, and that turned into a serious grudge. Something about you blowing her off and her forwarding your personal emails to your parents or something."

Her lips twitch and she shifts her gaze. "I don't talk about it for a reason, Kay," she says softly. "We were friends. It didn't work out. I don't feel comfortable talking shit about her now."

"But it's true?"

She straightens up. "Yes, it's true. And it's my business. And the extremely private information she stole from me and showed my parents before I was ready to tell them was my business, too. I'm sorry she died. But I don't need to talk about what went down between us. With anyone. It was painful and it's in the past."

I lay my hand palm up on the armrest between us as a peace offering. "Okay. You don't. I'm sorry."

She closes her hand around mine. "Being away from

everyone the past few days has been really helpful. I feel like everything is finally coming into focus."

"You didn't seem to care before."

"How would you know? You weren't answering my calls. I think I know who the killer is. But before I say it, you tell me. Who do you think killed Jessica?"

"Santa Claus!" a high-pitched voice cries from somewhere above.

I let out a shriek. There's a small, sticky child dangling over my head from the seat behind me. An annoyed-looking woman yanks him up and away and hisses at me, "Can you talk about your adult shows in indoor voices, please?"

I look down at my notebook. "The police have narrowed it down to me and Spencer."

"I think they're wrong," Brie says.

"I never thought I'd see the day when Brie Matthews offered to defend Spencer Morrow pro bono."

"We'll see about that."

I eye the paper curiously. "What have you got?"

She unfolds the piece of paper she placed on my notebook and I look down at it. It's a list of evidence, like the one I made, but much neater, arranged in sections of notes in a nexus around a central word, all pointing to a name written in large, black, all-capital letters: NOLA.

Brie's face glows in the overhead reading light. "It all makes sense."

I roll my eyes. "Of course it does. Because you don't like her."

"She's not one of us."

I turn away from her and draw a heart on the frosty window as we pass a series of abandoned buildings. I'm not sure why a heart. It stings to hear words like that coming from Brie's mouth, especially after I've just come from my little leprechaun house and she's waltzing back from her precious mansion. Because I'm the one who's not one of us.

"Just look." Brie points to her paper. "It's all here."

"Do you have any idea what I've been going through? I've been getting phone calls in the middle of the night physically threatening me. I've tried calling campus police to file a report, but they won't help me. I know you've at least seen my Facebook wall. I've been going through hell, and Nola's been a real friend."

Brie's eyes fill up, and when she speaks again, her voice sounds thick. "I can never apologize enough for abandoning you."

"And I said okay. But you're not going to throw Nola under the bus for killing Jessica." I push my hair back from my face. I'm starting to regret cutting it. It's harder to get out of the way now.

Brie takes her headband out and hands it to me. "I have a million of these."

"Thanks." With my hair out of my face I feel a little more in control, a tiny bit less chaotic. "What about Spencer?"

"He's a possibility. But I have a feeling about Nola."

I cock my head. "A feeling. Then let's go straight to the cops, shall we?"

"Let's play lawyer," she suggests.

"I'm not in the mood for games." The train seems to be speeding along more carelessly than usual, its frame rattling like it's about to collapse.

"I'll prosecute. You defend."

"Fine."

Brie looks to me for permission, and I nod and gesture for her to make her case. "Nola Kent is a brilliant girl. She has the capacity to memorize massive amounts of information, hack into school databases, and frame innocent classmates for murder. She also has the ability to kill, and to befriend the person she frames for that murder. When Nola first came to Bates Academy, she had a hard time making friends. One group of girls in particular were pretty nasty to her. She vowed revenge. And she was patient. Two years later, she killed Jessica Lane in cold blood and framed the ringleader of those girls, Kay Donovan, for the death. She used her computer skills to set up a website that would turn Kay against her friends and vice versa, before delivering the final blow: sending her to prison for murder. Nola Kent killed Jessica and she did it to frame Kay."

I look out the window through the sheen of frost, my eyes focusing and unfocusing on the gray blur of fog-obscured mobile homes we're passing, neat little rectangles firmly planted in the dirt, sideways graves. Nola forgave me the night after the confrontation with Cori, the night we kissed. Hearing Brie bring it up makes me feel like a terrible person again.

"Defense?" Brie prompts.

I look at her wearily. "You haven't suggested a single reason why she would have killed Jessica. Why Jessica? In court your theory would fall flat. Because you need to prove that Nola killed Jessica, not that she has a grudge against me. And Nola's theory against Spencer wins. And you know what else you have to admit? The case against me beats them all. That's the best case right now."

Brie closes her eyes and leans her head back against the seat. "I know she did it. I know it."

"Knowledge isn't evidence," I say.

"Then let's talk to Spencer." She looks up at me. "Both of us. Just to be on the safe side."

I look out the window again. I'm not sure he'll agree to it after everything that's gone down. But at this point, it might be the only way left to get any kind of resolution.

"I have to go alone. Just keep your phone on."

26

*n*ola texts me throughout the day and I write back, but just terse, fluff answers. She didn't return any of my texts on Thanksgiving, and I wonder what happened with her family, but don't want to pry. I hate that Brie planted this seed of doubt in my mind. Yes, Nola had a reason to hate me. I'm sure she did for a while. And when we first started spending time together, she wasn't exactly the warmest, fuzziest personality. But she's proven her loyalty. Or maybe I just don't want to believe anything bad about her. Maybe it's Todd syndrome. I call Spencer as soon as I get to the train station, and I'm actually surprised when he picks up.

"Still hate me?"

"Since you asked me if I killed Maddy to hurt you?"

"And you called me a killer and said everything I touch gets ruined?"

"I'm pretty sure Charlie Brown said that. In the Christmas

special. Surely I was more original." I hear him take a sip of something.

"Are you drinking?"

"Just chocolate milk. Be sure to drink your Ovaltine."

"Wow, you're really getting into the Christmas spirit."

"The Christmas *special* spirit," he corrects.

A gust of wind whips a newspaper into my face and I crouch behind a garbage can—all the benches are full. "I'm at the train station."

"And you need a ride."

"And I wanted to see you, or I would have shared a cab back to campus." I wait.

I hear him gulp the rest of his chocolate milk down. "Five minutes."

We stop at a Dunkin' Donuts—there are no cutesy cafés or Starbucks near Spencer's house, and the truth is, I prefer their vanilla coffee with a glazed doughnut. It reminds me of home, of the few good parts of home, of when Todd would bring home leftovers from practice, or the way Dad's truck always smelled. Dad is a house painter and he usually left for work before I woke every morning and returned with a dozen empty Dunkin' Donuts cups in the passenger side of the cab. When I was a kid, I got a quarter every week to clean Dad's truck inside and out. So Dunkin' is one of my happy associations with home.

After we order, I try to find an isolated table, but it's pretty crowded. We settle for one at the side of the building with a view of a busy side street. It's the opposite of Cat Café. Packed, overheated, a little sweaty. Nineties Christmas songs blare from a speaker positioned right over our heads. Around us, everyone is engrossed in their own lives. There are couples laughing (and one fighting), mothers struggling with toddlers flinging food, and groups of younger teens chatting over coffee.

"So, Katie D. Are we actually going to talk this time?" He grins, and I notice how much better he looks than the last time we met. Like he's slept for a long time and left his nightmares behind him for good. I wonder if he's moved on from me, and even though I was kissing Nola just days ago, it pisses me off. It automatically makes me want to touch him. I'm messed up beyond repair.

I can't stop the words from coming out of my mouth, though. "Are you seeing someone?"

"Maybe."

"Oh. Me too." I try to look casual, but I can feel my face morphing into pre-crying mode.

"How can you possibly be upset about that?"

"I'm not."

He takes a sip of coffee. "Maybe part of our whole problem was that we went all in on this Brie-and-Justine-versus-Kay-and-Spencer thing."

"I shouldn't have turned it into a competition."

"God, Katie, give Brie some credit. The pedestal thing is disturbing." He sighs and reaches his hand across the table, but mine feels too heavy to meet him halfway, so he leans his chin on his elbow and gazes up at me. "I really am always going to love you."

"As a friend," I say, rolling my eyes.

"As you," he says seriously. "No matter what either of us ever does."

I do know. It's how I keep loving Todd, even after what he did. Todd took Megan away. My Megan. The trivia champ of John Butler Junior High, a cookie connoisseur, and a champion snuggler. We had, between us, seven secret identities, and we could communicate in Sindarin, one of J. R. R. Tolkien's elven languages. And Todd destroyed her. And I still love him.

I push Spencer's hands away. "I don't want you to."

His eyes cloud up and he looks down, shading his face with his hand. "Why do you keep calling me?"

I feel stuffed and sick but I force myself to keep eating just to have something to do. "I don't want you to love me out of habit. I don't want you stuck with that. It'll ruin you, Spence. I am not worth holding on to."

He looks up at me with the grin that used to make my heart

jump. He was my secret keeper. Marked as mine. But now his eyes are shining wet, and it just makes me want to rewind to the day we met so when he sat down beside me I could tell him, "Run, Spencer. Don't look back. Run."

"Don't smile at me."

"Why?" He presses his lips together.

"Because it's weird. You're crying and smiling and it's weird."

"I'm happy and sad. Deal with it. So, what is this, our seventh breakup?"

"We weren't together."

"Now we're not allowed to be friends? Is that why you wanted to meet? To tell me that?"

"No. God." Shit. If I shine at one thing, it's making a bigger mess of an already spectacular screwup. "I wanted to see you. Everything's really messed up right now. But you keep telling me you love me, and that reminds me why we can't—"

"You're right. That's my fault." He wipes his eyes on his sleeve. "I totally failed to pick up on that. Katie, you will not be loved by me ever again. My good opinion of you, once had, is lost forever."

"Were you watching *Pride and Prejudice*, too?"

"It's long. But it taught me it's okay to marry beneath my station."

"Did you catch *Death Comes to Pemberley*, too?"

"Come again?"

"It's another book. The gang gets back together and a minor character is killed off. It's a murder mystery."

"Is it on Netflix?"

"Spencer, we have to talk about Jessica."

He chokes on his coffee. "I thought you were done with this murder thing?"

"Do you realize how serious this is? We are now the police's only suspects."

"How is that possible?"

"I was at the scene of the crime, have no alibi, they found something of mine in Jessica's room that night, and it turns out I did something pretty mean to her a couple of years ago." He tilts his head, interested. "And the police may think she slept with you to get back at me."

"Well. Doesn't that make me feel precious."

"It makes it look like Jessica and I had an ongoing feud or something."

"And I'm presumably a suspect because of my deadly sex curse. What about Greg?"

I take a second doughnut and scrape off some of the glazed sugar absently. "He has no link to Maddy."

He takes a cautious sip of coffee. "Her death could be unrelated."

"Greg told me something else that's interesting. The police

think they have the murder weapon. And someone tried to frame him by taking one from his house and planting it in the lake. But now they have the real one and they're running DNA tests."

He looks at me evenly. "Sounds like we're in the clear, then."

"You're not going to ask what the weapon was?"

He holds my gaze for a moment. "Sure."

"A broken wine bottle."

I GRIPPED THAT bottle so tightly the night of the murder. I don't actually remember putting it down from the moment I left Tai and the others and went looking for Spencer. It seemed like we had been kissing for hours when his phone rang the second time, but it couldn't have been more than a few minutes. In that time we'd made our way into his car, clothes off, underwear on, heat blasting, music pulsing. The buzz from the alcohol was fading into a smoother, steadier blur of desire and determination. I was determined not to think of Brie, not to picture Spencer with another girl, not to remember the look on his face when he saw me with Brie.

I was so determined.

And then his phone rang, and he pulled away.

I grabbed it from him, breathless. "What the fuck?" It was an untraceable campus number. All Bates landline numbers are untraceable for security reasons.

He reached for it. "Just let me answer."

I sat up. "Why?"

"Because I was supposed to meet someone. You know I didn't just randomly wander here looking for you. I'll blow them off; just let me answer the phone."

I pulled the *Gatsby* dress off the floor, feeling like an idiot. "While you're with me?"

His eyes turned pleading. "It wasn't like a date. She was freaked out and she wanted me to stop by and check on her."

"Stunningly original." The phone stopped ringing.

Spencer threw himself back against the seat. "Nothing's ever good enough."

I punched the side of the car. "You do not pick up the phone in the middle of a hookup. Ever."

The phone started ringing again. It was the same scrambled campus number. I answered.

"Spencer? Please hurry. I'm locked out of—"

"Fuck off." I hung up.

Spencer grabbed his phone, threw on his clothes, and stormed out of the car. I grabbed for the bottle of prosecco and realized that I must have left it outside when we moved things into the car. But when I went back to the path to look for it, I couldn't find it.

I leaned against a tree and sighed. My buzz was totally gone and the night was ruined. There was no way I was going to tell any of my friends I went crawling back to Spencer to be humiliated after the night started with them hailing me as a campus hero, so I had to put on a bright, shiny, everything-is-awesome face and meet them on the green like nothing had ever happened. I decided to take the long way through the village to cool down, and I began to walk away from the lake toward the darkened shops.

"Katie."

I turned back toward Spencer.

"Can I fix this?"

"I said everything I have to say to you."

"I can't undo what I did. I can't make her disappear."

"I can make myself disappear."

As I walked away, I heard the sound of shattering glass somewhere behind me.

I WATCH SPENCER carefully across the table. "Where did you go after I left you that night?"

"Home." He doesn't break eye contact.

I decide to put all the cards on the table. "I think my bottle was the murder weapon."

"It crossed my mind."

"That I killed Jessica?"

"You were pretty adamant that I get rid of her."

It suddenly hits me that this whole time everything I've been trying not to think about because it makes him look guilty has been weighing on him, too. Except to him, I'm the one who looks like the murderer. I was the one who kept insisting that she had to go. "I didn't know who she was yet, Spencer. I heard you say the name Jess, but that could have been over a dozen people, and I'd never heard of Jessica Lane."

"What about that prank?"

"It was anonymous," I say desperately. The tables just turned on me dizzyingly quickly.

"And Maddy? You just happened to be there to find her? You happened to be there to find both of them?"

I feel my eyes welling up. "Spencer, you think I did this? I thought you would be behind me."

"No, you thought I killed them." His eyes harden.

"I didn't think it. I just don't know what to think. It's you or me."

"Just because that's all the police have come up with doesn't mean that's all there is. Are you sure Greg is out?"

I gnaw on the lip of my cup until it begins to crumble in my mouth. "He says he is." Spencer rolls his eyes. "I trust him. He has no link to Maddy, no easy access to campus. I've ruled him out."

"And how do I apply for that status?"

"How about one more game of I Never?"

"It could be arranged."

I kick my suitcase at him. "I'm staying at your place tonight. Too many enemies on campus."

"Does that mean I'm officially cleared?"

"It means all things considered, I think I'm safer with one potential murderer than a campus full of them."

"I'll take it."

27

i feel like a fugitive revisiting the scene of the crime as I sit on Spencer's bed in my pajamas. I haven't been here since the night he walked in on me and Brie. So much has happened since then. This used to be such a safe and familiar place. I lie down and press my face into the pillow and inhale deeply. It smells like the apple-scented hair product he pretends not to use. I miss that smell. Then I notice another smell, something like patchouli. I wonder if he and Jessica had sex in his bed, and I sit up abruptly. Just then there's a knock at the door.

"Yes?" I always use my super-polite voice at Spencer's house. I want his mother to love me. I don't know why. She's just this adorable woman and you can tell she has a tough time of it. I want her to think I'm perfect. I guess it doesn't matter anymore. I hope his next girlfriend kisses her ass accordingly.

I'm fairly let down when Spencer walks in instead. "Have everything you need?"

"Actually, I was wondering if I could borrow a new set of sheets?"

He blushes. "Oh. Sure, yeah."

"Thanks."

He disappears into the hallway and comes back with a mismatched top and bottom flannel sheet set and pillowcase, and we work together to make the bed.

"We totally made out here," he says with a juvenile grin.

"That's a collective we, right? You and all the ladies of Easterly."

He rolls his eyes. "Yeah. All." He places the pillow at the head of the bed and sits on the floor with his legs crossed. "You were the cutest, though."

"Agreed." I sit on the bed and draw my knees up. "You may pour."

He takes a bottle of vodka and carton of lemonade and mixes my favorite drink in two equal portions and sets them in front of us. I choose the one in a Care Bears glass, leaving him with Snoopy.

"Before we begin, I would like to bring up a past game foul. The night we met, when we played, I said 'I never killed a person' and you drank."

He rolls his eyes. "You did, too, and you never killed anyone either."

My eyes fill up unexpectedly. "I told you my story."

"I'm sorry." He leans over and hugs me. "I drank as a joke. I thought we both did."

"No jokes tonight. We're playing for truth."

He clinks my glass. "May the worst player win."

I open to the point. "I never killed Jessica Lane."

No drink.

"I never killed Maddy Farrell," he hits back.

"I never slept with Jessica Lane."

He drinks. "I never slept with Brie Matthews."

I raise an eyebrow.

Spencer looks relieved. I kind of want to punch him.

"I never slept with Maddy Farrell."

He takes a sip. "You know all this."

"Lie detectors always ask control questions."

Spencer stirs his glass. "I never still love someone in this room."

We stare at each other. He takes a sip and I dip my pinkie into my glass and taste it.

"It's complicated," I say. "I never had sex with Jessica in this room."

He puts his glass down. "You don't want those details."

"I want all the details. That's why we're playing this game. You were one of the last people to talk to her. The police just don't know it. There's no way they could."

"No, I didn't have sex with Jessica in this room. My turn. I never heard of a suspect besides me, you, and Greg."

I drink. "They aren't serious suspects. Greg thought it might have been Brie for about five minutes because Jess and Brie didn't get along first year."

"Oh, I would have loved that."

"And Brie thinks it's my friend Nola. Which is also possible but I don't like it."

"Why possible? Why don't you like it?"

I sigh. "It's possible because Tai and I were bitches to Nola her first year, so she has a sort of motive for framing me. The killer also set up a blog threatening me if I didn't get revenge on Jessica's behalf for this prank we all pulled on her a couple of years ago. But Nola was one of the targets, she has zero connection to Maddy, and she's also been a really good friend while the campus has decided all at the same time to get back at me for every shitty thing I've done to every student. Which adds up to a lot. I have a few things to atone for."

"Not murder, though."

I glare at him.

"Double checking."

"I never let a loved one off easy because I wanted them to be innocent," he says softly.

I drink the entire glass down and get up. "You made your point."

He takes my hand. "Katie, I'm being serious. It's not just about Todd. Why didn't you come to me sooner if you actually thought I could have killed Jess? You mentioned Maddy to me, but you went out of your way to avoid talking about Jessica, and I think it's because you really thought I might have done it, and it was your fault for telling me to get rid of her and then vanishing into the night. Todd, then me, now Nola. Is there any chance Brie's right? As much as I hate to say those words?"

I sit again and rest my chin on my hands. The vodka shot straight up to my brain, and the lemonade is making my mouth feel sticky. "Brie made her best argument, and all she could really say convincingly was that Nola was motivated to frame me. Not that she actually killed Jessica or Maddy."

Spencer shrugs. "You're just as smart as Brie and Nola's your friend, right? What do you think?"

"I think there's no evidence." I pause. "I went home with her and she acted a little weird around her family. She lies a lot. Fights with her parents. But so do most of the people I know. I've met killers. No one else gets it. There are no obvious tells. It's not always a certain kind of person. It's not someone who's more or less loved. It's just something someone decides to do. Or it's an accident. Anyone could be a killer under certain circumstances. That's what no one else gets."

Spencer pours me another drink, this one almost all lemonade. "So who was it?"

"There's a detail somewhere that's going to make something click." I tap my fingers on the side of the glass, then stop abruptly. The sound of it makes a shiver run down my spine. "What happened to my bottle that night?"

Spencer takes a thoughtful gulp. "Gotta catch up with you there. I left right after you did."

"And you didn't see anything?"

"How could I?"

"I heard glass breaking as I was walking away. What if that was—"

"What if it was?" He gazes up at the stars on his ceiling, and I turn off the light so we can watch them glow. "You'll drive yourself crazy if you think that way. There was no reason to do anything other than what we did."

"Jessica called you because she thought someone was following her."

"Yeah."

"Greg? Because of their fight?"

"Maybe." He sits up. "No, she said *she* at one point.

Something like '*she's* still out there,' or 'she's still back there.' It was definitely a she."

I punch a pillow. "Oh my God, Spencer, why wouldn't you tell me this before now?"

"Because you flipped out at me when you answered the phone and heard her voice."

"That was before I was suspected of murdering her." My mind races. "*She.* Tell me everything else she said."

He pushes his hair back from his forehead. "I don't remember every word. I'm sure the police have my written statement. 'Blah blah can you come? Blah blah scared. Blah blah thee thou whatfore. Blah blah hurry.'"

"Thee thou what?"

"Whatfore."

I furrow my brow and shake my head, uncomprehending.

"There was some old-timey English mixed up in it. I had my phone on speaker in the car; it was hard to make out."

"Jessica talked to you in Old English? Like *Beowulf*?"

"No, like Shakespeare or something."

"That's not—never mind." But I have a sinking feeling in my stomach already.

He chews his lip nervously. "That was the last thing I heard. The freaky thing is, she suddenly sounded so calm. What if it wasn't Jess speaking?"

A chill runs down my spine. "'For in that sleep of death what dreams may come'?"

He points at me. "That's it."

I close my eyes and rest my forehead on his chest. "Shit."

---

i leave the next morning before Spencer wakes up and take a cab back to campus. The sun is just beginning to rise over the towering pines when we pull up to the dorms, spilling golden light onto the surface of the lake. It's not frozen over yet, but it will be soon.

Brie is an early riser, and I can smell strong coffee and hear strains of Schubert when I knock on her door. She looks pleasantly surprised when she sees me, and then a little puzzled as she notices my suitcase.

"Late night?"

"I stayed with Spence."

She opens the door, and I walk in and sit on her bed as if the past month never happened. Brie places a bookmark in her copy of *Othello* and leans back at the edge of her desk. "I could use a study break."

"How long have you been up?"

"Too long."

For the first time I notice Brie has come to resemble me in these past few weeks. She's dropped weight, there are circles under her eyes, and her smile is three-quarters strength. I feel a pang of guilt for ignoring her calls. She offers a box of pastries from the good bakery and I take one. Buttery flakes and smooth chocolate center.

"So, you and Spencer?" Before I can protest, she pours half of her coffee into a second mug and hands it to me.

"Just friends. I'm not stealing your coffee."

"I insist. Have you given any more thought to our conversation yesterday?"

I take a sip of the aromatic French roast. "Quite a bit."

"And?" Brie tosses me a sugar packet and I catch it without breaking eye contact.

I study her placid face. "What if I told you I killed Jessica?"

She doesn't hesitate. "We'd hire my parents."

"Did you ever really think I might have done it?"

"Not for a second."

"You questioned me with a hidden mic," I remind her. "Yesterday, you said doubt was the cornerstone of faith."

"It is." She doesn't look as confident as she did then.

"I don't know how we got here."

She takes a long sip of coffee. "I have a couple ideas."

"You hurt me. I hurt you. You're never going to leave Justine."

"I love her." She looks at me almost guiltily. "She's always been there for me."

We abandoned each other, I realize. It was a two-way street.

"Then before I destroy my friendship with the one person who's been here for *me* the past month, tell me why you asked us all to split up the night Jessica was murdered."

"Don't make me," she whispers.

"If you want me to turn against Nola, give me a sign of good faith."

Brie's cheeks flush and she bites her sleeve. "You can never tell."

"I won't."

"I was with Lee Madera. Ask her."

"So it's not really Justine. It's me."

"The timing never worked," she says in a hoarse voice. "First you told that homophobic joke about Elizabeth Stone right before I was going to ask you out. Then you pulled that Dear Valentine stunt, just when I thought maybe you weren't like the others. And then the cast party, which I thought was supposed to be a date, when you threw yourself at Spencer. You have broken my heart so many times. When you finally kissed me and then yanked your hand away and went back to Spencer . . . I mean that was it. Even after that, at the Skeleton

Dance, when Justine and I had a huge fight, I went looking for you and found you all over that junior. It just never worked."

The picture rearranges itself in my mind. She hasn't been holding my heart hostage all this time. I've had chance after chance to get things right, and I never did. "I'm so sorry, Brie. I didn't realize."

Brie raises her eyes to mine tentatively. "I don't want to lose you again."

"I'm not lost. Maddy and Jessica are dead. They have nothing to come back from. Cori has a shield of nepotism and Tai and Tricia will manage to deal with public school. You and I are going to recover. Or not. It's up to you."

"I miss you."

I smile, but my lips feel twitchy. "Me too. You're my one good thing."

"You're my very bad habit." She grins and brushes the back of her hand over her damp eyelashes. "Tell the police about Nola." She places the paper outlining her theory of Nola's guilt in my lap.

I open the window a crack, breathing a wisp of frozen air. "It doesn't matter what I tell them. There's no evidence against Nola."

That means I have until the DNA testing is complete before I'm arrested.

Twenty-four hours or less.

NOLA RETURNS THAT afternoon. I meet her at the train station, and she fills me in on the rest of her Thanksgiving break. Her parents flipped out and begged Bianca to come home, which she finally condescended to do, and then of course once the other guests arrived, they all acted like nothing happened. The rest was blah: Bordeaux, cliff-side golf, cranberry vodka.

We stop in the village to pick up some food, but she wants to go back to her dorm to eat it. This works out pretty well because I'd love the opportunity to sneak one last look at her journals before making any accusations. Luck is on my side; as soon as we walk in the door, she puts her food down and heads out to use the bathroom and I dive for the journals and start flipping through madly.

It's mostly pages and pages of boring accounts of daily routines in that practiced calligraphy. There are some copies of poetry and Shakespearean sonnets and speeches. I see one or two famous ones that I recognize, but most are obscure, at least to my eye. I finally find one that's dated this year and my heart stops when I read the first line in that delicate, studied handwriting:

Tai Burned Chicken

I snap the journal shut, my mind racing. She could be back at any second. I dive across the room and stick the journal hurriedly behind my back and underneath my coat. Most of those pages, nearly all of them, are copies of things other people have written. I didn't catch the exact date on this entry, just the year. For all I know, Nola used the revenge blog as source material to practice her calligraphy. Even so, how twisted is that? Emily Dickinson, Shakespeare—that's one thing. But this?

Nola opens the door and floats back into the room. She looks like an old-fashioned doll, dressed in a short black velvet dress with a lacy collar, white tights, and black Mary Janes, her hair tied with a sleek black ribbon and her eyes made even wider than usual with black liner and dark mascara. She's back to being School Nola.

I hang back by the bed, the journal stuffed into the back of my jeans, hidden under my coat. Part of me wants to take it and run, but I can't bring myself to do it. After everything we've been through, if Nola really did this, I need to hear it from her. To my face. No more guesswork and no more connecting dots. I need a confession or a refusal.

"You want to hear something awkward?"

"Always." She sets down her tray and drizzles an amber dressing on her salad, then looks up at me with sparkling eyes. "Spare no details."

"I ran into Brie on my train home."

Her expression darkens, but she doesn't say anything, instead taking a prim bite of strawberry and swirling her tea with a plastic spoon. Then she waves her hand as if granting me permission to continue.

"She was actually pretty apologetic about how things blew up."

"I bet."

"She sounded like she meant it."

"Ha!" Nola snorts.

I sit down on the bed hard and bounce my knees up and down nervously. I don't want to get off subject. "She had her own ideas about the whole Jessica thing."

"Dare I hope you had an opportunity to record them?"

"Of course not. She ambushed me."

"Are you okay? Why didn't you call me?" Nola seems truly concerned, which just makes this all the more painful.

"It was fine. I went to Spencer's just in case." She gives me an uncertain look. "He's out. Multiple alibis. And he slept on the couch. He thinks it was Greg."

She relaxes. "I should have come back sooner. My parents are so obsessed with my sister, they wouldn't have noticed if I left." She shakes her head and waves her hand.

"I'm sure that's not true."

"It's never enough. They want me to *be* Bianca," she says with a sad smile.

I'm getting sidetracked. I look at her, determined. "Brie had a really interesting theory."

She sighs loudly. "Will you shut up about Brie?"

"Excuse me?"

"I get it. You're in love with her. You always have been. You always will be." She adopts a mocking tone. "She says the sky is yellow and you say, gosh, I never realized that, Brie. You're so brilliant."

My mouth drops open. "You don't know the first thing about my heart, Nola. And that doesn't shock me because I'm not sure you have one. You act like we're so close and then you say things like that to my face?"

She laughs, completely undisturbed. "Kay, get over yourself. I'm just speaking your language. This is how you talk to people."

"Not anymore. I hate that I was such a bitch to you."

"And . . . ?"

"And I apologized."

"Did you?" She tosses her empty salad bowl in the trash can and starts on an oversize chocolate chip cookie. She holds it out to me, but it doesn't feel like a peace offering. More like a ritual that marks the beginning of a brutal competition, a coin toss at the start of a game.

I shake my head uneasily. "I thought I did. I'm getting way off track. I need to just get this out of my system and have it over with and done."

"Rip the Band-Aid off, Donovan," she says, smirking.

"Brie is pretty convinced—no, she's almost positive," I correct myself. "She thinks there's only one person who fits all the pieces of the puzzle. The cat, the website, me, the investigation. Everything but Jessica."

"There goes your brilliant theory."

"I know. We've been thinking of Jessica as the central piece. But when you're solving a puzzle, you can't get obsessed with a missing piece. You connect the pieces you do have, and then sometimes the picture emerges."

"So what if the other pieces are unconnected?"

"The thing is, they fit together pretty well."

She pauses for a moment. "Okay. Hit me."

I take a deep, shaky breath and knot my fingers together. My heart is fluttering and I feel light-headed. This must be what it's like for those doctors or police officers who tell family members that their loved one just died. It's unreal and dreamlike and I'm afraid of what comes next. "Brie thinks the only person who could possibly have done all of those things is you."

She looks at me, perfectly still, mid-bite, like a deer who's just heard something out of place and doesn't know if it is in danger yet. She swallows, takes a delicate sip of her tea, and folds her hands on her desk. "What do you think?" she asks.

I don't know for sure until the words leave my lips. "I know she's right."

_n_ola doesn't move a muscle. "Go on."

My heart is beating so fast now, it feels like a humming in my chest. "What do you mean?"

"Tell me. Tell me how I did it. Because from where I'm standing, it looks like you're the one going to prison."

I draw a deep, shuddering breath. "You're not denying it?"

"I'm asking you to tell me what you think. And how you're going prove it."

I slip my hand into my pocket and hand her the recording device she bought me. It isn't turned on, of course. She wouldn't speak to me if it were. She eyes it curiously. "I think you're a liar. I think your parents can vouch for that. I think you're capable of cruelty and killing. You proved that when you stole Hunter from Dr. Klein's house and killed him and then buried his body in the woods. You didn't find him kidnapped and tortured by someone else. You tortured him yourself. Just to see what it felt like to torture a cat."

"Wrong," she says, sounding bored. "I didn't torture Hunter."

"But you did take him. And you did kill him."

"So?"

"Some people would say that's pretty twisted. Some would even say killing animals is the natural precursor to killing people."

"Well, for the record, Kay, I didn't plan to kill the damn cat. The original plan was to heroically find him and return him to Dr. Klein. But he was such a jerk about it." She speaks so casually, it makes the hairs on the back of my neck stand on end. "Violent little freak."

"So there's that," I say. "Then there's me."

"It's all about you," she says softly. She smiles a marionette smile, as if strings have lifted and then immediately dropped the corners of her lips.

"I think maybe this time it is. The revenge blog. You blackmailed me into turning the entire school against me. Jeopardizing Tai's chances of going pro. Forcing Tricia out. Humiliating Cori, if that's possible. Almost sinking the soccer team. And I don't even know if you ever had anything on me."

"Police records are easy to hack. Even the sealed records of minors."

"Not for most people."

Nola nods graciously.

"But you're better than most."

"And you're worse. Not many people would brag about lying to protect their creepy-ass dead brother. But you went ahead and did all this evil stuff to your friends to keep that secret, and then you told me anyway. What were you thinking?"

I shake my head. "I trusted you."

She smiles mischievously and bites her lip. "Oops."

"You got me. The revenge blog was a mind game. Your mind game." I take the journal out from behind my back and show her the entry. "Oops."

She shrugs. "That website no longer exists."

"I'm no computer genius, but I'm pretty sure police detectives can find deleted web pages."

"Only with a warrant. And there's no reasonable cause to issue one." Her eyes remain on the journal, though. I grip it tightly, like a weapon.

"Which brings us to Maddy. Who you also killed, just before you came to my room to unlock the clue about her so we could find her together. My guess is that you crushed a lethal dose of sleeping pills into her coffee just before she took her bath, then pushed her under the water to finish the job. But this time—and here's the part Brie doesn't get but I think I do—you did it to shift the blame *away* from me."

Her mask of smugness freezes, and I see her lower lip twitch uncertainly.

"You did, didn't you?" I take a step toward her, but also toward the door, because I don't want to be trapped in her room with no escape. I don't know what she's capable of right here, right now, without witnesses. "You had second thoughts about framing me, and you wanted to backtrack. You went as far as killing Maddy when you saw a picture of her with Spencer because it was the perfect opportunity to set up someone else. You're one of my only friends, Nola. I know I'm yours, too. It's not too late to do the right thing."

She looks at me, her eyes glassy. "Of course it's too late. There is no right thing anymore."

"Turn yourself in. No one else has to get hurt. There's a body count. Nothing can be done about that. We can't turn back time."

"Would you?" she interrupts. "Would you take back what you did?"

"Of course I regret being shitty to you."

She looks at me with wet eyes, her lips trembling. "You were more than shitty. You tortured me."

I try to remember singling her out. We cracked those jokes about necrophilia, devil worship . . . Not nice stuff. But I don't remember anything more pointed than that.

She hands me the wooden chest from her desk and I open it to find a dozen envelopes marked *Dear Valentine* along with a little glass jar filled with tiny dried orchid petals.

And then the horrible, jagged truth crushes me.

Nola wrote the revenge website, and she made up the connection between me, my friends, and Jessica. She knew all about the Dear Valentine incident. But she wasn't the delivery girl.

I stare down at it for a moment, speechless, and then open one of the envelopes. *All of me.* I pick up the smooth bone and then stuff it back inside and slam the lid back on the box.

"Dear Valentine," she says quietly, in her soft singsong voice.

I raise my eyes to hers. "I'm so sorry. I would do anything to take it back."

She nods slowly, as if underwater. "No amount of sorry can ever erase how you made me feel. My first time away from my family. They were in pieces and they sent me away, and then you all treated me like I was worthless. I was so fucking isolated. I thought you would understand, Kay. You weren't like the others either. But you pretend so hard. And you crushed me."

"That's not fair. You weren't allowed to know about my life before Bates."

"Well, I did, and I thought—"

"You were wrong. I made myself fit here."

"You made yourself a bitch. And you made me what I am. You ruined my life."

"I didn't even know who you were," I say weakly.

"What difference did that make?" Her eyes well up, but her expression doesn't change. "You still destroyed me."

"Did you ever even speak to Jessica?"

"I didn't know her," she says.

"What difference did that make?" I echo quietly. "You still killed her."

"I had no intention of killing her. I wanted to hurt you and I was supposed to be the victim. That was the whole point of the website."

"*Your* website."

"I planned it perfectly. You would have been able to access it after you entered enough incorrect passwords. You didn't need me at all. Just your own paranoia and time to self-destruct."

I nod. "And you needed a victim."

"Well, the plan was to frame you for murder. It's not like I was excited to kill someone. Even less enthusiastic about dying. But framing requires a body. I chose Halloween night, by slitting my wrists and hurling myself into the lake. Because I knew you would be the one to find me."

"But that's not what happened."

She spins a hanging ivy plant and then halts it suddenly and places it on the floor. She begins to take down all of her hanging plants. "No, it's not. Because I had to watch you in the weeks leading up to murder, to make sure every move you made was accounted for in my plans. And you deviated from what I expected. You broke up with Spencer. He slept with this girl I'd never really noticed before. Most people hadn't. Jessica Lane. And the fact is, you had a motive to kill her. She was a much better frame than I was."

"So you decided to kill Jessica when I broke up with Spencer?"

"No. I mean I thought about it. But killing is . . ." She makes a face. "Yikes."

"Then what happened?"

"Skeleton Dance happened. I went, just like everyone else. I was determined to stick to my plan, and I went to the lake and stared down into the water. And I started to doubt myself. I didn't deserve to die. But I wasn't alone. Jessica was there, pacing back and forth, texting, and she wouldn't go away. And I finally turned to her and asked if she was okay, and she told me to fuck off. I asked her nicely if I could be alone, and she repeated herself. So she took my place. It's not like I enjoyed killing her, but I'd be lying if I said I wasn't grateful. No one wants to die. So I got to live. Jess had to die. And you had to take the blame. You even left me a murder weapon. It was like a sign." She holds a cactus in her hand, gently tapping the thin needles with her slender fingertips.

THE HENLEY COLLEGE LIBRARY

I lean against the door, stunned. This whole time we've been grasping for the link between the killer and Jessica, and it's so tenuous it's almost random.

"Maddy was an adjustment, too. Like you said. I decided to change things up."

Maddy was an adjustment. I feel light-headed.

"I did it for you, Kay," she says with a humorless smile. "So now you know what I did. You know I tried to reverse it to clear your name. And you've said you would do anything to take back what you did to me. It's the moment of truth. Are you going to turn me in, or let me go? Because right now, you are the only one who can put me in prison. And after everything you've done to me, you need to ask yourself if you can live with that." She sets down the cactus and folds her arms over her chest.

Lie for me like you did for Todd.

But the lie I told for Todd was a killing lie. The chain reaction it caused ruined so many lives. And I want to make up for hurting Nola, but Jessica and Maddy deserve justice. They won't get it this way. And I won't get atonement for killing two people I didn't kill.

"Nola, I am never. Ever. Going to forgive myself for what I did. But lying for you won't make any of that go away. You killed *two* innocent people. And then you framed me for murder."

"Please, Kay." Her eyes have begun to swell with tears

again, bright blue pools with dark, jagged edges. "You're the only friend I have."

"I'm still your friend. Maddy was my friend, too. There *is* still a right thing to do."

She rolls her eyes and the motion edges the tears out, spilling charcoal tracks down her cheeks, matting her lashes together. "Right thing to do," she says in a mocking tone. Then she leaps forward at me shockingly fast, grabbing a thin glass vase from her desk and slamming it down on my head.

The pain cracks like lightning and sends a burst of adrenaline through me. A thousand thoughts run through my mind in a split second. I'm going to die. I must be bleeding. My skull is probably rent in half. My brain is broken. But I don't have time. I only have pain and the choice between fight or flight.

The glass splintered in her hand, sending shards to the floor and ribbons of red running down her fingers. We both dive down at the same time, but the fragments are so jagged, she cuts her hand again and curses. I try to shout for help, but I feel weak and my voice comes out small and shaky.

As I pull myself to my feet, she turns and grabs one of her pen-sharpening tools from her desk, sliding the blade out as she faces me. I try to open the door, but I don't have time, so I brace myself against it and kick her in the ribs.

She flies backward, but since my back is against the door,

I need to step toward her in order to escape, and she grabs my arm and pulls me close to her. She jabs the blade into my stomach and I cry out from the impact but it thankfully doesn't break through the thick Burberry wool coat.

"I killed for you. You owe me," she shouts, her face white with rage.

I grab at the desk and my fingers close around the ceramic pot that houses the cactus plant. I smash the pot against the side of her head and she lets go of me and stumbles to her knees, clutching her skull. I whirl around and swing the door open, and run down the hall and out of the dorm.

When I reach the sidewalk, I keep running. I'm dizzy and nauseous, and I keep checking my head for blood, but all I feel are tiny pieces of broken glass in my hair. Nothing sticky. I'm afraid to look back, that she's somehow right behind me, that she'll slash me down in the middle of campus and no one will lift a finger to help because everyone hates me so much. I don't go to campus police. I go straight to the town police and ask for Detective Morgan. Then I remove my coat, lift my sweater, and take off the microphone I've been wearing—the one Nola had placed in my pocket the morning after Maddy died—and hand it to her.

"Here's your killer," I say.

She hands me a tissue and a glass of water without a word, but there's a trace of a smile on her lips.

"Now tell me. What did you find of mine in Jessica's room?"

She pulls a sealed plastic bag from a filing cabinet and places it on her desk. "It's evidence," she says. "So we need to hold on to it for a while."

Tears fill my eyes as I smooth the plastic over the lost photograph I had kept hidden in the inner pocket of Todd's coat.

30

*b*ianca was the original victim.

After turning the evidence in and giving my witness statement, I was taken straight to the emergency room to have my head checked out. Apparently, I was very lucky. No broken skin, no sign of concussion. Just a mess of broken glass in my hair and a massive, aching bruise.

I called Greg first from the hospital to tell him it was over. He held his breath while I told him who killed Jessica and then he cried into the phone. I keep forgetting how much he loved her. I sent two short texts to Spencer and Brie letting them know I was alive but out of commission for the time being. Then I called Bernie and Mrs. Kent. I don't know why, but I felt guilty. Bernie had paid me, basically, to be Nola's friend. To keep her out of trouble, maybe. And I'd delivered her to the police. Whatever the reason, I called them on my walk back to campus and let them know Nola was being arrested for murder and it was partially my fault.

They apologized. To me.

Then they asked me what I really knew about Bianca, and of course, I said nothing.

If I'd been there when they made the arrest, I would have found out that Nola *is* Bianca. She started calling herself Nola when she came to Bates. Completely changed her clothes, her hair, even her accent. She was tired of being Bianca, I guess. The way the Kents told it, it was some terrible secret.

But it's kind of the story of my life.

Nola is also a pathological liar. There's basically no way to know if anything she told me, ever, is true. The Kents invited me to come visit them again, whenever I like. It was weird.

I spend the rest of the afternoon hiding out in my room until I see the last of the police cruisers leaving campus. Part of me wants to find Brie and tell her how everything went down over coffee and croissants, and part of me wants to flee campus and drive around aimlessly with Spencer all night. But I don't feel up to facing either of them. Both of them have the luxury of going back to normal now. I've been jolted off orbit and I'll always be running to keep up.

Nola did manage one final act of revenge between the time I left her room and her arrest, and this one is going to leave shock waves. She emailed the Dear Valentine girl story to the entire school, to the press, and to Jessica's family, claiming that Jessica was the victim. I read the story on seven news sites within an hour of returning from the police station. I've decided that I'm not going to defend myself. The real story is known to me, my remaining friends, Nola, and the police. Jessica's parents will find out as the case unfolds. It's not important that the community knows the truth. I did what I did, and so did the rest of us, and the fact that we did it to someone who ended up being a killer doesn't lessen the fact that we did it. There will be fallout, too. I'm not going to get a top draft. My rep is for shit. My parents are just going to have to deal with that. Jessica is dead, and so is Maddy, and that's an indirect result of my ego and lack of judgment. I'm going to carry the weight of what we did to Nola, of the repercussions it had on Jessica and Maddy, for the rest of my life. I'll take comeuppance for $800, Alex.

By the time I finish the last of the articles, campus is still nearly deserted and I decide to go for a walk in the cold twilight. Most of the students will return tomorrow night, milking Thanksgiving break for all it's worth. I'm glad for every moment of solitude. The sun is just gone by the time I reach the lake, with wisps of icy blue lining the horizon, the final remains of daylight. The dirt crunches under my sneakers, not frozen, but just on the cusp. My breath floats out in clouds. I pause at the place where we found Jessica and look down into the water. You would think there would be some marker, but there isn't.

It would be unsightly. It's just water over water, next to water. I only know it because of the thornbush I decimated trying to rescue Brie from unknown horrors. Unknown at the time. Now we know.

I take my coat off and tuck it under the bushes. It's a windless night, and the lake is smooth as polished stone. Stars scatter over the surface like snowflakes. I take off one shoe and sock and dip my foot in up to the ankle. It's so cold, the pain is paralyzing, hypnotic. I kick off my other shoe.

I may not have killed Jessica, but I've done other things. Bad things. Maybe worse. And I've always been able to begin again, like I did when I came to Bates. It's like Tricia said: *Everyone has secrets.* And truths are things you make, not things that happen. Like when I created Todd's alibi when the pictures of Megan were sent on his phone.

And when I created Rob's alibi when Todd was killed.

There are so many truths in tragedy. One truth that is indisputable is that the football game ended at ten, and the only reason it is indisputable is because so many people agree. A truth is only a truth because people say it, and continue to say it. Our car was parked close to the school, but I asked Todd to walk me to my bike, which I'd left at the playground, because that was the plan.

Rob and his friend Hayden were going to beat the shit out

of Todd. It was fair. After Rob had shown me the evidence in his truck, he had said that everyone on that list killed Megan. I killed Megan. And I realized I had one chance to redeem myself. Rob agreed immediately. He and Hayden would wear ski masks, and I would run for help so it wouldn't look like a setup. No weapons. No one would ever know. It was the perfect plan.

Of course Todd offered me a ride with his friends and I insisted that we walk because it was a nice night. Because that was the plan.

The march across the dark and deserted parking lot, away from the field where people were laughing and celebrating, was endless.

My brother put his arm around me and ruffled my hair and called me kiddo, and my stomach tightened slowly until it was the size of a bullet. When we reached the playground, I stood by my bike and waited. But only for a moment.

Because as Todd and I stood there in the dark, someone shouted, "Move, kid!" and headlights suddenly beamed at us from the side of the playground. Rob's truck shot out from the darkness and smashed into Todd, and my world exploded into infinite microscopic pieces.

I tried to scream, tried to look for Todd, but Hayden tossed my bike into the truckbed and grabbed me, and then we were skidding down the street. I shook violently on his lap, unable to pry my gaze away from the sharp beams of the headlights as they swung over the dirt roads, the back roads, crunching twigs and bark and maybe bones.

Rob spoke calm and low and dangerously. "Listen to me. You came straight to Megan's to help her mom make cookies. You came straight to Megan's to help her mom make cookies. You came straight to Megan's to help her mom make cookies."

A truth is only a truth because people say it, and continue to say it.

I'd left the game right at the end and rode my bike to Megan's house to help her mom make chocolate chip cookies, Megan's favorite. Her brother, Rob, and his friend Hayden were there, eating pizza and playing Dungeons & Dragons. They were about six hours into a ten-hour campaign when I arrived. A half hour later I got the call that stopped my world on its axis for the second time. Todd was dead, had been killed by a hit-and-run.

I STRIP THE rest of my clothes off and stare down at the water. When I dove into the lake my first year, I was Katie, the girl who failed to stop her best friend's suicide and then killed her own brother. I emerged Kay, the social powerhouse who fought her way to being within inches of having everything she ever wanted. The girl, and then the guy of my dreams, more friends than I needed, a college scholarship, the illusion of a perfect life.

I wade in knee deep, the cold scraping my skin raw. Now I

enter the water as a person with essentially nothing and no one. Brie and Spencer, and even Greg I think, will be there when I need them. But they don't know me. They don't know what I've done. What I'm capable of. And for all Spencer's pretty words, he has no idea what it takes to love a person who does bad things. It changes you.

A cloud passes over the moon, and the water seems to deepen.

Who will I be when I emerge this time?

In Tranquility, I was Katherine. Nola named me.

I only have one more half year to ride out at Bates, and if I can manage to bring up my grades and get back in the game, I might still have an outside shot at a scholarship, though it won't be to the kind of school my parents envisioned for me. Maybe I'll take up the Kents on their offer to visit. Of course I could never replace their daughter. But their house will be empty for a very long time, and despite what my father says, he sent me away for a reason. He doesn't know I helped Rob, but he knows I know more than I say I do. And he will never forgive me. I don't blame him.

I killed his son.

You never find closure for that sort of thing, even if it wasn't what you intended. It settles into you and absorbs through your skin and worms its way in until it's in your marrow, deep in your bones. It moves when you move, it's still when you are still, but never, for a single, solitary instant, does it sleep.

Nola and I aren't the same, exactly, but she wasn't entirely wrong about me either. I didn't make her kill Jessica and I didn't make Todd or Rob do what they did, but I played a role. I spoke.

What if I'd spoken different words to Megan?

Refused to lie for Todd?

Written no valentines?

If I could talk to any of them right now?

I like to believe I'd know what to say. But I think I'm done lying. Maybe that's the kind of person Katherine will be.

I don't feel cold anymore. I take a deep breath, prepare for a long submersion, and plunge into oblivion.

Acknowledgments

t here are too many people to acknowledge than there is room left in the book.

The first thank-you must go to my agent, Andrea Somberg, because without her, I would still be practicing my acknowledgments in the bathroom mirror, Oscar speech style. Andrea is a fierce advocate, a patient hand-holder, and an expert defuser of writer anxieties.

My second thank-you goes to my amazing editor at Putnam, Arianne Lewin. Ari is ridiculously brilliant and it was an astounding honor to watch my book evolve and grow into itself with her edits. She is tireless, lightning fast, and her enthusiasm is dangerously infectious. It is thrilling to work with Ari.

I owe many, many thanks to Amalia Frick for reading endless drafts, talking through changes with me over the phone, and sending me my beautiful ARCs.

I am so very grateful to Maggie Edkins for designing the perfect cover for this book.

Thanks to everyone at Putnam and at Penguin Random House who has spent time, or will spend time, working on my little project that has turned into a great big one.

I am grateful for the invaluable comments and critiques provided by Katie Tastrom, Chelsea Ichaso, Jessica Rubinkowski, Sa'iyda Shabazz, Michelle Moody, Joy Thierry Llewellyn, Kate Francia, and Jen Nadol. In the later rounds of editing, I would most certainly have dissolved into a pool of tears and melted Klondike bars if not for the advice, feedback, and encouragement of Kaitlyn Sage Patterson, Rachel Lynn Solomon, and Jessica Bayliss. I also owe thanks to the Sisterhood, who gamely read my terrible fanfiction aloud in the basements of the new dorms many years ago.

Thanks to my family for celebrating my successes and supporting me through my struggles, and who made it possible to continue working this year when life interrupted, as it does.

To my husband, David, for going all in on the writing gamble. I am grateful to my partner, co-parent, and friend for supporting me through long nights and busy days of scribbling, plotting, and adulting. This book would not exist without his help.

Finally, I am most grateful to my son, Benjamin. To and for.